L'Orté Point

THE AWEN CHRONICLES: BOOK 1

J. A. GIBBENS

FriesenPress

One Printers Way
Altona, MB R0G 0B0
Canada

www.friesenpress.com

Copyright © 2021 by J. A. Gibbens
First Edition — 2021

All rights reserved.

No part of this publication may be reproduced in any form, or by any means, electronic or mechanical, including photocopying, recording, or any information browsing, storage, or retrieval system, without permission in writing from FriesenPress.

This novel is a work of fiction. Businesses, characters, incidents, names, and places are either the product of the author's imagination or are used fictitiously. Any resemblance to actual persons, living or dead, events, or locales is entirely coincidental. The facts concerning historical events, including the relationships of historical figures, and geographical locations have been modified to fit the narrative.

ISBN
978-1-03-911291-9 (Hardcover)
978-1-03-911290-2 (Paperback)
978-1-03-911292-6 (eBook)

1. Fiction, Thrillers, Crime

Distributed to the trade by The Ingram Book Company

AUTHOR'S NOTE

I invite readers to visit with me at www.gibbensauthor.ca, on Facebook as J. A. Gibbens (www.facebook.com/gibbensauthor), Instagram (gibbensauthor), Linked-In (J. A. Gibbens), and Twitter (@gibbensauthor).

Readers are urged to refer to "Maps" on page v, "Generations" on page 286, and "Glossary" on page 287 for additional information.

Many thanks to Joyce McCombe for taking her time to read an early manuscript and provide me with feedback. Much appreciated. Thanks as well to Donal Carey for his linguistic insight.

The Awen Chronicles: Book 1 – L'Orté Point (2021)
The Awen Chronicles: Book 2 – Cow on the Ice: ko på isen (2022)
The Awen Chronicles: Book 3 – Epitaph: Full Circle (2023 est.)

DEDICATION

For my husband, Greg,
with love and thanks for your support and understanding.
You have brought song into my life.

*Where music is, pause and listen;
evil people have no song.*

–Unknown

MAPS

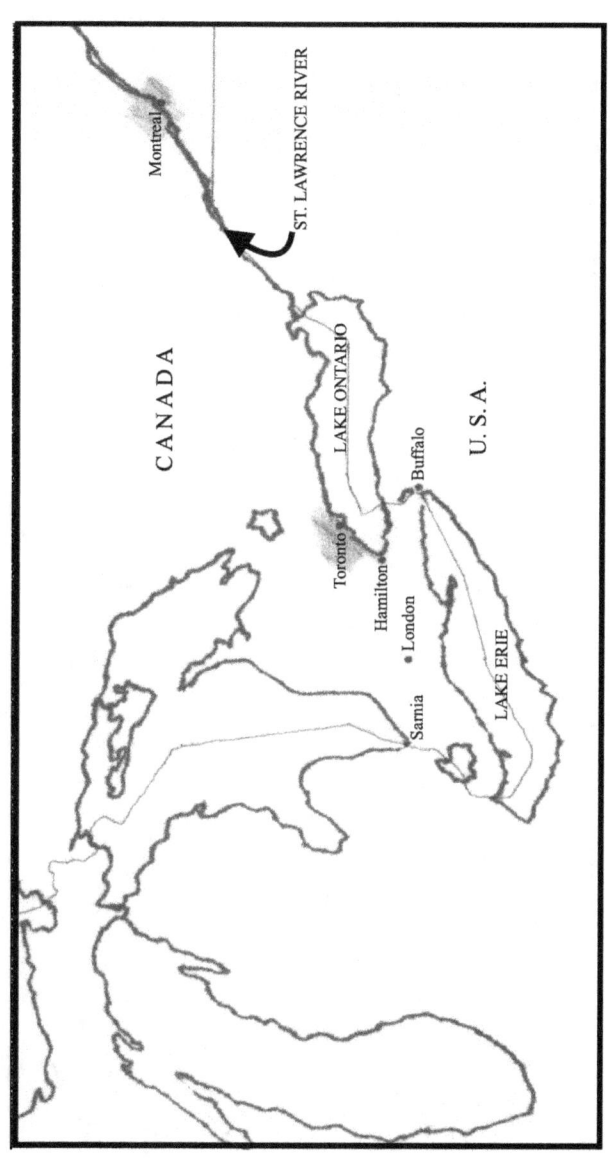

Map A

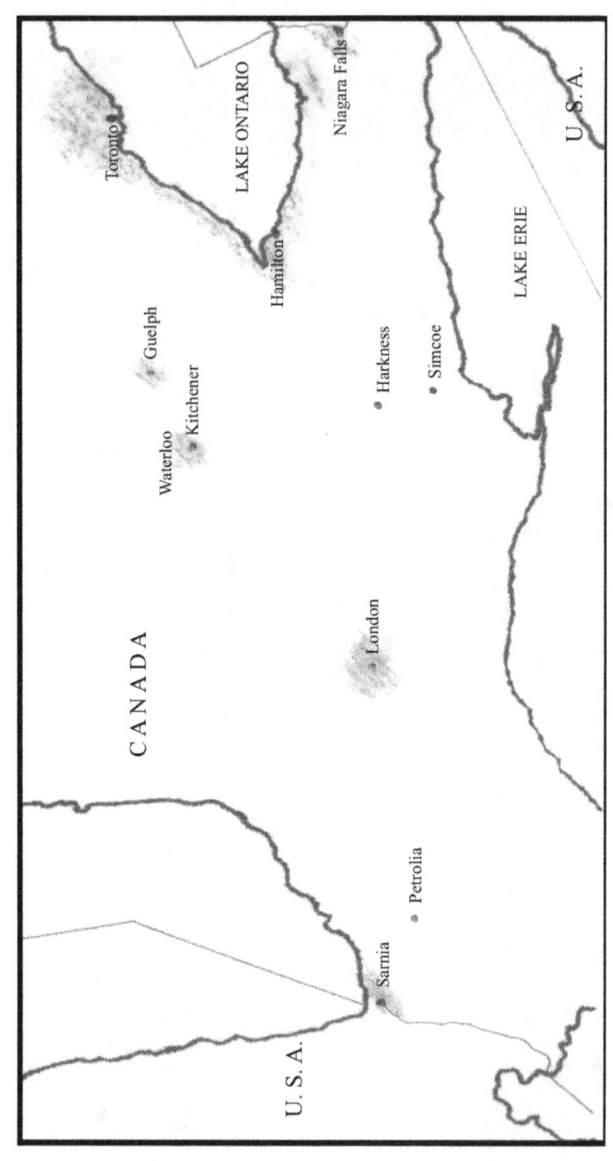

Map B

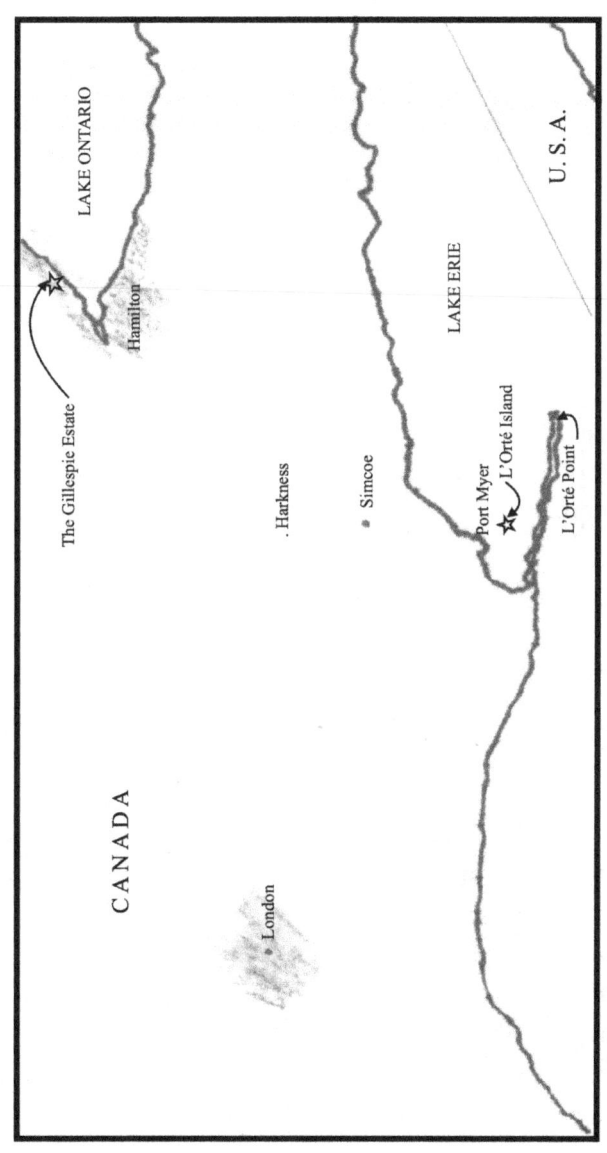

Map C

TABLE OF CONTENTS

AUTHOR'S NOTE .... *i*

DEDICATION .... *iii*

MAPS .... *v*

PART I
    Chapter 1 .... *1*
    Chapter 2 .... *9*
    Chapter 3 .... *13*
    Chapter 4 .... *16*
    Chapter 5 .... *22*
    Chapter 6 .... *31*
    Chapter 7 .... *34*
    Chapter 8 .... *41*
    Chapter 9 .... *45*
    Chapter 10 .... *47*
    Chapter 11 .... *55*
    Chapter 12 .... *59*
    Chapter 13 .... *67*
    Chapter 14 .... *72*
    Chapter 15 .... *83*
    Chapter 16 .... *96*
    Chapter 17 .... *103*
    Chapter 18 .... *111*
    Chapter 19 .... *122*
    Chapter 20 .... *126*
    Chapter 21 .... *135*

Chapter 22	*144*
Chapter 23	*149*
Chapter 24	*161*
Chapter 25	*170*
Chapter 26	*186*
Chapter 27	*190*
Chapter 28	*193*

PART II

Chapter 29	*205*
Chapter 30	*214*
Chapter 31	*223*
Chapter 32	*227*
Chapter 33	*230*
Chapter 34	*233*
Chapter 35	*238*
Chapter 36	*245*
Chapter 37	*253*
Chapter 38	*258*

PART III

Chapter 39	*277*
Epilogue	*282*

GENERATIONS *286*

GLOSSARY *287*

PART I
2015

CHAPTER 1

Bbrrrinngg...

It was late morning and the natural light streaming through the expanse of glass in Lucy's studio was perfect. She had just become immersed in her painting, picking up from where she had left off the previous day. Daubs of various hues of heavy-body acrylics dotted the white surface of her palette.

Bbrrrinngg...

Uncertain that the sound she heard was emanating from outside her head, she hesitated. Even when she confirmed that indeed the sound was real, she remained unenthusiastic about answering the phone. Her painting had been going well, and the disruption was not welcome. Without using a retardant, the acrylics would rapidly dry.

Bbrrrinngg...

Of course, the ringing continued because Lucy had not arranged for messages to be taken on that line. The studio's wall phone rarely rang. People used her cellphone number if they needed to speak with her or leave a message. The wall phone had been installed as a safety measure because she spent so many hours working in the studio by herself, and well into the night. A cellphone or a portable could get lost amid the clutter, which took hold in the studio periodically and—truth be told—rather frequently. But a black phone in the white-walled studio was a different matter.

Bbrrrinngg...

The studio was located on the second floor of the house Lucy shared with her husband, Kent, and he had insisted on the house phone. Helen and Albin were usually on the property as well, but with Kent travelling so very often, the phone sounded like a good idea at the time. *But not now.*

Bbrrrinngg...

Very few people knew the number. *Probably some marketing company doing a survey,* she thought. *Or enquiring about the cleanliness of my ducts. Or warning me about the apparent use of my credit card halfway around the world, and would I please confirm the information by providing my card number, expiry date, and CVC number. Yeah, sure—no!*

Lucy was increasingly frustrated by the intrusion. The sound imposed itself upon her creative thoughts, obliterating them for the present. She used a damp cloth to cover her palette, then gave a quick rinse to the brushes she had been using and put them aside for later.

Bbrrrinngg...

And still with the ringing, enough already! Her mood had turned foul. She walked toward the phone, expecting the ringing to stop as soon as her hand touched the receiver. It didn't. *As soon as I figure out how to set this for messages...*

"Hello," she said, acknowledging the caller yet unwilling to identify herself.

"Is this Elizabeth Szabo?" queried the masculine voice at the other end of the line.

"No, you've got the wrong number," Lucy snapped, then immediately returned the handset to its cradle, disconnecting from the call. She couldn't get rid of the caller fast enough. Somewhat shaken, Lucy returned to her painting. She stared at the canvas, but her mind remained elsewhere. *Coffee...*

Soon, the soothing aroma of the magic beans spilled from the Nespresso machine. Already, she could taste the much-needed double espresso. She selected her favourite chair, among the few in the room, and sat with her legs tucked under herself. As she enjoyed her coffee, she looked up at the second row of tall windows, angled toward the roof in the manner of skylights. The height of the ceiling, the abundance of natural light, the coffee—these were all things that made her happy, usually.

She sat, oblivious to the passing of time. She could still hear the ringing, but this time it wasn't the phone, merely her brain playing tricks on her. It did that ever so often, as if attempting to distract her, yet only succeeding when she wasn't painting or sketching.

She took her empty cup to the counter, and placed it in the sink. Then she returned to continue work on her most recent painting.

Sometime later, Lucy realized she was no further along than she had been at the time of the telephone call. She saw that some of her brushstrokes had been so poorly chosen that she had actually set back her artistic endeavour rather than advancing it. She couldn't help but wonder why she had responded so forcefully to the caller's query, and why the call itself was still affecting her.

She wished she had handled it differently. Her curiosity was getting the best of her, and the distraction was something she did not appreciate. Moreover, the entire matter left her unsettled and unproductive. *Perhaps the party who called will call again.* She hoped they would, if only to ease the torment she had been experiencing since the call. Lucy was now plagued by curiosity.

Rather than frustrate herself further with this particular painting, she decided it was time to add her signature to one she had completed earlier. Then she planned to suspend work for the day. Her mind wasn't where it needed to be.

Taking up a dagger striper, she signed 'Awen', written boldly and in black. Yoichi, her agent, would appreciate this one. Yes, perhaps she would phone Yoichi.

Yoichi and Lucy were roommates and became fast friends during their first year at Queen's University, where they had been students in the Fine Arts Department. Whereas Lucy went on to produce art, Yoichi opened the Song Gallery and produced little of her own artwork, primarily acting as Awen's agent. Their relationship worked well over the ensuing years. Yoichi Song was well-connected in the art world through her parents, who were tremendously supportive of the Fine Arts. Lucy had never developed the facility or interest in marketing her artwork, but Yoichi found the business end particularly satisfying.

Lucy remained in her studio to phone Yoichi, settling once again into her favourite chair with a second espresso in hand. She glared at the black wall phone across the room as if it were responsible for having started *this*, whatever *this* was, and called Yoichi on her cellphone.

"Just thinking about you. Done?" Yoichi queried, getting straight to the point.

"Mostly, but they'll be done when they're done. And that's not why I'm calling you anyway. Sorry, that sounded all wrong. I'm frazzled . . . something really weird happened."

"Okay, no problem. Tell me." And Lucy did.

Only Yoichi and Kent knew her personal history and how she had struggled. Lucy had been named Elizabeth Lucille Taylor by her parents who had planned to call her Betty-Lu because Betty was her mother's name. Betty died when Lucy was only eight years old, and Lucy's father, John, took his own life ten years later, just before she began her university studies.

Even as a young child, Lucy had known that her father had a different surname prior to her birth: Szabo. He had an older brother, Laszlo, who used that surname, as did that entire branch of the family.

"So you see, when he asked for Elizabeth Szabo, he might have been looking for my mother if he knew her back when she was married to Dad. But I don't think anyone ever called her anything but Betty. And if he's looking for me . . . well, asking for Elizabeth Taylor would be more accurate. He didn't mention Lucy at all," she explained, while still trying to understand why she had responded so adamantly to the caller's question.

"But it doesn't sound like you gave him much of a chance to do so, did you?"

"True."

"I understand how this might unnerve you, but your phone number doesn't necessarily provide him with your address, right?"

"Oh my god, I hadn't even considered that! I'll let Albin know to be extra cautious. Helen as well, just in case he shows up unannounced."

"He's not going to get in through your gate, is he now? Although, sometimes, you leave that gate open. It's a security feature, Lucy, and you really should use it as such."

"Perhaps it was something official. I could kick myself for the way I handled it. My curiosity is getting the best of me, and I really don't need this distraction. I'm unsettled, unproductive, and pissed off with myself. I don't want to discuss this with Kent. He's got enough on his plate right now and won't be back for at least a week anyway. I'll handle it differently if they call again, and I kind of hope they do so promptly. Thinking about it, the possibilities—I'm just digging myself a hole overthinking this."

"Well, I think you should tell Helen and Albin immediately. Then I think you should go down into the gym and work out. Besides, it doesn't sound as if you're going to be in the right frame of mind to complete the final canvas anyway. Right?"

"You're right. I'll do just that. Now, get off the phone and let me accomplish something today!" she said, trying to lighten her mood. They exchanged goodbyes and disconnected.

Lucy took the time to return her painting supplies to their proper locations, used the brush washer, and placed the canvas she had signed with others of the series. She hoped that by putting herself in a position where she would have to take out her supplies again for tomorrow's session, she might be provided with a fresh start and not a continuation of today's frustration.

Helen would tidy the area around the sink, making sure that coffee pods were available, and that there was water in the cooler. She was careful when she cleaned in the studio, never moving any art-related materials or equipment. Lucy appreciated her unwavering diligence.

Lucy left the studio, secured the door behind herself, and made her way to the main level of the house before heading for the lowest, where the gym was located. As she reached the main floor, she heard Helen knocking about in the great room so took the opportunity to share her newfound security concerns with her as Yoichi had urged. Once the matter had been discussed, she returned to the stairs and made her way to the lower level.

When Lucy entered the gym, she saw Albin running on the treadmill. He had the television tuned to a political talk show, but as soon as he saw Lucy, he turned off the television and stopped running. As an employee in her home, Albin was welcome to use the equipment.

"Did I misunderstand, ma'am? I thought I was doing self-defence training this evening for you and Eve. Did you want it now? It'll just take a moment for me to dig out the martial arts gear." Although Albin preferred a style known as Jiyu Ki Do Ryu, he was skilled in several styles of martial arts, and sparred regularly with Kent.

"No, Albin, you're right about that. I just need to take my frustrations out on something. The heavy bag may be in trouble shortly, as long as it doesn't hit back. Eve will be over later, as usual."

Eve was a neighbour and one of Lucy's very few close friends. For the past several months, Eve tended to dominate their conversations with her various dating escapades, all of which added to Eve's frustration and resulted in further wear and tear on the heavy bag.

Lucy shared her security concerns with Albin as she had with Helen. He nodded his head as he absorbed the information, and she trusted that he would take the appropriate action. He didn't make her feel that she was overreacting, nor did he say anything to increase the level of her concern. Shortly thereafter, he left to tend to his responsibilities, and Lucy found herself alone.

The room was large, with mirrors along one wall; a television was suspended from the ceiling and visible from the treadmill, the elliptical, the stair climber, and the smart bicycle. Another wall of the gym had been painted by a friend who was a graffiti artist specializing in 3-D effects. The mural depicted woodland creatures exercising in a fantasy forest. Along that wall were various pieces of equipment including kettlebells, dumbbells, and a cable multi-gym.

The wall opposite housed various miscellanea hidden behind cupboards and doors: a water cooler, small change room, and access to the tunnel leading to the pool house, where a swim spa was located.

Lucy's favourite was the fourth wall, the outer wall of the house, which Kent referred to as 'animated architecture'. The wall was self-luminous and covered with integrated LED polycarbonate panels. In some ways this was equivalent to a giant television screen, but instead of streaming the standard fare in supersize, it was most often used to provide light therapy. It could also be used as an alternative to the LED pot lights on the ceiling. Albin maintained the solar panel system, which provided energy for the home, so power from the grid was minimal.

Lucy changed into her workout clothes and shoes. She selected a light therapy program for the wall and some audio to suit her mood, adjusting the volume to accommodate her sensitive hearing. As she did her floor exercises in the area in front of the mirrors, she noticed that her mood was already lifting. The well-used heavy bag hung suspended from the ceiling in a corner of the room, and a ski training machine was in another. Lucy would get around to using both before breaking for a light evening meal.

CHAPTER 2

He reached across the centre console, taking in hand the gift box sitting on the passenger seat. After a final check in the mirror, he emerged from the black luxury sedan wearing a smile set to dazzle the ladies. The parking lot was nearly full, which suited him just fine. *All the better, another reason to smile,* he thought. It put a glint in his eyes and a spring in his step.

L'Orté Park Assisted Living and Long-Term Care Home sat amid a mini-forest. Many of the trees had been planted, rather than occurring naturally on-site, but the result was a vibrant forest of assorted birch, chestnut, oak, and other species. The seasonally decorative trees and shrubs surrounding the building itself hinted that they were awakening from their state of winter dormancy. The building was three storeys in height and a central portion jutted forward, defining the entry. The effect was acceptable but tending to serve some practical need, rather than pleasing aesthetic. As he crossed the parking lot, he wondered how far into the back of the property the complex might extend and surmised that it would contain a garden with a fountain, a feature common to such establishments, especially upscale ones such as L'Orté Park.

He approached the front entrance at the same moment as an elderly man arrived at the door pushing a walker. The aged resident was accompanied by a younger but mature woman, probably the resident's daughter. She smiled and thanked him for holding the door, allowing them to pass. He considered the possibility that he, too, might take a resident from the facility for a short trip. But first, he must introduce himself to the staff.

In the lobby area, reception had been designed to resemble a hotel check-in counter, rather than a nurse's station in a quasi-medical facility. *Appearances are important,* he observed. A young blonde woman with wispy hair and a too-pale complexion sat at a lower portion of the counter, putting her at the same level as a resident who was using a walker or a wheelchair. Other employees busied themselves, eventually moving down one of the facility's several hallways. Apparently all the employees working that day were female, though it was unlikely this was actually the case. Although no security guard was visible, the position was commonly filled by a male staff member. Perhaps he had a pattern of walking the floors, or was socializing with another staff member in some private alcove. The man wished the guard were present. *Perhaps next time.*

He was aware that the young blonde woman had immediately noticed him upon his entry into the lobby. He smiled as he approached, then introduced himself and requested the room number of a resident. As expected, there was hesitancy on her part. He explained that he was the elderly woman's grandnephew-in-law, dropping by at the behest of his cousin to enquire about any current requests the resident might have. He placed a wrapped box on the desk in front of the young woman, with the gift card visible for her to read:

> *Gran, here are the cookies you wanted—all the way from home! See you soon. Love, J.*

Whether it was the small box wrapped in floral paper, his personal grooming, his expensive scent, or the cut of his suit, the delicate blonde generously shared the floor and room number he had requested. She told him her name was Ashley. He thanked her, and was beginning to turn toward the elevator when she pointed to a bound register and asked that he sign in and return to do so again upon his departure. This too had been expected; security was important. He smiled and did as Ashley had requested.

He took the elevator to the next floor, where he found a visitor's washroom near that floor's laundry facility. There, he removed the wrapping and card, placed the card in his pocket, and left with the box. He returned to the elevator and pushed the button for the correct floor. Her floor matched the previous one he had visited—the carpeting and painted walls were a different colour, though part of a unified colour scheme. Each room featured a small display recessed into the wall near the resident's hall door. The displays contained memorabilia of significance to the residents, such as photos and keepsakes. He wondered what the old woman's might contain.

Soon, he found her room and noted that her display included a few photographs of people but, other than the resident herself, there were no faces familiar to him in the photos. It also contained some typically Irish-themed kitsch, possibly the result of St. Patrick's Day the previous week. Her door was closed. He tapped lightly, and when he heard no stirring from within, he cautiously opened it. She had a suite of rooms. There was no one in the first room, but the door to the bedroom was ajar and he could see she was napping, a knitted throw covering her small body on the bed. She stirred. Quickly, he took a series of photos of her room then returned to the display in the hall, carefully closing the door behind himself.

He located the stairwell, walked down a flight of stairs, and then followed the hallway into a different section from which he retreated onto a raised deck in the garden. He found a secluded spot to sit and began to snack on the shortbread.

He was pleased with the quality of his photographs and was able to enlarge them sufficiently to examine the various photos and trinkets in her room, as well as its furnishings. The contents struck him as being sparse. It would be easy to commit the details to memory.

After a while, he returned to the elevator he had used earlier and descended to the lobby. He placed the cookie box near the register and noted his departure time, rounding up the time just as he had rounded down upon his arrival. When Ashley glanced at the cookie box, he offered her one of the few remaining shortbreads, mentioning that the resident had insisted that he remove them and he had complied, ever dutiful. The elderly, he assumed, were notorious for suddenly becoming irritated with things—even those they had specifically requested—and increasingly obstreperous with their demands. He gave Ashley a sad smile and left the home. The delicate blonde would remember him *just enough*.

CHAPTER 3

It was mid-morning and Lucy was in her studio, her special place. She spent some time sitting in her favourite chair, espresso in hand, enjoying the morning light, and marvelling at the myriad shades of green, increasingly abundant with the advance of spring. Flower buds were just beginning on the branches of the trees, and soon the daytime temperatures would be pleasant. Before long, she might find it comfortable to sketch and paint on the terrace.

Recently, the final canvas for her current series of paintings had been covered in gesso and given adequate time to dry. The canvas itself was too big for the elevator and she was planning to go even bigger for the next series. For a moment she considered a second coffee, then she chastised herself for her caffeine dependency and rose from her chair to place her cup in the sink. A second cup could wait.

The black wall phone rang just as Lucy was preparing to immerse herself in her creative process once again. "Hello," she promptly answered.

"Hello, I'm calling from the law office of Garner and Garner in Toronto," the voice said. "My name is Juliette Garner. I'm trying to locate one Elizabeth Lucille Taylor. With whom am I speaking, please?"

Lucy remained silent. Although she had been hoping for this call, she hesitated.

"Hello," the feminine voice queried. "Are you, or do you happen to know Elizabeth Lucille Taylor, or perhaps, Szabo? It's a matter of some importance."

Lucy paused. She took a deep breath. "My given name is Elizabeth Lucille, and my maiden name is Taylor, but the surname I now use is Gillespie . . . Lucy Gillespie," she answered. Lucy decided that the lawyer, if that's indeed what she was, didn't need any more information.

"Might we meet in person in order that I might verify your identity, Ms. Gillespie? That would be necessary before I am permitted to discuss the matter with you in any great detail. You are welcome to come to our downtown Toronto office, or, if you prefer, I could meet you somewhere convenient to your location—a quiet restaurant, perhaps. This initial meeting would merely be to verify your identity. If everything is confirmed as I expect it will be, then I would like you to accompany me to another location to meet with our client. That could be done either immediately upon verification or on another day if that's more agreeable."

Lucy considered the matter, not so much bewildered or intimidated by the situation as she was intrigued. It verged on cloak-and-dagger in the manner of the mystery and thriller novels she enjoyed at bedtime. She arranged for the lawyer to come to the house, reasoning that because the lawyer knew the number for the landline, there was little doubt that she already knew the address; Lucy had merely confirmed it. By having her come to the house, Lucy would not be inconvenienced. Moreover, she would make certain that Juliette Garner knew there were other people in the house; she planned to have Helen and Albin each make their presence known.

Immediately after disconnecting from the call, Lucy googled Garner and Garner. She noted that the firm's trademark employed an ampersand rather than the word 'and'. She regretted not having asked the lawyer for a confirmation email but planned to request a business card upon meeting Juliette. If the full word were written out, she'd know it was all fakery.

It was then that she received an official-looking email confirming their meeting. The email used an ampersand; it looked legitimate. She wondered for a moment how they knew her email address, then shook her head, as if to clear away any remaining doubts.

According to her web search, the pedigree of the firm was impressive. Garner & Garner had been established in 1900; they had offices across Canada; and Juliette Garner, though youthful, was a senior partner. Her face was tagged in many photos associated with corporate moguls, and a variety of charitable and artistic pursuits. She wasn't an unattractive woman and in all the photos she had been conservatively coiffed and styled, projecting a business-like image. The meeting next week would indeed be interesting. Lucy began to wish she had arranged to meet earlier.

Then again, if the Juliette Garner who arrived for the meeting didn't resemble the photo, she would know it was an attempt at deception. Lucy found it hard to trust others— she trusted herself.

CHAPTER 4

The traffic on the drive from Toronto was slightly heavier than Juliette had expected; nevertheless, the traffic moved well in the westerly direction for much of thirty minutes. She pondered the case and how fortunate she was to be in a position to deal with it. Fortuitous timing indeed. Both Kyle and Langston wanted the account, but Edwin and Frederick had agreed that Juliette was best-suited for the task. She wished she could present everything to Lucy Gillespie during this initial meeting, but it was probably best to withhold certain information from her, at least at the outset. Moreover, that had been one of the client's instructions.

After turning off the Queensway, Juliette followed the instructions from the disembodied voice of her GPS. The traffic thinned and she found herself in a wooded community of upscale homes high on the bluffs overlooking Lake Ontario. While the view of the lake was apparent from the roadway only intermittently during this part of the drive, it would have been spectacular from any of the residences she passed. The houses were architectural masterpieces, and each was unique in its design. While Juliette admired such structures architecturally, she found her condominium penthouse apartment in downtown Toronto better suited to her needs. She had no spouse or children and little time for, or interest in, a social life outside work. She had been groomed since childhood to take the reins at Garner & Garner, and the firm was her only family.

Soon, she arrived at the address Lucy had confirmed for her—not that she had needed confirmation. The firm's investigators were certain this was the residence of Elizabeth Lucille Taylor, also known as Lucy Gillespie. However, it was good to have had Lucy confirm the address, as it might have been unsettling for her to have a new visitor to her home who did not require it. She sensed that Lucy had been left uneasy as a result of the firm's initial abortive attempt to contact her. Juliette had discussed the sloppy work with the male associate, though now she felt that she herself had been excessively casual in leaving the initial contact to an associate, especially in this case.

The gate was open, and Juliette wondered if that had been done in anticipation of her arrival or if the gate was perhaps rarely secured. By habit, she made a mental note of this as she steered her anthracite-blue Mercedes-Benz through the opening and toward the house. Once inside the property, she noticed a man trimming some small shrubs just within the perimeter.

The architecture of the home was distinctly modern, yet somehow organic, with much glass and stone. A three-car garage was located to the right, and where it was attached at an angle to the main house, there was a service door. Her eye caught sight of an herb garden just outside the door. The driveway was tear-shaped and passed through a dramatic portico that sheltered the main entrance from the elements. There seemed to be a second-storey over sections of the structure, including the garage, and a terrace extended over part of the portico. In one area, the second-storey looked as if it had additional height, but whether it was that or a third-storey, Juliette wasn't certain.

Decorative plantings near the house were minimal and rather stark, matching the sleekness of construction. Although an area had been cleared around the house, most of the property had been left in a rough and natural state, or at least that was the impression. While some of the trees of modest size may have been planted more recently, the larger ones—to all appearances: maple, oak, and black walnut—were native species and placed there by nature rather than landscapers.

A fine spring rain began just as Juliette parked her luxury sedan, taking full advantage of the protection provided by the portico. She collected her purse and briefcase, and approached the massive, solid walnut door set into the stone structure of the entrance. It was then that she noticed the security cameras positioned at the entry. Although the residents would be well-aware of her arrival by now, she rang the doorbell and prepared to identify herself to the person who answered.

The door was opened by a middle-aged woman who introduced herself as Helen. She wore black trousers, a white polo shirt, and sensible shoes. On her right hand she displayed a single piece of jewellery—a signet ring, which Juliette recognized as that of the Royal Military College in Kingston. Helen's hair was cut very short and she wore no make-up. She ushered Juliette through a small anteroom and into the foyer. To the left was a short hallway with two doors facing one another and a third at the end of the hallway They were all closed and provided no satisfaction to the ever-curious Juliette. To the right was a wall of glass overlooking a small patio with an avant-garde cascading fountain, comprised of polished stone balls on a rough-hewn plinth. The area had lain hidden behind a stone wall and Juliette had been unable to see it from the driveway.

A large open staircase with a sizeable landing encircled a glass elevator directly opposite the entry. Just beyond the foyer, in front of the staircase, a wide hallway looked to run the entire length of the house. To the left of the stairway, Juliette could see an expansive living room with several significant pieces of art—both paintings and sculpture. A grand piano gleamed in a corner. The back wall looked to be entirely made of glass and provided a dramatic view of Lake Ontario from the bluffs, just as Juliette had envisioned. Other walls were clad in substantial sheets of stone; even at a distance, Juliette could see that the stone contained large fossils. The dining room, furnished with a lustrous Italian-modern dining table and credenza, was located to the right of the staircase. Helen brought her down the hallway to the right, past a Euro-styled butler's pantry on the left and an additional view of the patio with the fountain to the right.

She was led into a great room with an open kitchen and a casual dining area set in a glass alcove. Juliette admired the sunny view of the vast treed backyard overlooking the lake. The colour scheme of the room combined the greys of the stone features with plain black upholstery, white quartz countertops, and dark walnut cupboards. In Juliette's opinion, the effect was predominantly masculine. It looked as if there were other rooms to the right, in the direction of the service door Juliette had noticed earlier.

In the great room, a younger woman of medium stature, with shoulder-length auburn hair, walked toward them and extended her hand to Juliette in greeting. She introduced herself as Lucy Gillespie. After the niceties of introduction were concluded and a business card had been provided, Juliette noticed that Helen had quietly disappeared from view. Both coffee and tea had been set out upon a tray on the island.

Lucy directed Juliette toward the casual seating near the stylish ultra-modern fireplace and enquired what the lawyer would prefer as a beverage. She brought Earl Grey tea and a few biscuits, setting the tray upon the coffee table. Then she sat, looked at Juliette, and waited.

After a sip of tea, Juliette began, "You have a lovely and rather unusual home, Ms. Gillespie."

"Thank you. I don't mean to be rude, but I'd really prefer to get to the point of your visit, if you don't mind."

Juliette repeated what she had said over the phone, emphasizing that she needed to verify Lucy's identity. Lucy had prepared ahead of time and presented her with documentation—originals and copies—of her birth certificate as Elizabeth Lucille Taylor. She also had her diploma from Queen's University, which showed her name to be E Lucille Taylor. Then Lucy presented the Certificate of Marriage of Lucy Taylor to Kent Gillespie, and finally her driver's license showing that Lucy Gillespie lived at that specific address. Lucy even had a copy of her father's change of name from Janos Szabo to John Taylor, dated in early 1980. Then Lucy handed her a brochure for an upcoming art exhibit at the prestigious Song Gallery in Toronto, pointing out that she was also known as Awen.

"Now please tell me what this is all about, or do you require something further?"

Juliette smiled—warmly, she hoped—and replied, "This will be sufficient to allow me to provide you with some of the information, but unfortunately, I'll also need a DNA sample. Just swab the inside of your cheek." With that, she handed Lucy a cotton swab encased in plastic—somewhat resembling a ballpoint pen in a clear case.

Lucy was becoming irritated, but she was even more intrigued. It was akin to a game, but one in which she had no idea of the stakes. Garner & Garner was a highly sought-after law firm by all appearances, so she acquiesced and provided the requested sample.

"Now can you tell me what this is about?"

"Our firm was established in Montreal over one hundred years ago by Andrew and Bennett Garner, known as A and B.

They were my great-granduncles. They hired a young man by the name of Giovanni Sarto. He wasn't a lawyer, but over time he became more of a colleague and moved with B to Toronto when the office opened here in the 1920s. Eventually, the firm also became his legal representative. It was rather a two-way street, you see."

"Yes, and . . ."

"Giovanni Sarto established a trust prior to his marriage and the birth of his child, but died before either occurred. He never saw his child. The woman died during childbirth, as was more common back then, and within days the child was fostered by the Szabo family and soon thereafter adopted by Jozsef and Erzsebet Szabo. That child, we understand, was your father. Currently, the trust provides for our client, Gracie Hogan, and we believe you are her sole relative, and therefore, the trust's legal heir upon her death."

Lucy was waiting for the drop of the second shoe, as was her habit. "What exactly are we talking about here? I sense a *but* or something ominous hanging over this information."

"Well, you are somewhat correct. Unfortunately, that's information which is best shared by our client. When would you prefer to meet?"

"Now, if possible. But I should tell you that I don't recall ever hearing the name 'Gracie Hogan'."

CHAPTER 5

A short time later, they were heading westward in Juliette's Mercedes, away from Lake Ontario and toward Lake Erie and Simcoe, a sleepy town of 14,000 located in Norfolk County. Juliette decided to avoid the traffic on the controlled-access highway, choosing instead to use a lesser-used two-lane roadway that followed a winding path through a number of smaller communities. In the more rural areas, farm machinery being driven from one field to another sometimes blocked the flow of traffic. As a result, the trip took longer than expected.

During the drive, Juliette provided additional information, but nothing that Lucy considered significant. However, Lucy was feeling sufficiently comfortable in the lawyer's presence to answer all questions to the best of her ability. As a result, Lucy didn't have much to say because she had little recollection of her early years.

Over the course of an hour, Juliette learned that Lucy and Kent had met at Queen's University in Kingston. Kent had completed a degree in architecture at the University of Waterloo, and had subsequently earned his law degree at Queen's. They married shortly after graduation. Lucy explained that he was now an entrepreneur and property developer. He worked on major projects such as Monroth, which required the formation of consortia and involved significant investor financing. As a result, the house in which Juliette had taken such interest was quite often the site of investor gatherings. Juliette knew of the Monroth project and that the key individuals involved were held in high esteem.

"And the woman—I believe her name is Helen—is she an employee?" Juliette was sincerely curious, as it was her nature, but she realized that her questions might have become too intrusive. She would need to pay more careful attention.

But Lucy answered quite willingly. "Helen and Albin live with us and take care of the house and grounds and whatever. You could say 'everything' and you wouldn't be far off. Kent's busy and sometimes away, and I'm busy with my art, so we couldn't make it work without the two of them."

"Interesting."

"How so?"

"Oh, I was just thinking aloud. I find it particularly interesting the way people assemble their families. For years, we had what they liked to call the traditional family, where the husband worked and the wife stayed home to take care of the house and two-point-whatever children. Now, people are revealing that, for many, their blood relatives do not necessarily define their family. Family is more what you choose to make it. It's as if it's carved out of one's personal life experiences. There are those for whom life is their work and their family consists of colleagues." The final comment was a veiled reference to herself, but Juliette would never let that be known.

The patches of old Carolinian forest became increasingly prevalent the closer they got to Lake Erie. Although Lucy couldn't name most of the trees, she loved the sight of new growth and imminent budding on the cucumber trees nestled among the rarer species of hickory, oak, and walnut.

"I provided my client with a sound-activated portable audio recorder," Juliette stated. "While it's possible there will be all sorts of attendant chit-chat for you to plough through, she finds it pleasant to talk aloud and reminisce. You may find some of the information interesting and even helpful. Before we leave the residence, we'll exchange the recorder that's there now with another I've brought with me. I suggest you alternate between the two with each visit, assuming the visits continue in my absence. You can download the files onto your computer at home and exchange recorders at the close of the next visit."

L'Orté Park Assisted Living and Long-Term Care Home, at least from the outside, had features which hinted at its high-quality construction—not that Lucy found the design particularly appealing. She smiled at the thought of Kent's expected commentary on the architecture. He might be highly critical of the lack of originality and forward-thinking, though it was equally plausible he would recognize that for such a residence, construction with a nod to the past might be more appropriate for the clientele.

The building echoed French Country architecture and it was fair to assume that the name had been derived from a nearby spit of land known as L'Orté Point. The rooflines were tall, sloped and hipped, and featured a black tile roof, likely the product of modern manufacturing techniques. The windows—at least those visible along the front of the building—were tall and rectangular, and set within a natural grey stone façade. Adhering to the architectural style, the windows of the first and second floors aligned in perfect symmetry.

Lucy smiled upon remembering that the round arches of the windows were called eyebrow arches. She wondered if Kent had learned as much about flatwork art as she had about architecture and law over the years.

As they turned from the driveway and into the parking lot, Juliette added, "I would also suggest that, while it's not advisable to tire my client, at ninety-six years of age it might be best to assume that any visit could be the last. You say you have few memories of your early years and even fewer mementos from those years. Well, this might be an opportunity to fill in some of those gaps with the missing pieces of your family story."

Juliette parked the car, and the two women approached the main entrance. An old tree towered over the walkway. As she passed, Lucy looked at the little sign, which identified it as *Liriodendron tulipifera*—not yet in blossom, though budding had started. On the other side of the walkway, a small tree was already displaying some tiny, pink flowers—its sign stated that it belonged to *Cercis*, the genus of the Judas tree. Other trees, primarily chestnut, oak, and birch dotted the park-like setting.

At the reception desk, the delicate blonde Ashley smiled and welcomed Juliette as she signed the register for their visit. As it was late morning, Juliette arranged for her client's lunch to be brought to her room. She and Lucy made their way to the elevator, then down the hallway to a room with an Irish-themed display in the hallway memory case, just outside the door. Lucy hesitated . . . none of this felt familiar.

Juliette knocked on the door, then entered, calling out, "Gracie, where are you?" A small but clear voice responded in acknowledgment of her visitor just as Lucy entered the first room of the suite. Juliette then announced, "I've brought someone with me, Gracie."

The diminutive woman who emerged from the bedroom had a full head of fine white hair and wore such a big smile on her face that it reached her clear blue eyes and made them twinkle. She seemed poised to dance with excitement. Lucy was reluctant to believe that her own presence could engender such an enthusiastic response, yet it made her happy as well. Juliette made the formal introduction.

"Gracie Hogan, it's my pleasure to introduce you to Lucy Gillespie, your grandniece."

The women embraced, Lucy taking particular care not to break her visibly fragile, elderly aunt. She noticed that Gracie smelled like baby powder and smiled at that. Gracie looked up into Lucy's green eyes and smiled in recognition. "You've Annie's eyes! And her hair too, unless you've coloured yours. You haven't, have you?"

"No," she assured her and then added, "But who is Annie?"

Gracie looked shocked, as if she might burst into tears. Juliette interceded and encouraged the women to sit while they talked and began to resolve the many years which had finally brought them to this point.

"Annie was my sister, four years older and, like you, a bit taller. I was the runt— feisty, but a runt," she chuckled, then solemnly said, "Annie was your grandmother."

"I thought my grandmother's name was Erzsebet."

"Oh, no, Erzsebet Szabo was a very sad woman who became your grandmother only because your father came into that family."

"Did you know my birth grandfather?"

"Didn't Juliette tell you? *Tut-tut*. Oh my, yes. He had many names, but was born Giovanni Sarto in Quebec about 1900. We called him Gianni."

"Juliette mentioned something, but I'm rather overwhelmed by all of this and don't recall what she said about this name business."

"Well, it *is* complicated. Juliette would be the best person to provide you with the details. Would you please do that for me, Juliette? And please provide Lucy with whatever other information she asks for, or that you think she should have, alright?"

Juliette nodded. It was clear that she would not take precious time away from the women's reunion.

"Tell me, Lucy dear, what do you remember of the time before your father died in 1998?"

"Not much, I'm afraid. Sometimes some sound, or some thing will trigger a flashback of sorts, but pretty much everything up until the death of my father is indistinct; jumbled. I'm not even sure what's an actual memory and what's a dream. I paint, and sometimes I think that my painting is a form of searching for those missing memories. I've brought a brochure from a gallery showing my work. Would you care to see?" Lucy withdrew the Song Gallery brochure from her purse and Gracie examined it carefully.

"Awen," whispered Gracie.

"Yes, that's the signature I use for my paintings."

"How interesting," Gracie mused aloud. She appeared to have stopped listening, got up from her chair, and made her way across the room to a bureau. From one of its drawers, she withdrew a photo and presented it to Lucy. "You should have this."

Carefully, Lucy accepted the photo from Gracie's hand. It was a very old black-and-white portrait of a darkly attractive man, mature yet possessing a boyish charm, and beside him, a young woman who looked remarkably similar to Lucy. "Gianni and Annie?"

"Yes," Gracie softly answered.

"I have something to show you as well, Gracie." Lucy dug into the contents of her purse and retrieved a gold pocket watch on a gold chain. As she presented it to Gracie, she explained, "I know nothing about the origin of this watch. What I do know is that my father got it from his brother's widow. I think it's the only thing from that side of the family that came his way."

Suddenly, Gracie's demeanour changed. Lucy thought that the elderly woman had become catatonic. But Gracie reanimated and, with a quizzical look on her face, enquired, "Why do you sign your art, 'Awen'?"

Lucy thought about it awhile, then answered, "Actually, I'm really not sure. I knew I didn't want my actual name on my work. My father would sometimes relax by doing deep breathing, and as he exhaled it sounded like 'awen' to me. At least that's what I remember. It was probably 'ah, when', but I shortened it into a name. It sounds the same."

"I'm pleased that the watch has made its way to you. It's Gianni's. He always wore it. You can see the 'GS' in fancy script and notice this—" she said, drawing Lucy's attention to a symbol that looked as if it might have been an afterthought in the decoration: three concentric circles containing three dots and three lines radiating outward from the dots. "That's an awen, Lucy. Your grandfather had it added to his watch shortly before his death."

Gracie breathed in deeply, closed her eyes, and then continued, "It's a Celtic symbol of the balance of male and female energy. Some say it represents mind, body, and spirit, and others earth, sky, and sea. I used to use the word, much as your father did, to centre myself and deal with the stress of living in the Szabo household. Perhaps he picked up my habit."

With a confused look on her face, Gracie asserted, "But you say that Janos got it from Laszlo's widow, Goldie. That must have been about 1993. It would have come into Laszlo's possession when Jozsef died back in 1979. Jozsef wouldn't have let that watch out of his possession during his lifetime. I wasn't permitted access to any part of Jozsef's estate; Laszlo was in charge."

Lucy didn't want to disrupt Gracie's thoughts, but she had to know, "Why are you so certain that Laszlo would have gotten the watch only after his father died? Why is that so important?"

"Oh dear, Jozsef must have killed Gianni! It's the only explanation!" Gracie looked horrified. "Gianni's body was found in the charred remains of L'Orté Point Lodge. The police had suspected foul play, but there were plenty of shady characters in the mix around there at that time, so they assumed it was a robbery gone wrong and the case was never solved."

There was a knock at the door, and it was opened by a server who brought Gracie's lunch into her room and placed the tray on the small table. Gracie remained quiet, her attention on the server. She continued only after the server had left the room and the door had closed behind her.

"Jozsef either killed Gianni or had him killed. There is no other way that the watch could have come into his possession. The watch was not with Gianni's body when they found him. I remember because there was some question about identifying the body. Annie had suggested the watch, but it wasn't with his body. We just assumed someone had stolen it, perhaps even one of the officers. I haven't seen that watch in over eighty years."

Lucy and Juliette remained quiet, hoping Gracie would continue, but Grandaunt Gracie had an appetite and apparently relished today's quinoa salad. From her experience, Juliette knew that shortly after lunch, Gracie would be ready for a nap. This visit was drawing to a close. They remained with her while she ate, and tried to keep the conversation lighter.

"What can you tell me about Jozsef and Erzsebet Szabo?" Lucy asked.

"Well, I started working for them when I was very young; I kept house and then took care of the children. There was Janos, and Laszlo who was just a few months older. I was fond of Erzsebet, but then she lost her mind and you couldn't really tell what, or if she was thinking.

"*Lost her mind*, Gracie?" Lucy asked, dumbfounded.

"Even before Erzsebet found herself with child—that's how we referred to it back then—she often became very upset. I thought it was because she was taking care of Jozsef's father, Peter. Peter was a nasty man and to protect me, she wouldn't let me tend him alone. He used to spit at me and called me *slaba* among other things. I thought it was some sort of pet name at first, but Erzsebet told me that in Hungarian, 'slaba' means 'weak'. I don't know how old he was. I was only ten years old and children aren't a good judge of such things."

"But I digress. Erzsebet . . ." Gracie paused to collect her thoughts. "I remember Peter visiting doctors with her, in Toronto and even in the States. I assumed Peter was the patient, but later I found out that I was wrong about that. You see, one day they arrived home after several days away—perhaps it was a week—and Erzsebet had bandages on her head and two holes that needed healing. I can't think what they call that." Gracie repeatedly tapped her head, as if to dislodge a memory.

"A lobotomy?" Juliette suggested. Gracie nodded her head and continued eating her quinoa salad.

"She was different after that. Being pregnant didn't make her happy—though she did perk up a bit when Peter died."

"Can you tell me more about Peter's death?" Lucy asked.

"Oh, he died in his sleep. He'd been ill. He was old, or so I thought then, though I'm sure I'm much older now than he was then. Slaba indeed! That was the same year that Gianni died and Laszlo was born. But Peter never saw his grandson." A moment later, she added, "Well, dear, I'm pretty tired now, so I think I'll take a nap. Please come and see me again soon."

They left shortly thereafter, having exchanged the recording device Juliette had left on a previous visit with the new one she had given to Lucy. Gracie was reminded to relate any stories, thoughts, and recollections so that Lucy might have a better grasp of her family connections and the years since Gianni was killed.

Lucy held tightly to Gianni's gold pocket watch before transferring it to her purse for safekeeping, along with the treasured photograph and the audio recorder.

CHAPTER 6

Lucy was stunned by the information provided by Gracie, and there was silence in the vehicle for most of the return drive. She tried to reason away Gracie's conclusion that Jozsef had been responsible for Gianni's death but could not. There was also the matter of Erzsebet's apparent lobotomy. *What kind of people were they?*

"Gracie instructed me to give you all the information I have, and there is something you should know. Gracie stayed in the Szabo household, taking care of the children and the house, and Erzsebet when she became ill—it may have been ovarian cancer—until she died in 1958. Gracie married Jozsef the following year."

"How could Gracie have married Jozsef? But of course, she didn't know until I showed her the watch. How terrible for her! Let's see," Lucy did a quick calculation, "she would have been forty when she married him. For how long were they married?"

"Until his death in 1979, so that would be twenty years."

"That's about the time my father changed his surname from Szabo to Taylor. Do you think there's a connection?"

"You might get some ideas about that from Gracie, but keep in mind that Gracie was out of the country for about twenty years. She returned to Ireland after Jozsef died. Not right away, of course, but shortly thereafter. She went to live in a place called Ballynacally in County Clare, which sounds as idyllic as her photos make it look."

Nothing else was discussed for the duration of the return trip. As Lucy expected, Juliette declined her invitation to stay for dinner. Neither of them had much of an appetite, despite having missed lunch, but Lucy called ahead and requested that Helen bring a couple of protein bars to the car for Juliette's drive to Toronto. As before, Juliette reminded Lucy to contact her about any matter or any question she might have concerning Gianni, the Szabos, and the Hogans.

By the time Juliette made her right turn back onto the roadway outside the gate of the Gillespie estate, she had formulated a plan. The file concerning Gianni Sarto was one of the oldest in the firm. The fact that he may have been murdered by Jozsef Szabo, who then raised Gianni's son Janos, was something she was motivated to investigate further. She felt that she owed it to Lucy to help clarify her family lineage—not as a professional obligation, but rather a duty paid by one human being to another.

She was confident that the DNA would help confirm that Lucy was a direct descendant of Gianni Sarto. The geneticist had explained that the match would not be as good as was obtainable by comparing mitochondrial DNA to trace the maternal line, but that, unfortunately, didn't apply in this case. Using the DNA that had been obtained from the few items of Gianni's—which were in the possession of Annie Hogan and kept for safekeeping by Gracie—they had already confirmed a geographic connection for Gianni specifically to Italy. Juliette suspected that Lucy would show some strong degree of connection with the same region of the world as Gianni, as well as a connection with Ireland through Annie Hogan, whose family was deeply-rooted there. She wondered if Lucy had anything with her father's DNA on it. That would confirm his maternal lineage to Annie and Lucy's link to Janos, and, indirectly, to Annie as well.

This hadn't been in her plans until Gracie mentioned the word murder. Murder changes everything. It would take a few days to locate the oldest files, but Juliette was confident that the information could be found.

The research took longer than expected—Juliette kept getting side-tracked. She found it fascinating to review the careers of her ancestors and felt that by skimming their files she was getting a sense of the persons themselves, beyond that of the names and faces presented in the portraits adorning the office.

The documents proved to be more difficult to examine than Juliette had anticipated, but she considered each to be a challenge and it heightened her resolve to collect the facts pertinent to Gianni Sarto. The papers were sometimes brittle and discoloured with age, and the ink was often faded. The cursive writing was beautiful, but at times it was difficult to read for that reason alone. However, the more she familiarized herself with the material, the easier the task became. Dogged determination got her through law school and it was proving its worth yet again. She planned to provide the information to Lucy the next time they visited Gracie.

CHAPTER 7

The sunlight promised crocuses, daffodils, tulips, and hyacinth, but up in her studio, Lucy found herself drawn into the darker scene which was developing on her canvas. The scene itself was undecided; she didn't know where it would take her. It demanded to be painted, and Lucy was merely its instrument. She did as she was compelled, painting all day until the light dimmed; finally she was released by her canvas.

Kent had been away for just over two weeks, meeting with potential investors elsewhere in Canada, abroad, and in the USA. He was expected to return home from his travels later that same day and in time for an evening meal. Once an investor was secured, further contact was generally by electronic communication, except when they would all gather to celebrate the opening of a completed project. Kent would be occupied with the organization of such an event for Monroth in the very near future, but once the project party was over, they would celebrate with some 'we-time'—just the two of them.

Lucy covered her painting with a cloth, cleaned her brushes and palette, and stored the paints, extender, and medium. She had accomplished much and looked forward to sharing her painting success and news with Kent.

She left her studio on the second floor and walked down the hallway, past the guest suites and games room, and then descended the stairway to the main floor. The elevator was rarely used, except when items such as paintings needed to be transported, or if a visitor was using a mobility device. The house was certainly more extravagant than Lucy felt she required, but it was efficient and served them well given their lifestyle. Kent had enjoyed designing and overseeing its construction. Because Helen and Albin took care of the house and gardens, neither she nor Kent was ever burdened with the maintenance of the property. Lucy focussed on her painting and Kent on his business. He often said that while he was away, he slept better knowing that Albin would maintain extra security to keep Lucy safe from harm.

Generally, Lucy was comfortable with Kent being away, but the meeting with Gracie Hogan had left her somewhat unsettled. Lucy accepted change intellectually while struggling with it emotionally. Kent being home would help her sort through that.

She walked past the living room, with the broad expanse of glass providing a view of the deck and the lake off in the distance. City lights shimmered on the distant shore. She passed through the foyer of the master suite and entered the bedroom on the right. Given their highly variable hours, Kent had designed the house with two master bedrooms connecting both in the suite's foyer but also opening onto the shared hot-tub patio at the far side of the suite. Through Kent's bedroom, there was access to his office, which had a second door opening into the hallway to the main foyer of the house.

After a quick shower, Lucy walked to her wardrobe and selected a long-sleeved silk blouse with washes of colour that brought out the green of her eyes, knowing it was one of Kent's favourites. She picked a pair of skinny, black tapered pants and a pair of comfortable slip-on sneakers. Then she set about fixing her shoulder-length auburn hair and, after checking herself in the mirror, decided to apply a bit of lipstick. It was as if she were preparing for her first date with Kent, which had been over sixteen years ago. When he was away, she missed him terribly and looked forward to welcoming him home again—she was confident that he felt the same.

Traffic slowed to a crawl, the result of a vehicular accident. While it was tempting to complain about being caught in the rapidly building backlog of cars, it was still preferable to being in one of the vehicles directly involved in the accident. The driver of the limousine expected that his passenger could pass the time doing something productive and might not even notice the delay. He observed that the well-dressed man, possibly a businessman, busied himself with phone calls.

"Hi, I'll be arriving soon. Anything in particular you need to tell me?" the businessman enquired.

Of course, the driver couldn't make out the reply. One-sided conversations were intriguing to him, and he'd heard many. To pass the time as the traffic crawled along the eight-lane controlled-access highway, he wondered about who the other party might be and what that person might have said in reply.

"U-huh, when was this?"

"Where exactly?"

"Can you deal with it yourself, or will we need to call someone to come in?"

"Okay.

"Does she know?

"Oh, that's interesting, Albin.

"Other than that, has everything else gone smoothly?

"Good.

"Yes, as soon as I arrive. Should be very shortly .

"No, I'll let you know when I'm ready. Soon though, very soon."

The driver looked in the rearview mirror. Having completed his conversation, the passenger adjusted his expensive-looking tie and ran a comb through his dark hair. The traffic cleared just as they approached the exit. Soon, he had dropped off his passenger and was headed back to the garage for the night.

Just as she was debating whether to spend some time on the phone with Yoichi, she heard the front door close and a familiar voice call out, "Lu–cy! Honey, I'm ho–ome!" She hurried out of the master suite and down the hall to greet him in the foyer.

Kent smiled at her and his blue eyes twinkled. He gave Lucy a big kiss and a long hug, and she felt the tension of travel leave his body. "You do know that your Ricky Ricardo shtick is pretty corny, right?" Lucy teased.

"I could always sing the chorus of 'Betty-Lu's Gettin' Out Tonight', but that's more appropriate for sometime when we're actually planning to leave the house, don'tcha think? Besides, that song is far more energetic than I am right now."

"Good trip?"

"For the most part, yeah, I think so. Only time will tell. You know how it unfolds; this one won't be any different from the rest. What about you? Got any 'splainin' to do, Lu–cy?" After a brief pause, he added, "Okay, that's the end of my Ricky Ricardo for the night, but I do love my Lucy!" With that, he gave her another big hug, punctuated by a kiss.

"How about I tend to dinner while you freshen up a bit and I'll see you in the great room?" Lucy had a big grin on her face as she headed toward the kitchen while Kent picked up his portfolio case and made his way toward his office and the bedroom beyond. At some point, Albin must have taken care of Kent's suitcase, which wasn't in the foyer, though she wasn't clear when that might have occurred.

Helen had already set the table and there was little for Lucy to do but serve the portions. The welcome-home meal was always one of Kent's several favourites and tonight it was a hearty boeuf bourguignon, a small green salad with a light vinaigrette, a fresh baguette, and a Chateau Margaux '95. There would be no dessert, at least not with the meal. Lucy couldn't help but smile.

"Well, that was quick," she exclaimed as he entered the room. She hugged him once, then once more, taking in the pleasant scent of his cologne. They toasted to being together again and enjoyed a satisfying meal. He didn't speak of his business trip, and she didn't mention Gracie Hogan. There would be plenty of time for that later.

The following morning, Lucy looked for Kent in his bedroom. She noticed that he was no longer in bed and the door to his office was open. She entered and spied him in his library on the second floor of his office.

"Hey, up there," she called out, "Good morning! You're up early. Had breakfast yet?"

"No, thought I'd wait for you. We didn't talk about our time apart, and I want to hear what you've been up to," he said, as he descended the small spiral staircase to the main floor.

As usual, Helen had organized breakfast. The great room was once again pristine and Helen was nowhere to be seen. They sat at the kitchen island, its white quartz top gleaming brightly in the morning sun and for a time just looked into each other's eyes—well, until the coffee was brewed.

"So how did you spend your time with me out of your hair? Was it productive?" he asked.

"Yes, this series of paintings has gone well and I think Yoichi will be pleased. They will all be done, I think, by the cut-off date she gave me for her next gallery show. You?"

Kent shrugged and sighed in apparent frustration. "The site seems perfect and the project is the type that appeals to many of my investors, but . . ." he paused and sighed again, "I'm having trouble acquiring the property. It's just bizarre. It's a derelict property, but the current owner might be hesitant to sell. It just makes no sense and it's frustrating as hell!"

Lucy made supportive noises—at least she hoped they sounded supportive—but thought that she just might have Kent beat in the *bizarre* department.

He continued, "And I've yet to actually meet with the owner. There was a directive that all contact must be made through the owner's lawyer. I suspect that my message isn't reaching the owner intact, so I'm less effective in securing the property. If I could just get in front of the owner, preferably without the lawyer—initially, at least—you know I could close the deal." After a short pause, he added, "If this plan falls through, I've devised a back-up and they're willing to stay with me for that, but I'd really prefer this property in Harkness."

"Well, if there's nothing to be done at this time," Lucy suggested, "why not just put it aside awhile rather than spinning your wheels, and focus instead on the positive—your project party for Monroth? When are you planning to do that? I'm sure that Helen would appreciate a heads-up. And if you can provide an outline as you did last time—that'd be great. Best if we're all on the same page."

"Ah, that reminds me I've a final fitting at Roman's for a new suit. Julius has offered to come all the way out here, but I'd rather not. I dunno," Kent reflected, "he's offered more than once, until now I'm actually noticing pressure—from my tailor, no less. I'll give him a call and arrange something for tomorrow in Toronto. Perhaps that trip just took more out of me. Never used to, maybe I'm just . . ." He closed his eyes and whispered softly, "I just need some down time at home with you. Anything else while I was away?"

"Well, now that you mention it . . ." Lucy told Kent about the phone call she had received shortly after his departure, as well as her meetings with Juliette and then with Gracie Hogan. By the end of her tale, Kent's eyes were starting to resemble those of the big-eyed characters painted by Margaret Keane.

"So this Juliette, lawyer-person, what firm is she with?"

When Lucy said, "Garner & Garner out of Toronto," the look on Kent's face was impossible for her to decipher. While there was amazement, and even optimism, she also sensed something else.

Kent put down his fork and brought his face close to hers. Staring intently into her eyes, he said, "That's the firm I've been told to deal with on that frustrating property deal! That's some coincidence. What the hell is going on?"

CHAPTER 8

With Kent occupied with the Monroth party and pre-occupied with Garner & Garner's involvement in the property he wanted to acquire, Lucy focussed on completing the series of paintings for the showing at the Song Gallery. She was in her studio positioning the new paintings for Yoichi to view, when the gallery owner tapped on her door and entered the room. They hugged and did a double cheek peck, then got down to business.

Quiet at first, Yoichi finally spoke, "These are quite different, Lucy. They speak to me of a searching, a darkness yet an optimism, a dichotomy of sorts, yet they are well-balanced, and each forms an integral piece. Your technique, as always, is flawless and the colours are bolder and richer than some of your earlier series. There's greater saturation and the end result is that they're more dramatic than usual."

"And I continue to evolve," Lucy declared.

"Some of these are too large for your elevator," Yoichi noted. "How would you prefer we move them from here? We could go onto the terrace, then lower them to ground level, and have them carried around the side of the house, or we could take them up the hallway, through the games room, and out via the terrace over the portico. Which would you prefer?"

"Last time we went through the games room for the larger ones and Helen said she found no damage in the room once your crew was gone, so let's do that again. Now that they're done, how soon can you get them out of here?"

"You mentioned Kent's party is next week. Do you want me to move them before or after the party?"

"Well, how about you arrange to move them before the party and then, of course, stay for the party? Your manager can take care of unloading, right?"

Yoichi nodded before adding, "I thought I'd bring someone to the party, but this one's smart, so he could make his way out here to the boonies on his own." Yoichi's most recent boyfriend had been an intellectual disappointment to her. "Are you having overnight guests, or can I claim my room, in which case I'll schedule the move for the day before the party."

"The room is yours, but tell me more about this *someone*," Lucy said teasingly. "Who, what, where, when, why, and may be even how? See, I remember my one and only introductory course in journalism."

Yoichi didn't need much encouragement. "His name is Donald Gallagher and he's a linguist. Speaks a zillion languages. He's well-travelled. His father was a senior civil servant in the External Affairs Department, so he was born in London, England, but he's Canadian. He grew up and went to school all around the world. He just walked into the gallery one day because he admired one of your paintings, surprisingly enough. And yes, he bought it. Regarding *how*, well, that I can't explain. Consider it in progress but going well." Then she took a deep breath, looked at Lucy, and smiled, "It feels right."

"I'm so happy for you, Yoichi. I'm really looking forward to meeting him, and I'm sure Kent will be eager to meet Donald too. It'll give me someone else I'll really *want* to talk to at Kent's party. You know they're really not my thing—I much prefer the more intimate gatherings. Fortunately, the projects take a long time to complete so it's not as if we do this sort of thing with any great frequency—at least not big parties like this one."

They withdrew from the studio and walked down the hall to the games room where Helen had arranged a light lunch. Lucy told Yoichi about the telephone call, meeting Juliette, and travelling to L'Orté Park to meet Gracie Hogan. She decided not to mention Gracie's comments about Jozsef having killed Gianni, nor her having married Jozsef. Nor did she share Kent's frustration with Garner & Garner. Lucy didn't talk about Kent's business dealings with anyone.

"The law firm is really old, I guess. The founders were Andrew and Bennett, so they refer to them as A and B. That makes the lawyer who contacted me, J. I don't know what they expect will happen when, at some point in the future, they reach the end of the alphabet," she chuckled, spearing a morsel of chicken with her fork.

"And some letters of the alphabet aren't really used in popular names," suggested Yoichi, "I mean, names beginning with X or Z aren't popular, are they?"

"You're right, but I think Z for Zelda or X for Xena would be great. Maybe I'll ask J."

Lucy became more serious and explained, "I'd prefer to meet with her and Gracie again before the party, but we're waiting on the DNA results, so it might not be until after. I guess that, for legal reasons, she needs to present Gracie with the results of the test. I'm just curious about the whole story. I really don't have a coherent family story—unlike you and Kent. His parents are gone, but at least he knows their stories. Your parents are alive and you've mentioned cousins and aunts and uncles. I don't even have many photos." Lucy returned to considering a piece of romaine lettuce in her Caesar salad.

"I get it. It's possible that all this has impacted your painting. If so, I think it's a good thing. It'll be interesting to see where this leads, both as your family story unfolds, and also as it reveals itself in your paintings. You said that Gracie was old. How old is *old?*"

"At least ninety-six, but she's in great condition, both in body and mind. She just tires easily, maybe a bit drifty when she's telling a story—that sort of thing."

"No matter how wonderful you think her health is, it could change quickly at that age. You'd better get as much information as possible. I can't think she has too much time ahead of her."

Lucy nodded in agreement. Yoichi and Juliette had both advised her to make the most of this opportunity with Gracie Hogan. It was time she took their advice to heart. The two women chatted amicably, enjoyed their Caesar salads with grilled chicken breast, and soon it was time for Yoichi to return to Toronto and her Queen's Quay condo apartment.

CHAPTER 9

"Well, hello gorgeous!" Lucy said, doing her best Barbra Streisand imitation. "Let's see that new suit."

Kent had just arrived back from Toronto, and was organizing some documents in his office. He smiled at her and his eyes lit up.

"You remind me of a kid with a new comic book," Lucy added.

"Now that's—yeah, actually, that's pretty much spot-on." He grinned, "Wanna see it?"

"Absolutely. Lead the way." She had always known that Kent was a bit of a clothes horse, though he might have denied it. Lucy followed him out of the office and directly into his bedroom, specifically his dressing room.

Kent made a grand gesture in presenting his new suit to her, withdrawing it from the protective garment bag and displaying it with a flourish and a smile. "My cashmere and silk, single-breasted *comic book*, madam. What dost thou think? Julius has a great eye for fabrics and colours, doesn't he?"

"That medium grey is great with your colouring. I recognize that it's Italian; I'd say Ermenegildo Zegna—even if I hadn't noticed that tag. Could be that Julius is a good influence, even if you think he's a bit pushy sometimes—I can't wait to see you wear it."

Recently, while exercising on the treadmill during Kent's absence, Lucy had viewed a documentary on the history of Italian tailoring. "Next time you visit Roman's, ask Julius to compare the tailoring of Naples with that of Milan or Rome, I'm curious what he'll have to say."

Thinking she had no doubt impressed Kent with her broad knowledge of such things, she decided to quit while she was ahead and so changed the topic. "Did I tell you— Yoichi's bringing a plus-one to your party? She's found someone special."

"No, you didn't tell me. I hope this guy's got more on the ball than that last one she dated. Yoichi is an attractive, intelligent, and very accomplished woman. Where or how does she find these duds? Are you going to tell me about him or do you want me to form my own opinion?"

Lucy nodded, paused, then asked, "I can tell that you're tense, Kent. What's up?"

He breathed deeply. "When are you planning to meet with Juliette Garner again? I ask because I'd appreciate it if you would mention to her that I want to discuss Gold Farm, the property just outside Harkness, with someone at Garner & Garner as soon as possible. I hate to involve you, Lucy, but I've tried every way I can think of to move this along and it's just not budging. Really, it's highly unusual. You know the number of these deals I've done over the years. Sure, there can be snags, but never before have I encountered such a roadblock on what is clearly a derelict property."

Before he got his second wind and continued to bathe in frustration, Lucy cut-in, "Sure, no problem at all. I guess I have a pretty good connection with Juliette, in part because she knows my grandaunt much better than I do, but also because I've found her so easy to talk to. Tomorrow, I'm planning to listen to some of the audio recordings Gracie made and start to outline a chronology, a summary of who did what, when. Maybe Gracie has more photos."

There was an audible uptake of air as Kent breathed in, then sighed in relief. "Thank you," he said, his eyes revealing the sincerity of his appreciation.

CHAPTER 10

The following day, Lucy spent considerable time trying to download the audio file from Gracie's recording device. Its Bluetooth wasn't compatible with her laptop and it took considerable time before she could locate the proper cable in their junk drawer, which was crammed with bits and pieces of all things electronic. It didn't help that she wasn't particularly tech-oriented, but she was finally able to listen to the recording collected from Gracie. Much of the audio wasn't informative, which was very disappointing. There were merely random sounds as Gracie or one of the caregivers worked in Gracie's room. During this time, Lucy browsed her wardrobe, trying to decide what she would wear for Kent's party later in the week.

Having decided on the dress she would wear, Lucy then entered the alcove in her room where her desk and Corbusier fainting sofa were located. She spent a moment admiring the white, pink, and purple blooms on the *Phalaenopsis* lining the window shelves. Moth orchids were her favourite. Clearly, Helen had a green thumb. *Are plant whisperers a thing*, she wondered. Just as she decided she'd had enough of listening to essentially nothing, the audio recording suddenly became interesting. Gracie began to reminisce.

Quickly, Lucy paused the audio, grabbed a pen and pad, and stretched out upon the sofa, taking a few notes as she followed the story being told by Gracie.

"Annie and I, Mam 'n' Da came to Canada from County Clare in Ireland after the terrible Spanish Flu ripped around the world. Mam's family were in County Kildare and many of her brothers and sisters—my uncles and aunties—and my cousins perished within a week's time, I was told. Annie was born in 1915, just before it all happened, and I was born in 1919, just as it finally ended. I guess that they needed a change and were trying to provide Annie and me with a better life. But as they say, 'Man plans and God laughs'.

"Da got a job here working on the Welland Canal. The work was dangerous and he was killed in an accident on the job. I don't know what happened, exactly, except that he was suddenly gone. Mam found employment at a convent. Again, I don't know what she did there. Not long after, we were told, she was hurrying on a work errand when she was hit and killed in a car crash, would you believe. In Ontario, people drove on the right-hand side of the road, as they do now, but in certain other parts of the country that wasn't the case back then. I guess the combination of Mam not being all that familiar with vehicles being on the road, being in a hurry, and the driver of the truck being from somewhere where they still drove on the left-hand side of the road all came together and resulted in her death. Truth be told, I wouldn't be surprised if alcohol had something to do with it as well, though I couldn't say for certain.

"So as young girls, Annie and I were sent to live at the convent's orphanage. My guess is that it was somewhere near Hamilton. I think it was above, and not below the escarpment, but again I can't be certain.

L'Orté Point

We really didn't care where we were as long as we were together and had food, shelter, and some clothes. The nuns provided that and more for us, and for a time I thought we might have ended up as sisters in more ways than one, but that never happened.

"For some reason, we were sent off to the Szabo household. At that time, they lived in a large house in Simcoe. I looked for it when I returned to Canada after Paul died. I couldn't recognize the area at all; I think the house has been razed in favour of an apartment building. But, no matter. There was old man Peter, his son Jozsef, and Jozsef's wife Erzsebet. Annie was supposed to take care of Peter—I don't know for certain what his problem was, but my guess would be severe gout—while I helped Erzsebet take care of the house, even though I was but a child of ten. We quickly learned to watch ourselves around Peter and Jozsef. Peter was what you'd call a dirty old man and he was mean. Jozsef, his son, was just mean. Somehow Annie became acquainted with Gianni, I guess, because she began to work for him as his secretary. I remember being relieved when Erzsebet stepped up to take care of Peter, and I did more of the regular housework. I didn't want to have much to do with him. Erzsebet was good to me—I think she was a good friend to Annie as well.

"Then Erzsebet was with child and lost her mind. Laszlo was born in 1933. That was the same year that Gianni was killed in the fire at L'Orté Point. Peter Szabo died at about the same time as well. Can't say that anyone in the household mourned his loss much. He had been a horrid man. Foul. Behind his back, we used to refer to him as the emperor—he thought *highly of himself and relished wielding whatever power he had over people.*

"Annie returned to the convent near the orphanage where we had grown up, and gave birth in their infirmary to a baby boy. She died giving him life, as was more common back then. I wanted her near me, so they arranged for her to be buried in Simcoe. That was 1934. With some help from Erzsebet, I managed to convince Jozsef to bring Annie's baby boy into the family. He wasn't told that the child was Annie's. I merely suggested that the two boys would occupy each other. I think Jozsef liked the idea of being able to control the number of outsiders little Laszlo interacted with. I don't know if they adopted my nephew, or if he was their ward—I'm really not sure. Perhaps dear Juliette could sort that out for you, if you're interested. Anyway, they named the wee lad, Janos."

Gracie stopped there and announced that she was going to her room to take a nap. Soon, Lucy could hear soft snoring off in the distance. *Gracie must have gone to her bedroom, forgetting the recording device in the outer room of her suite.* Lucy smiled to herself. Clearly, Gracie had expended a lot of energy in telling her tale. Lucy let the recording run for awhile longer. There was the sound of the hall door opening, then some odd sounds, but no additional storytelling by Gracie. Lucy paused the recording, planning to continue it later.

Returning to her studio later that day, Lucy spent time organizing the paintings, which Yoichi and her employees would collect the day prior to Kent's party. Yoichi was right about them; the colour palette was less muted than her usual style.

Lucy accepted that such things were autonomous. The subject matter and choice of hues, textures, and values just happened; they weren't planned. She was the artist, but the identity of her muse eluded her.

Lucy prepared additional canvases—larger than her usual—with gesso, and checked her supply of quality brushes, as well as the paints, gel media, and powdered pigments she would need for her next series. It was always best to be prepared well before inspiration lit its fire within her.

Once she completed her studio tasks, she gave Kent a quick phone call. It was preferable to wandering around the house looking for him. The house had several ways of getting to the various floors.

In addition to the central staircase and elevator, there was a set of stairs in Kent's office going up to its second level, the library, which subsequently gave access to the corridor outside the games room. A small set of stairs was located between the two master suites near their hot-tub on the patio and provided access to the lower level with the gymnasium. Another set of stairs could be found near Helen and Albin's apartment on the opposite side of the house, providing them with ready access to all levels of the house. And because there was a tunnel from the gymnasium out to the pool house in the backyard, there were stairs at the end of the tunnel, which also led up to the pool house. Her call to Kent revealed that he was in his office and would join her shortly in the games room.

The games room contained a well-stocked bar, a table with chairs for games or sometimes a meal, a billiard table, a sizeable wall-mounted television, and comfortable seating. Lucy opened the door to the portico terrace and thought about going outside to wait for Kent, but it was a bit chilly in the late afternoon air.

Helen arrived promptly with the evening meal and set it out on the games table. As if on cue, upon Helen's departure, Kent arrived.

"Sorry, I got a bit wrapped up putting together the photos and documents for the Monroth project. But I'm all done now and ready for the party. It's always such a relief when everything is done yet, oddly enough, also some sadness."

"Yeah, I understand. You dedicate yourself to your projects and then when everything is done, they don't need you anymore. I think you end up feeling abandoned in some way, set adrift again. I see that in you, you know." Lucy moved the arugula and goat cheese around on her salad plate and pierced a section of mandarin orange with her fork.

"It strikes me that it's been quite a while since our last party. I think we should have them more often and make more use of the house. Besides, I like people," Kent announced as he tore into a rustic roll and began to butter it.

"You're more of an extrovert than I am, but I can tolerate most of them . . . I guess. So, sure," Lucy agreed. "And I promise to ask Juliette Garner about Gold Farm. Hopefully, she'll be helpful. She's certainly been a help to me, and clearly to Gracie. I considered just emailing her, but because you find the situation so odd, I think I'd prefer to see the look on her face and her body language when I ask her about it."

"About Gold Farm, thanks again. And that's a good idea about doing it in person, too. When do I get to meet the mysterious Gracie Hogan?"

"Soon, I promise. I'll be returning to L'Orté Park with Juliette soon. We're still waiting on the DNA results. Feels as if we've been waiting forever. Once it's been confirmed that I am indeed Gracie's grandniece—something that's quite apparent to both of us, by the way—we can visit her together whenever you have the time. But it sounds as if there's more paperwork or something, I dunno."

Lucy then told Kent what she had learned earlier in the day, listening to the audio recording of Gracie reminiscing.

"Fascinating. Peter must have been a real piece of work, eh? I can't think that Jozsef would have been much different from his father, living in such close quarters with him right up until the old man's death," suggested Kent. "How did he die? I mean if, as Gracie says, he was a nasty guy and he's old and then he dies—maybe he had some help. I mean, gout won't kill you, will it?" He turned his attention to his salmon.

"Well, Gracie is a sweet thing, and she describes Erzsebet as having lost her mind. It was apparently due to a lobotomy early in or prior to her pregnancy. From what I've read, that sort of operation renders the patient—or the victim—rather compliant, but it's also inexact, especially back then. That doesn't sound like someone who could kill anyone, does it?"

"Maybe it was an accident on Erzsebet's part, especially if she was still taking care of Peter." Kent mulled over what he had learned about the Szabos so far. "Sounds as if she didn't think it was safe for Gracie to take care of the old man."

"I doubt we'll ever know how Peter's death came to pass. Besides, I'm not related to him by blood. I'm more interested in Gianni Sarto, my grandfather."

"That's not official."

"Yet."

Lucy and Kent moved to the sofa with their coffee, put their feet up, and enjoyed a quiet evening. Lucy was content having completed her most recent series of paintings, and Kent was content with the completion of the Monroth project. Neither spoke of their unease—Lucy in finding out more about Gianni Sarto and the Szabos, nor Kent in dealing with the frustration surrounding what he hoped would become his next major project: Gold Farm.

When Kent caught Lucy trying to stifle a yawn—one that he then caught himself— clearly it was time to call it a night. "Get a good night's sleep, sweetheart, and I'll see you in the gym tomorrow morning before breakfast, okay?" He hoisted Lucy from the comfort of the sofa, where she feigned complete exhaustion, and accompanied her to the master suite.

CHAPTER 11

When she returned to her bedroom, Lucy decided to listen to more of the audio. She wondered if it might be a good idea to ask Gracie to turn it *on* and *off* instead of leaving it *on* all the time. Much housekeeping audio was being collected each time Gracie coughed or snored or shuffled about, and each time any of the caregivers entered her room to provide a service. However, she was also concerned that much could be lost if Gracie forgot to turn the device *on*. Lucy resolved to discuss this with Gracie. Much of the audio acted as white noise, and Lucy was soon asleep.

"Lu–cy . . ."

Her name sounded loud and clear, and with some sense of urgency. She arose from her bed but didn't slip her feet into her fuzzy slippers, nor did she don her silken robe with its pink sash.

Lucy left her bedroom, then the little foyer beyond. She walked down the hallway with her bare feet cool against the polished stone floor, and followed the main stairs to the upper level. There, she continued down the hallway to her studio.

She approached a large canvas and instinctively reached for a charcoal pencil, which was upright in an old can on the table beside the large easel. She began to sketch.

Enshrouded by the dark of the room, she continued to draw on the prepared canvas with only moonlight and starlight filtering through the large expanse of glass—not hesitating, not considering, not aware. Of anything.

Lucy persisted in her artistic frenzy. No longer was she holding the charcoal pencil. In its stead was a brush. Other brushes had the earmarks of being used as well, as did the various paints dotting the large palette. The hues were organic with browns and golds and greens—their values deep and intense. The scene developing on her canvas evoked a manic Rembrandt with lighting as in *The Night Watch*, or imaginably, a cross between Van Gogh's *The Starry Night* and *The Potato Eaters*. If there had been anyone else in the room, they would have found it difficult to judge, as the morning was far too young. As the light of dawn began to leak over the horizon, she maintained her frenetic pace, unencumbered by conscious thought or decision.

Finally, it was done. Lucy collapsed to the floor, exhausted. She slept deeply, restfully.

"Lucy!" Kent's voice rang out in the distance.

Too tired to rise from—not her bed—Lucy once again fell into a deep sleep. Some time later, moments, minutes perhaps—it might have been hours for all she knew—she found herself on the studio sofa, covered by one of Helen's knitted throws. Kent sat scrunched next to her, his concern providing even more warmth than the throw. Gradually, she awakened, and as she became aware of her surroundings, she was struck by the unusualness of it all.

There was full morning light flooding the studio, and for the first time, Lucy saw the completed painting. The expression on her face caused Kent to refocus his attention toward the large canvas as well. While their attention was turned toward the canvas, Helen re-entered the studio carrying Lucy's fuzzy slippers, and her silken robe with the pink sash.

The huge painting depicted a derelict stone-and-wood building overgrown with vegetation. Although the brush strokes were bold, there was significant detail, which became apparent as one studied the painting. It was easy to get lost in it. Kent and Helen were beyond words, and Lucy was reluctant to accept that she had produced the scene, though the technique used was clearly hers. Unable to fight the urge, she arose, selected a dagger striper, and in black acrylic signed the painting, Awen. Only then did she actually assume ownership of it.

Normally, Helen would have withdrawn, giving the two of them the opportunity to enjoy a quiet and private breakfast together, but today she hovered. Her concern was palpable. Lucy explained what she could, "I was in bed and heard my name called. It happens that I hear such things for some reason when I'm stressed. I can never tell if the sound is real or comes from inside my head—you know that. Anyway, I don't remember anything after hearing my name called. The next thing I knew, I was partially asleep and dreaming that I heard you in the distance calling my name. And then I was on the sofa with you looking all concerned for me. I swear—seeing that look on your face unnerved me more than anything!"

"So, you don't remember anything about going to the studio to paint?" Kent asked, while Helen hovered.

"No, I don't remember *deciding* to go to the studio, nor do I remember going *to* the studio, and not even *doing* all of that painting. I mean, that's a huge canvas and it's finished! I signed it because it felt right to do that, but I don't remember painting it. It's not even a subject I thought of painting. I had no plans to start another series." Lucy was befuddled; she paused, looked at Kent, and continued, "Series . . . hmm, I wonder if this will happen again."

Kent suggested a doctor's appointment, which Lucy declined as he expected she would. Lucy had developed a dislike for medical intervention in the event of such things. Her odd hearing had variously been assessed as tinnitus and an auditory perception disorder and not only was it a condition of little interest to the medical profession, there was no real treatment. Lucy wondered if it might be a form of synesthesia, but the issue wasn't generally of concern to her, either—until now. She was irked that *it*—whatever *it* was—had upset the household.

"Well, take it easy today. You sure didn't get much sleep last night. Then again, I don't know if you do, or don't when you sleepwalk, or whatever that was. I mean, you had some sort of sleep, but clearly you worked during much of the night. It took time and effort to create that painting. I think that it's absolutely incredible, by the way. Yoichi is going to be blown away by it."

Then he added, "Next time you don't show up in the gym for a workout, I'll know where to find you. Honestly, the studio was the last place I considered."

"Duh, it was the last place because that's where you found me, so you stopped looking, silly."

CHAPTER 12

Kent was ready for his guests. Assisted by Helen and Albin, and the staff they had hired for the evening, the Monroth party was finally happening. Although she was still in her bedroom, Lucy could visualize the gathering taking shape outside the master suite. She had the perception of having done this often—it had a pattern, a predictable sequence. Kent was a natural when socializing at such events, and Lucy felt she wouldn't be missed, so would take her time in getting ready.

She selected the silk V-neck brocade sheath. In her opinion, the sleeveless, black dress with gold brocade required little jewellery; dangly gold earrings and her wedding rings would suffice. The dress barely covered her knees and had short slits on either side. She slipped on the two-tone gold and black high-heeled sandals with double ankle straps, and hoped that the combination gave her the semblance of having longer legs. Lucy felt short. Kent had tried to reassure her, saying that she was a perfect height because her feet touched the floor, but the feeling persisted.

Lucy looked at herself in the mirror, wondering what to do with her hair. Then she rummaged through her collection of cosmetics. She strongly disliked being a canvas, applying make-up to herself. Lipstick was all she could normally muster.

A moment later, as if on cue, the entry system to the master suite politely chimed, and a quick glance at the screen confirmed the presence of Yoichi. Lucy opened the door to her friend. Yoichi wore a long-sleeved, silk dress with a crew neckline, and ostrich feathers adorning the hemline. The dress was very short and featured a large floral motif: a huge pink flower. Because she was wearing extremely high stiletto heels, Yoichi's long legs looked even longer than usual. Now Lucy felt downright stubby.

"You look stunning, Yoichi. Dare I say that you have dressed to impress a certain Donald person?" Lucy smiled, happy for her friend, before adding, "How did you know I needed help?"

"Lucy, you always need help with your hair and make-up. I'll never understand why someone with your artistic ability finds the application of make-up to be such a challenge. Gimme." And with that, Yoichi launched Lucy's metamorphosis.

The task took very little time, but when completed, Lucy was transformed. Her thick, shoulder-length auburn hair was shiny, showed just a bit of a natural wave, and provided an excellent backdrop to her dangly gold earrings. Her skin glowed with vitality and Yoichi's application of eye shadow, liner, and mascara helped emphasize Lucy's deep green eyes. After a moment's thought, Yoichi selected an intense red lipstick to balance the look. "I'm so happy you went with my suggestion regarding your manicure. The black and gold fleck is perfect for this dress and is just edgy enough for Awen, the artist. Your hands are usually such a mess, Lucy. You really should treat yourself better and get a manicure more often."

"Generally not a priority for me," Lucy smirked.

Lucy thanked Yoichi for her help and the two women walked out of the master suite to join the party, which was spreading throughout much of the house: from the living room, dining room, great room, out onto the deck, and upstairs to the games room.

"I'll give Donald a call and find out if he's here somewhere, or still in transit," Yoichi said, looking around at those in attendance. Lucy nodded and went off to greet guests and locate Kent.

Kent introduced Lucy to the guests she didn't already know. In this situation, she saw herself as a supportive wife and not an artist, but she was delighted that many mentioned Awen. A few had already added an Awen to their collections, and others declared they were keen to attend the next showing at the Song Gallery. Lucy took note of who among them she would introduce to Yoichi later in the evening.

It wasn't long before she saw Yoichi entering the living room, hand-in-hand with a pleasant-looking bald man. He was approximately her height, except that due to her stilettos, he was now looking up at her. Lucy noted that the look was one of adoration. *So, this must be Donald Gallagher,* she thought.

Although Lucy wanted to get to know Donald better, clearly that wasn't going to be easy during the party. Conversations consisted of light banter and pleasantries. Other guests would join in periodically as they mingled. Eventually, the topic turned to bad jokes, the kind sometimes referred to as dad jokes.

One of the guests offered this gem: "'I've started dating a twin,' says this guy, so his friend asks him, 'How do you tell them apart?' And the first guy says, 'Well, Suzie has a mole on her cheek and Willie has a beard.'" The comic's little audience groaned and dispersed.

Lucy had forgotten the name of the slightly inebriated guest, but even when he was completely sober, this investor could butcher a joke. Sometimes he would forget the punch line, and other times he would switch the sequence of statements. This time it was merely his presentation—he had chuckled his way through his own joke. Fortunately, having delivered of his wit, he wandered off to regale another group. Lucy caught Helen's eye. They would be restricting his alcohol intake rather slyly for the rest of the party.

A loud and dramatic cackle sounded from the foyer. Lucy and Yoichi looked at one another and smiled broadly. Donald looked both curious and perplexed. "Ah, that would be Eve," explained Yoichi.

"A neighbour," Lucy added.

At that moment, a towering blonde woman wearing just a tad too much perfume swooped into the room, greeting first Lucy, and then Kent most effusively. Eve could be counted upon to be the life of any party. She had been a dancer and choreographer in her younger days, and had maintained her flexibility, strength, and stamina—and love of the stage—ever since. She stubbornly lied about her age and admitted to merely forty-five years, though the depth and breadth of her professional career suggested she was conceivably ten years older. She wore a robe-like midi dress, striped in black and dark green. On anyone else, it might have looked like loungewear, with its oversized shawl lapels and knotted tie at the waist. Eve's stature and bearing meant that she could carry off the look—on her it was dramatic and elegant. For footwear, she had selected an older pair of flesh-coloured, satin ballroom dance shoes with classic Cuban heels. Sometimes Eve would arrive wearing Mary-Janes and once it had been ballet flats. Lucy half-expected her to show up wearing satin ballet slippers. Eve's feet were at least a size twelve, but her generosity of spirit was even larger.

As expected, once Eve had announced her arrival to all in attendance, she returned to find out more about Donald. "Euphrosyne Vighild Ek," she announced, her hand extended toward Donald, "Eve to those whose tongues can't handle the real thing."

"Your parents were prescient when they named you, weren't they?" Donald said, a smile on his lips, and in his eyes. "A lovely Swedish oak. Would you prefer Euphrosyne or Vighild? Both are apt to describe you, I think."

Clearly, Eve was enraptured by Donald. Her interest persisted as he revealed his linguistic skill by teasing her in Swedish. It was apparent to both Lucy and Yoichi that Eve was vetting Donald, not flirting with him. They suspected that Donald was aware of this as well.

Lucy's attention wandered and her eyes lit upon Kent on the opposite side of the room, speaking with a group of his investors. Albin, looking highly professional in black trousers, a crisp white shirt, and black tie, had stepped away from the foyer and approached Kent. Lucy couldn't determine what the two men were discussing because Kent had turned his back to her to converse with Albin. It was then that Lucy noticed Helen who bore a concerned look, but given the placement of everyone she couldn't tell whether Helen was focussed on the encounter between the two men or the distraction caused periodically by Eve. Seconds later, everything returned to normal and Lucy abandoned the threesome while Eve continued pressing Donald for additional autobiographical details.

Lucy took a deep breath and continued to act in the role of the good hostess. She wandered throughout the house, where guests were enjoying themselves, encouraging them to continue to do so and sharing a few words with each grouping. There were a few people on the pool deck, though it was a bit early in the season for them to take an evening swim. These were Kent's regular contract workers and staff, who tended to be younger and disinclined to mix with the investors. Sometimes they would wander from the pool house and use the underground passageway to access the gym on the lowest level; however, they knew what was expected of them and didn't avail themselves of the equipment. It was merely part of the house tour some would provide to their plus-one.

Most of the guests remained in little cliques, some finding greater comfort in the more casual atmosphere of the great room, or the direct bar access provided in the games room. One of the guests was a talented amateur pianist and provided live music in the living room, while at other times a bit of recorded smooth jazz sufficed. Periodically, Kent would take a newer investor into his office-library for a short time and share memories of some of the past projects enshrined there. The Monroth project was the most recent of many. Helen ensured that food and drink were offered to the guests by the staff hired for the evening, while Albin maintained security. Eventually, Lucy happened upon Yoichi and Donald, this time in the games room.

When Donald offered to go to the bar and get a drink for Lucy, Yoichi took advantage of their time alone and asked her if the three of them might go into the studio so Donald could see Lucy's newest painting. Drinks in hand, the trio walked down the hallway and away from the partiers. Lucy coded in the entry for the studio door. "Security in the studio is at least as important as it is in Kent's office," Yoichi explained to Donald. "There's no point in chancing an inebriated guest to take a brush to one of her paintings. Once would be too often."

"I guess with the number of people, and given that most are business acquaintances and, of course, whomever they've brought with them, you can't take the chance," agreed Donald.

Lucy adjusted the lighting. The room looked quite empty now that Yoichi's crew had removed the paintings which would be featured at the Song Gallery. The large canvas, the product of Lucy's sleep-painting, dominated the room, commanding the visitors' attention.

Donald stood in front of it and maintained an appropriate distance. "Oh my, this is— powerful!" He was mesmerized and unable to remove his eyes from the painting. "Is this the first time you've included an awen in one of your paintings?"

"I always sign my paintings, Awen," said Lucy, somewhat baffled.

But Donald jumped right back into the conversation, "No, no, not your signature—the awen, here." He pointed to a small detail amid the branches of trees surrounding the stone building. "And here's another one, amid the stones."

"But how do you know about the awen, Donald?" Lucy asked.

"We Gallaghers have a deep love of history, particularly Celtic history. I think it took root in me when I was read James Stephens' compilation of 'Irish Fairy Tales' as a small child."

The trio managed to identify two more awen, yet none of them was convinced they had found them all. Even Lucy couldn't be certain. In four locations, they could make out three concentric circles surrounding a cluster of three dots, from which three lines radiated: an awen.

Lucy asked them to wait in the studio as she hurriedly made her way to her bedroom, returning to the studio a short time later with Gianni Sarto's gold pocket watch.

"This was my grandfather's pocket watch. He had an awen added to the engraving in anticipation of marriage to my grandmother, who was from Ireland." Lucy then outlined to Yoichi and Donald all that she had learned about her family from Gracie Hogan.

Donald was spellbound. And though Yoichi had already heard much of the story, Lucy shared more this time than she had previously. With some hesitation, Donald began, "If you wouldn't mind, it would be my pleasure to help you sort through your family tree— both the Sarto–Hogan side, and the Szabo side back to Peter, or beyond for that matter. I'm active in genealogical circles and find the challenge of tracing family trees to be very rewarding. It's just personal history after all, and I think yours is especially fascinating."

"Are you certain this wouldn't be a burden to you?" Lucy enquired.

"Oh, definitely not. I can't wait to get started, assuming you want me to, that is. And I don't foresee any problems arising should some of the records be in Italian or Hungarian because those are two of the languages with which I am familiar. Fortunately, it's easier to retain competence in the written word than in the spoken. If something is outside my area of expertise, I have friends who could assist—if that's okay with you, of course."

Lucy said it was and that she would email him any information she received about her familial connections, so that Donald might have as much information as possible. In return, he promised to provide her with information as soon as it became available, on the off-chance that tidbits might stimulate Gracie Hogan to recall additional details.

Lucy experienced a lightness, as if a burden had been lifted from her shoulders. She looked forward to sharing the information with Kent, but decided not to mention it to him until the gathering had concluded. *One thing at a time,* she decided.

Yoichi and Donald wandered off to mingle with the other guests. Lucy locked the studio behind herself, and went to find Helen to inform her that there would be two more guests at breakfast: Yoichi and Donald.

CHAPTER 13

Although there was an outdoor swimming pool with a whirlpool for entertaining and summer fun, the pool house contained a swim spa so they could enjoy aquatic exercise even in the dead of winter. Lucy was in the final minutes of her swim when Eve located her in the pool house. "Hi—I know I'm early, but I just had to get out of there!" Eve had already changed into her exercise attire but was clearly agitated, and not ready to exercise.

"Hi, I'm nearly done here," Lucy replied. The timer shut off the flow of water that had enabled her uninterrupted swim—that is, until Eve had interrupted it. As Lucy climbed from the swim spa and wrapped herself in a terry cloth robe, she asked, "What's up?"

While the two women took the stairs down into the tunnel and followed it to the main house, Eve expressed her frustrations to Lucy. Even as they emerged from the tunnel, Eve continued her rant. "I really can't make heads or tails of what you're saying, Eve. Let me change out of this wet bathing suit while you grab us some water and gym towels. It'll just take me a moment."

Later, as she vacated the changing cubicle, Lucy called out to the voice-activated control system, and the lighting and background music were initiated. She had selected something she hoped her guest would find soothing, as Eve clearly required it.

Then she joined her on the mat, where they began some gentle stretching moves.

"Okay, tell me again—what's up?" Lucy asked.

Eve took a deep breath and began, "I must have gnomes in the attic."

"Gnomes in the attic? Ah, that's 'bats in the belfry'. Well, we know you're neither stupid nor crazy, so tell me, why do you say that?"

"It makes me skogstokig."

"I can see that, Eve. Breathe deeply and tell me about it." Lucy spent so much time with Eve that she was picking up Swedish words and phrases. Eve had just revealed that she was *forest crazy*, which meant that she was raging mad—something that was quite apparent.

"Remember I told you I'd met a particularly attractive man a while back, not too long before Kent's party?" She paused, waiting for a response.

"Uh, no. Sorry, I don't."

"Well, I did. Face it, at my age, there aren't a lot of attractive, well-groomed, interesting, and attentive men lined up to court me, not at all as it was . . . well, you know, in my before life, on stage."

"Eve, I can't keep track of all your male friends—it's as if there's a new one in the wings every time we talk!"

Eve shook her shoulders and harrumphed, "Stor i orden."

"Okay, so you're saying they're all talk, right?" Lucy spoke more gently, trying to calm Eve.

Eve nodded, then continued, "There is nothing true, honest, or substantial about them. Lies. Always lies."

"So, what's happened?"

"He said his name was David Tremblay. He struck me as being quite lovely really, the perfect gentleman. In retrospect, I made allowances for his persistence, thinking it was just his enthusiasm for me. Stupid!" She looked both angry and hurt, and embarrassed as well, then breathed deeply to compose herself.

However, when she paused to take a gulp of water, it was clear that she remained agitated. "I now think he was just insistent upon getting his own way. I let him come by the house too soon, but he always had a good reason. He'd claim that the location of the restaurant made it convenient—therefore, it was logical. Or he'd say he was on his way to some place and had a gift he wanted to drop off for me—"

Eve took another gulp of water, and continued, "I thought I saw his car just up the street one day, but when I asked about it, he became indignant, said I was accusing him of spying. Then I got paranoid, I guess, because I thought I saw him in other cars, even an old piece of junk that passed me on the road when I was out walking." She paused then added, "Perhaps I shouldn't have done it. I think maybe I have shit in the blue cupboard."

"Ah, I don't know what that means, even though it's English. Done what?"

"Oh, it means—" She took another mouthful of water, "It means 'I think I may have made a fool out of myself'. I gave his name and whatever information I had to a private detective. I needed to know the facts. But I think that by the time you do this, the relationship is over, no?"

"My sense is that once you *think* you need to, then the lack of trust already indicates it's over. Trust your intuition, Eve. Hiring the investigator is just tidying up what is already a dead relationship; you're collecting facts to back up a hunch, perhaps."

"Perhaps. Anyway, David had been particularly upset with me—I'm not sure if he was angry with me or hurt that I'd not invited him to attend Kent's party as my plus-one. I had my reasons, but at the time they had nothing at all to do with any mistrust of him. I just wanted to attend alone. Anyway, that's when I decided to hire the investigator. I got his report just this morning and my David Tremblay doesn't exist! His BMW was rented— apparently with fake identification. The phone number I had was for a disposable. I wish I had a photograph of him, then I'd go to the police!"

"Well done, Eve!" Eve wasn't convinced, so Lucy explained, "No, really, you protected yourself sufficiently. There are things you wouldn't repeat doing in any future encounter, so you've learned a good lesson. I'd say you did yourself proud."

Eve remained stubbornly incredulous.

"Remember the Grimm's fairy tale about the princess and the frog? Well, sometimes you need to kiss a lot of frogs before you discover a prince. Sounds as if every so often you kiss a toad as well." Lucy smiled encouragingly at her friend and squeezed Eve's hand.

Eve chuckled a bit at the 'kiss a toad' comment, and considered what Lucy was saying. Soon she became more relaxed. "I guess you're right. Thanks. I appreciate you saying that, even if it's only to make me feel better." Though much calmer, Eve wasn't quite herself yet. "I'm just a dumbom, a ninny. It'll take a bit of time for me to bounce back, I guess."

"Perhaps it's time for you to revamp that list you have in your head, the characteristics you think you're looking for in a partner. At least reorganize it—consider what's the most important characteristic and go from there. It's possible that list in your head was more suitable years ago, before you met Lars. You and Lars were married for many years, but he's been gone for over eight years, so I think you need to approach your dating as a mature woman, not an ingénue. And there's nothing wrong with admitting that you're a widow."

Eve seemed more contemplative. Her blood pressure was down, as was the volume of her voice.

After another sip of water, they began to work through their routine for today—a bit of yoga and some positions at the ballet barre, both led by Eve. The soothing music and light therapy helped to relax them both. They spoke no more of David Tremblay, and though Lucy wanted to share her own personal news with Eve, she thought better of it and decided to postpone her storytelling to another time.

CHAPTER 14

Lucy was aware that Kent had a full morning planned elsewhere, but was surprised to learn that he had arranged for Albin to act as his chauffeur. She would be spending the time visiting Gracie with Juliette; consequently, Helen would be left on her own. Lucy suspected that Kent had become aware of the underlying tension between Helen and Albin, just as she had at the party two days earlier.

Juliette arrived shortly after Kent and Albin had departed. After a few words with Helen, Lucy climbed into Juliette's blue Mercedes and the two women departed for L'Orté Park. "I'd hoped to introduce you to my husband today, but he left earlier than I'd expected, I'm afraid," Lucy began. "There's a property he's interested in purchasing, and he's been advised to contact your office. I understand that, despite several attempts to do so, he's not been able to make contact with anyone who can provide further information. I was wondering if you might be in a position to provide some assistance, please."

"What property are we talking about?" Juliette asked.

"I believe it's in Harkness in Norfolk County. It's called Gold Farm."

Juliette shifted in her seat and Lucy thought she detected the hint of a smile, "I'll take care of that right away. When would Kent care to meet at the property?" But before Lucy could answer, Juliette added, "On second thought, have him call the number on my card to set something up, the sooner the better."

"Will do. And thanks."

Juliette reached into an inside pocket of her suit jacket, withdrew an envelope, and handed it to Lucy. "I did a bit of digging in our archives and made a summary for you of what I found pertinent to Gianni Sarto and the work the firm did for him back then, as well as the work he did for the firm. This might help you sort things out a bit more, or at least generate more specific questions for Gracie. Did you find the audio recording informative?"

Lucy interrupted her opening of the envelope to answer Juliette's question. When she reached into her purse to retrieve her notes and the questions she had based on the recording, she also confirmed the presence of the recording device she would leave with Gracie in exchange for the one Juliette had given her during their previous visit. She decided to postpone the opening of Juliette's envelope until the drive home and prepared herself to make the most of this visit with Gracie, ever mindful that at some point it would be the last visit.

The westward traffic flow was light and they made excellent time, arriving an hour earlier than on the previous trip. Juliette parked the Mercedes beside a BMW in the lot, near a small tree with tiny pink flowers.

Lucy noticed a gentleman who looked to be in his mid-fifties, impeccably groomed and wearing a dark, well-cut suit in a fine fabric, enter the parking lot through a side door of the residence. Although the sky was grey with clouds, he wore sunglasses. He nodded to them in acknowledgment and effected a slight smile before opening the door of the BMW.

Lucy and Juliette made their way into the residence, and Lucy signed the register, indicating her presence as well. "Oh, you must be Ms Hogan's grandniece," observed the young woman with fine blonde hair who was working at reception. Lucy noted that the young woman's name tag identified her as Ashley. Ashley showed every sign of saying something further, but she didn't. Lucy thought nothing of it, smiled, and left to meet Juliette at the elevator.

When they arrived at Gracie's door, Lucy knocked lightly, then opened it gradually. Gracie wasn't in the outer room, and Lucy thought perhaps she might have returned to bed after breakfast. *So much for trying to get some extra time with her before lunch and a nap,* Lucy chuckled to herself.

It was then that she spotted the sign on the bedroom door. It read: 'Do Not Enter, Medical Visit. Please Knock to Let Us Know You're Waiting'. Lucy thought it rather odd, but Juliette was familiar with such postings. "Medical visits are made by a doctor accompanied by a nurse." Juliette knocked, as instructed in the posting, then the two women took the same seats they had during their earlier visit. Lucy used the time to remove the audio recorder from her purse and exchange it for the one Juliette had given to Gracie previously. She took out her notes. Just when she thought she might read the information Juliette had prepared for her, the door opened and a nurse, a doctor, and Gracie emerged from the bedroom.

Gracie made introductions and informed the doctor that any information concerning her own health could be shared with Lucy. "Decisions will continue to be made by me, or by Juliette, if I am unable, but feel free to share information with Lucy—we are blood relatives." Turning to Lucy, she added, "Evidently, I'm as healthy as a horse and won't be off to the knacker's yard just yet, right, Doctor?"

"Right you are, Gracie. I'll check-in with you when I'm around again, but have them give me a call if you encounter a problem. And now I'm off!" With a nod to Lucy and Juliette and a "Nice to meet you" delivered with a smile, they were gone.

Juliette began, "Well, everything is in order. Gracie, Lucy—you are most definitely grandaunt and grandniece. I'm very happy for you both. Would you like me to remain, or would you prefer that I leave the two of you alone?"

Lucy and Gracie looked at one another and Gracie urged Lucy to speak. "If you have something you'd prefer to do, Juliette then by all means go and do it, but otherwise you are most welcome to stay for our visit." Lucy replied.

"Well, I have one call I need to make, but then I would enjoy joining you, if that's okay with you," Juliette replied.

When she had gone from the room, Gracie and Lucy took a moment just to hold hands and look at one another. Lucy brought up the question of whether to have the recorder turned on all the time, and they discussed the matter briefly. Lucy asked if Gracie had any photos of other family members or places, such as the Szabo house in Simcoe where Gracie had worked and lived. Gracie shuffled back into her bedroom, and, as she returned clutching a small box, Juliette rejoined them. She was accompanied by an attendant carrying a tray with tea and shortbread.

"Juliette, would you please take a few photos of Grandaunt Gracie and me?"

"Of course," Juliette enthused. Gracie and Lucy mugged for their photo session and Juliette captured it all on Lucy's smartphone. They posed more formally for a few photos but generally they were so happy that they couldn't refrain from acting silly.

After a quick look at the results of their photo session, Lucy began, "I listened to the recording you made prior to our last visit, and I have some questions."

Gracie indicated she was eager to hear them and urged Lucy to proceed.

"I was wondering when and why you migrated to Ireland, Gracie."

"I returned to Ireland in 1979, shortly after Jozsef died. The finances were all tangled in a trust that Peter had started and Jozsef had modified somewhat along the way. Jozsef was true to his word and provided an allowance for me, but his son, Laszlo, thought I shouldn't receive anything else. That's why I didn't even receive Gianni's gold watch, which has since found its way to you—I am so very pleased that it did. And Laszlo tried to deny me the house in Simcoe where I had lived for fifty years—since I was ten years old! That's when I contacted Juliette's firm, though I dealt with Henri Garner back then. I thought—no, indeed I *was*—threatened with bodily harm by Laszlo, so I entrusted Henri to do what he could on my behalf, and he came through with flying colours. The house became mine; a price was decided, and Laszlo paid me outright for it. I don't know why he wanted it so badly. He and Goldie had moved out when they married in 1960."

"When and why did you decide to return? I'm very glad you did, but curious about why."

"I returned in late 1998. Paul—that's Laszlo and Goldie's son—had died a couple of years earlier, but the estate wasn't settled until 1998. Juliette would know more about what was involved—she can tell you if you're interested. Anyway, everything came my way, and when I pass, it will all be yours."

"Don't rush it, Gracie! There are many more conversations to be had—and tea and shortbread to enjoy together." Lucy took a sip of her tea, then said, "I was wondering about photographs of the Szabos. I can't remember ever seeing any."

"There weren't many photographs taken. This wasn't a sociable, happy family," Gracie shook her head slowly from side to side. "I found Erzsebet burning photographs shortly after old man Peter died. She made a show of taking delight in it, though as I remember she was crying as well. That took care of the older photos and some documents, I expect. There weren't many photographs taken after that either, even with the two young boys at home. Jozsef became increasingly miserly and considered it a waste of money."

When Lucy didn't respond to the lull in the conversation with a new question, Gracie spoke, choosing her words carefully, "I understand there was considerable upheaval in your family in 1983 when you were three years old. Do you remember? Your mother wrote to me about it."

Lucy thought about it, but nothing came to mind. "I don't know what you might be referring to. What do you mean?"

"Actually, I'd rather just prick your memory. Probably best if you remember on your own now that I've mentioned it."

"O–kay," Lucy answered slowly, wishing that Gracie would just spit it out. "Do you know why my father changed his name?"

"Well, I had already departed for Ireland by then, but I can guess." She paused to take a sip of tea. "Janos was always trying to be a good son to Jozsef, but the more he tried, the clearer Jozsef made it that he preferred Laszlo. I think Jozsef thought himself a puppet-master and enjoyed manipulating people, toying with them. Janos was always working, and he would co-mingle his income with that of Laszlo and Jozsef, so it ended up in an account over which Jozsef held complete control. Allowances were doled out to Janos and Laszlo, even as they became mature men. Things didn't change when Janos married your mother, so I think he just became increasingly frustrated with the arrangement. When Jozsef died, it was clear that everything had been bequeathed to Laszlo—except for my allowance and the continuation of a small allowance to Janos."

"Why would he have turned over his income to them?"

"Remember that Jozsef exerted complete control over every aspect of their lives and had done so since they were babies. He and Laszlo were trained to accept that. Jozsef would promise fairness, and even generosity, sometime in the future. Janos believed him; Jozsef was the only father he'd ever known, and he trusted him. He shouldn't have. I think Janos eventually just had enough of all the nonsense, and his first step in exerting his independence was to change his name."

Gracie nibbled a shortbread, then continued, "Betty told me about the name change and later her joy at your birth. I was very sad to learn that she and your baby brother had died. Annie and Betty—both gone as a result of childbirth." Gracie sighed, remembering the young mothers.

"What can you tell me about my mother?"

"Your mother was a sweet girl, Lucy, and so very much younger than Janos. To look at her, you'd think she was just a delicate little thing, but she worked hard. She was a farm labourer and one of the better workers during the tobacco harvest. There were many young people who worked the harvest, but few who found employment earlier in the season. Because she worked so hard, Betty was always fully employed. I think that attitude attracted Janos because he was a hard-worker as well. There were other women, some closer to your father's age, but he was never interested—not until Betty."

Gracie finished her first cup of tea, then she poured herself a second cupful and helped herself to a second shortbread before continuing her story.

"I remember there was one about five years younger than Janos . . . Oh, what *was* her name? I can't recall it right now. Anyway, I don't remember whether she was interested in Laszlo or Janos, but she died by suicide about the same time as your parents married, which is why I recall her. I think she had a son. I'm sorry, I think my memory is going a bit fuzzy. I promise to record more about this for you. Assuming that I remember."

They spent a short time looking at the contents of Gracie's little box, but the photos were primarily from her time in

Ireland. One was a portrait of John, Betty, and baby Lucy. Others were annual portraits of Lucy as a child, until age seven. That was the last one.

Although it was nearly lunchtime, Gracie decided it was time for a nap. She pressed the Taylor photos into Lucy's hand and packed the others back into the little box. Then she gave Lucy a quick peck on the cheek and said goodbye. She picked up her little box of photos, and tottered off into the bedroom.

"Do you think I tired her too much?" Lucy asked, concerned.

"No, Gracie has her way of indicating when a visit is over. If she were tired, she would have closed the visit sooner."

Lucy nodded, trusting Juliette's judgment. Again, Lucy signed the register at reception, noting their departure time. And again, Ashley looked as if she wanted to say something, but didn't. Lucy was far too engrossed in her thoughts about Gracie's stories to catch Ashley's hesitation. Lucy and Juliette left the building, walking past the small tree with pink flowers and beneath the large tulip tree, as they returned to Juliette's vehicle.

Once they were back on the road, Lucy followed up on a suggestion that Gracie had made and asked Juliette, "So, what's the story regarding how the estate ended up going from Paul to Gracie and by-passing my father?"

"The trust established by Peter and then modified by Jozsef was tight and horribly unfair. It was designed to accumulate assets and very poorly structured to distribute them. While there was a male in a position to inherit, no female could. So, the assets were inherited by Laszlo and, upon his death, by his son Paul, by-passing his mother. She, such as Gracie before her, received an allowance upon the death of her husband and secured the right to live in her house while the house itself remained secure within the trust. In Gracie's case, Laszlo had been trying to evict her by his threats of bodily harm. This type of trust is now considered to be outside the public good because it's so unfair. If asked, we would have made that argument for Goldie, as we had for Gracie, but she was never our client. Unfortunately, the one matter that the trust was very clear about is that your father was not permitted to inherit or control any aspect of it. Save for his continued receipt of a modest allowance—the amount established many years before—he received nothing. Therefore, when Laszlo, then Goldie, then Paul, passed away in succession over a period of three years, Gracie, rather than your father, inherited the trust, which, by the way, has now been dissolved. As the beneficiary, you will receive the estate unencumbered upon Gracie's passing."

"And Gracie said you'd be better informed regarding whether my father was adopted by the Szabos or was a ward of the Szabos."

"I'm reasonably certain he was adopted, but I'll see if I can locate any documentation on that for you. It does sound as if Jozsef wasn't really in agreement with the spirit of adoption and treated him as a ward in certain ways."

A road crew had begun work and traffic slowed as Juliette negotiated the pylons, redirecting her attention to the road and away from the conversation.

Lost in her thoughts, Lucy suddenly remembered, "I should send a message to Kent so he can contact your office about Gold Farm." Lucy sent her message off to him and upon returning her phone to her purse, she saw the envelope Juliette had given her earlier in the day. She opened it, and began to skim its contents:

> *Giovanni Sarto*
> *Date of Birth: August 26, 1900*
> *Place of Birth: Latte, Quebec*
> *Work Experience:*
> *- uncertain, likely clerical*

- *Garner & Garner, Montreal*
    - *A. Garner's notes indicate a facility with languages, self-taught with a broad range of skills and aptitudes.*
    - *Facilitator and liaison with contracted Italian immigrant labourers.*
    - *First alternative identity created: Jean Couture*
- *Garner & Garner, Toronto*
    - *Providing translation services, B. Garner valued his opinion in a broad range of matters, apparently he was a quick study.*
    - *Additional identity provided: Johannes Schneider*
    L'Orté Island (101 ha) and
    L'Orté Point (3,278 ha)
    - *Named by Giovanni Sarto (previously parcels were only legal descriptions and sometimes informal local and inconsistent names).*
    - *Land transfers show that the properties were previously owned by a variety of people. There were 12 parcels in total, including one particularly large parcel owned by Peter Szabo, which was sold to Johannes Schneider and subsequently to Giovanni Sarto. Other parcels were sold to Jean Couture before being sold to Giovanni Sarto. (Note: this took time to sort out after Gianni's death/murder, but it was finally determined years later through court proceedings that Giovanni Sarto was the rightful owner of both the island and the point at the time of his death and had clear title.)*

– A trust was established in 1933 directing that upon his death, all of Giovanni Sarto's holdings were to be held and managed for the use of Annie Hogan. Annie made a will at the same time, naming Gracie her heir.

"I don't understand—there's another trust?" Lucy puzzled.

"Yes. The one you've discussed with Gracie has been dissolved and concerned only the Szabos. The trust mentioned in my notes, the L'Orté Trust, originated with Gianni and was both set up by Garner & Garner and managed by the firm ever since. It took many years to satisfy a variety of interested parties that Gianni was the rightful owner. When that was finally accomplished, I think someone dropped the ball on the file. It took ages to locate information on Annie and locate her will. It shouldn't have because it had been drawn up by our firm, but it did. A and B would have been very disappointed in us. However, I think this all worked out for the best for Gracie because by the time we had identified that Gracie was the rightful beneficiary of the L'Orté Trust, Jozsef had died. She was so frightened by Laszlo that she moved to Ireland and had us continue to manage the trust. She took a very small role in directing it."

"I'm eager to hear more, but I think I've pretty much hit information overload at this point. Would you stay for a late lunch so Kent can hear all about it as well?"

"Understandable. Unfortunately, I can't accept your invitation, but perhaps we could do that another day."

Lucy was disappointed, but she appreciated that these matters were not the only concerns for Juliette. *She must have other clients.*

CHAPTER 15

Upon returning home early that afternoon, Lucy found Kent in his office, looking very content. When he saw Lucy at his doorway, he arose and greeted her with a warm smile and embrace.

"I take it from the smile on your face that you were able to make first contact for Gold Farm," she said, rather pleased with herself.

"You take it correctly, my dear. All thanks to you, Juliette came through and I have an appointment to meet in Harkness at Gold Farm tomorrow afternoon. Do you want to come with me? A drive in the country on a lovely spring day might do us both a world of good. What do you say?"

"Are you planning to drive, or will Albin be driving?"

"If Albin drives, it'll be easier for us to talk because I won't need to pay attention to the road."

"That's what I was thinking. If there's time, and we still want to, after your meeting at the property, we could drive to Simcoe and do a quick visit with Gracie just to introduce you."

"Sounds like a plan."

Now that a major roadblock to his new construction project was gone, the old Kent was back. Lucy thought that sometimes he put too much of himself into his projects, leaving little in reserve for himself. She was looking forward to their drive together.

Helen had prepared salade niçoise. Lucy retrieved the two plates from the refrigerator and brought them to the table while Kent rummaged through a drawer looking for the corkscrew. Lucy pointed it out to him. "You can't see it for looking at it," she declared, laughing.

Having successfully located the elusive corkscrew, he selected a wine, paused, and then asked, "Do you want a glass of wine tonight or not?"

"Actually, not tonight, thanks. Just water for me. Have you checked what she's prepared for our dessert?" Lucy began to slice a baguette, which was still warm from the oven.

"Ah-ha, look what I've found! La tourte sucrée aux blettes." The pastry Helen had prepared contained Swiss chard and was one of Kent's favourites. "I don't think I'll have wine tonight either, just water. I'll have a double espresso after dessert."

As they started their meal, Lucy began, "You're familiar with hectares, right? You know I've no mathematical concept of distance or area at all, so I was wondering, 101 hectares—is that a tiny amount of land? Can you give me a sense of it?"

"Well, that's—give me a moment here—250 acres, if that helps. No? From the look on your face, I see it doesn't. Let's just say that it's a medium-size family farm for southern Ontario. Why do you ask?"

Rather than answering, Lucy pressed on, "So, 3,278 hectares?"

"Three-two-seven-eight hectares, according to my calculations, works out to 8,100 acres, which is— nearly 33 square kilometres. A piece of land 5.7 kilometres by 5.7 kilometres. That's ranch-size and you don't usually find that around here as a single parcel. That's the equivalent of more than 5,504 Canadian football fields. Does that help? Why do you ask?"

"Oh my," she murmured, then began to tell him about L'Orté Island and L'Orté Point with its lodge, or what now remained of it. "I'll need you with me when I discuss this further with Juliette. This is getting to be too much for me to process."

"I know nothing about either of those properties, Lucy, but I'll be glad to provide you with additional eyes and ears."

"And brain," Lucy interjected.

"And brain," Kent stated, his voice calm and reassuring. "Fortunately, you've time before you need to do anything about either of them, if at all. Are there any buildings on either parcel? You mentioned the remains of a lodge. Anything else?"

Lucy, who had just taken a forkful of tuna, shook her head and shrugged. "I haven't the slightest idea," she mumbled.

Although there was much to discuss, both were overwhelmed by the magnitude of the L'Orté properties and chose to put further discussion aside for the moment. The rich aroma of roasted beans filled the air and their focus shifted to dessert and coffee, and each other.

Later that night, when they returned to the master suite, they kissed goodnight and agreed to meet in the gym for a quick morning workout before heading off to Harkness and Gold Farm.

Alone in her room, Lucy withdrew the photo of Gianni and Annie from her purse and resolved to get a suitable frame or maybe an album, in the hope that more photos could be located. She glanced at the few notes she had taken while visiting with Gracie and the year she had written: 1983. She would have been three years old. How could Gracie have expected her to recall anything that happened when she was so young? Although curious, she decided against listening to the audio recording, saving it for another day. She needed her sleep, and tonight not even a late-night espresso could keep her awake.

"There you are!" Kent exclaimed from the doorway of the studio, the morning sun catching the look of concern on his face.

Groggy from sleep, Lucy reluctantly opened her eyes, increasingly aware that she was not in her bedroom. "Oh no, not again," she groaned.

For the second time, Lucy found herself on the floor of her studio, at the foot of an easel holding a large canvas with a completed, though unsigned, painting. In many ways, this painting was much as the first one—dark with dramatic lighting. But the scene was quite different and featured the head of a young adult male framed within what looked to be a doorway and viewed as a dog might, looking upward at its master. The young man was reasonably attractive and had dark hair and a ruddy complexion. Lucy was drawn to the intensity of his stare, but she wasn't certain what to make of the subject's expression.

As she had on the previous occasion, she took a dagger striper in hand and, using black acrylic, signed the painting, Awen. Although the painting was more upsetting in its subject matter than the earlier one had been, the fact of the painting and the odd process of its creation was less so. Nevertheless, she hoped this was not going to become her new normal.

Kent had come prepared with her fuzzy slippers and silken robe with the pink sash. As he helped her don the robe, her eye caught sight of an awen in the painting. She sighed, trusting that there were others as well.

"What do you want to do?" Kent enquired, prepared to follow her lead regarding their schedule.

"I sure don't feel like exercising now because clearly I didn't get much restful sleep last night, but that shouldn't stop you. I'll just potter about: shower, nap, breakfast . . . I'm really not sure. Just let me catch my bearings here. It's rather disorienting. The only thing I *do* know is that I still plan to go to Gold Farm with you. Oh, I don't have my cellphone with me. Would you, please, take a few photos of the painting? One overall and the other a close-up of just the face?"

Kent, disquieted, remained silent. He took the photos she had requested and sent the jpeg files to her in an email. They left the studio, and she locked the door.

"I've loaded the cooler with water, and you've got a thermos of coffee and some snacks, protein bars, and nuts in case you lot get peckish," Helen announced. "Anything else you think you might want to eat before I have Albin take this to the car?" Helen was fussing again, likely in reaction to the news of Lucy's new nocturnal wanderings. She hadn't seen the most recent painting, but Lucy and Kent both knew that once she did, there would be a significant uptick in her rate of fussing and hovering.

Albin deftly guided the red Tesla sedan through the traffic, which was somewhat heavy but moving well. He wore his usual uniform, consisting of black trousers and a white polo shirt, with aviator sunglasses to complete his look. He was fit and fifty, clearly having benefitted from having ready access to the exercise facilities available at the Gillespie estate.

Kent wore one of several suits he had recently purchased at Roman's, and Lucy thought he looked quite handsome. She thought he smelled wonderful too; the eau de toilette he wore was a blend of neroli, green apple, and bitter orange top note, with a rosemary, cyclamen, and thyme middle note. The back note was oriental cedar, tonka bean, and vanilla. These facts were not readily apparent to her, but she enjoyed being the beneficiary of their overall effect.

Despite her initial enthusiasm for the drive to Gold Farm, Lucy remained fatigued. Even her wardrobe selection had taken longer than usual. She had selected and then discarded several outfits before deciding to wear dressy jeans, a silk blouse, and a cashmere jacket. She wasn't planning to take part in any of the discussion Kent would have with the lawyer from Garner & Garner so could dress more casually. However, she made a bit more effort than she might have done otherwise because she expected to visit with Gracie. The scent of Kent's eau de toilette relaxed her and at various times she considered just curling up and falling asleep. Nevertheless, she was determined to push forward.

Lucy sent a quick message to Yoichi, attaching the photos of her new painting. Yoichi's response was rapid. Recently, she had become the agent for a photographer who did highly technical photographic modifications. He had access to prime equipment, and the knowledge to use it. Yoichi suggested that the photos be shared with the photographer, in the hope of accessing greater detail in a blow-up. Lucy thought it was a great idea and gladly gave her permission.

The sky was clear, a perfect spring day. As Albin drove, Kent began to entertain them with a recent anecdote. "So Roman's was having a heating problem when I was there before my trip. It was during that severe cold snap and the furnace was out. I thought Julius owned the building, but apparently he leases, so he calls in the landlord's caretaker, a guy by the name of Lincoln, to investigate the cause. Lincoln comes back to report that there's nothing wrong with the heating unit. He says it's because of all the metal—the racks and display shelving—which he claims are radiating cold into the store. A whole new theory of thermodynamics: radiating cold. Julius just looked at me when Lincoln said this, but I couldn't keep quiet. With a straight face, I told Lincoln I found that confusing—with all the warm fabrics, wools and such in the store, shouldn't that have counter-acted the cooling effect?"

Albin laughed aloud.

"Lincoln is now referred to as 'The Missing Link.' Not only does he lack a basic comprehension of such things, I understand he's also hard to contact and convince to come out to investigate problems. I wouldn't be surprised to see Julius move to another location."

Lucy was tired, and she wasn't enjoying the day as much as she had anticipated. While she had enjoyed Kent's humorous anecdote, she wanted to share with him the information she had garnered from Gracie the previous day, and bring him up to speed. She couldn't come up with a skillful way to steer the conversation in that direction, so she just launched into it.

She outlined the history of the Szabo Trust and how it functioned, and especially how Laszlo had attempted to frighten Gracie away from her legitimate claim to the house in Simcoe. And she shared the reasoning that Gracie had offered regarding Janos Szabo's change of name to John Taylor.

"Yeah, that would certainly do it. How old was he?" Kent asked.

"My father changed his name just before I was born, so Szabo was never my name. That would have been 1979 or 1980, I guess, and therefore, he would have been about forty-five-ish—that's an advanced age to finally make such a statement and change your name, isn't it? I mean, that's got to mess with your personal identity, your sense of self, don't you think?"

"Perhaps your father was particularly patient and trusting. I think that sometimes when people possess such attributes—positive attributes—in abundance, they find it especially difficult to recognize that other people they're dealing with suffer an extreme deficit in those areas. It just doesn't occur to them. Gracie's already told you that Peter and Jozsef were horrible people. It's logical to assume that Laszlo would be as well, both through nature and nurture as they say."

"Well, we know that my father's nature was totally different from that of the Szabos, but his nurture, his environment, his home life during his formative years in particular, would have been largely similar to Laszlo's, except that Laszlo was the favoured son. I wonder how conflicted he must have felt being who he was in his heart, yet living in an environment that was created by these horrible people and reflected their value system."

"Hmm-m. I wonder what Laszlo's son, Paul, was like," Kent pondered. "You must have met him, no?"

"I guess so," Lucy said, scrunching up her face, thinking. "Not really . . . Oh, I don't know. He was at least fifteen years my senior, male and a Szabo. So, there wasn't much overlap with my life. Now that I've focussed on it, perhaps some memory will bubble to the surface. Sounds as if I'm headed for another sleepless night."

"Maybe it already has," Kent offered, "bubbled to the surface, as you say."

"The face in the painting, you think?" Lucy settled deep into her seat and remained quietly thoughtful. Kent was silent.

Shortly thereafter, the GPS announced that they had arrived at their destination in Harkness, and Albin pulled the Tesla into the long driveway. Located in tobacco country, the community thrived while smoking was popular and considered a healthy pastime. With the recognition that smoking caused lung problems, many of the farms switched to other— albeit less lucrative—crops. Over the following years, some farmers sold their land for development. As a result, Gold Farm was situated amid properties which had been sold to other developers many years earlier. It was obvious why Kent sought to purchase the property, and less so why it should have been so difficult to get to this stage in the dealings.

The house appeared to have been built about 1960 and though large, suffered from serious neglect. This was a house completely lacking in aesthetics, even in its time. There was no reason for this building to continue to exist, unless practical use could be made of it for storage, or as a construction office instead of bringing a trailer onto the property. A more recent structure—a large garage—abutted the house. The garage showed signs of having been constructed about twenty years later, not that this was indicated by the style of the building because there was none. It was merely that the garage wasn't as dilapidated as the house itself.

A short time after they pulled into the driveway, an anthracite-blue Mercedes-Benz made the same turn. Juliette stepped from her vehicle while Kent exited the Tesla, holding the door open for Lucy. The women greeted each other, and Lucy introduced Kent to Juliette.

"Are we waiting for the owner, or are you speaking for the owner on the sale of this property?" Kent enquired.

"I'm here to provide specifics and am not authorized to make decisions about the property. For that, you will need to ask the owner of the property," she said, and then she looked at Lucy. "This morning, Gracie decided to sign Gold Farm over to you. What I need from you is one dollar, please, to secure the deal. The property is unencumbered, that I can guarantee."

Lucy looked at Kent and he at her, and he nodded. "Yes, I'm very familiar with the property, but I missed the Szabo connection somehow. If I recall, the property was owned through a numbered company."

"Yes, you are quite right. Szabo business dealings were awash in numbered companies, and tracing all of it has been quite a challenge. Here are the keys—one for the house, such as it is, and another for the garage. Also, an envelope containing copies of existing documents. Notarized copies of the newly-executed documents will be forwarded to you soon," Juliette explained as Lucy signed where it was requested, and dug in her purse for a loonie.

Juliette continued, "The house is completely full. Laszlo's wife, Goldie, lived and eventually died there. She was a hoarder, so the house is packed floor-to-ceiling with boxes, and stuff bursting from boxes. The same is true of the garage. Furthermore, she had purchased vehicles that were no longer road-worthy and used them for additional storage. The driveway and yard were cluttered with vans that had come here to die." Juliette couldn't hide her disgust as she described the situation.

"I certainly don't know what things were like when her husband was alive, but she was on her own from 1993, when Laszlo died, until she died in 1995. I understand that Paul dug through some of the stuff but didn't dispose of anything much, and then he died in 1996. Garner & Garner came onto the scene during the effort to locate Gracie, and, subsequently, Gracie arranged for the disposal of some of the more obvious waste. The entire process was filmed, and it was quite a mess. I had the film converted to a digital file for you," she said, handing a thumb drive to Lucy. "Gracie thought it would be best for you to have the opportunity to search through it all yourself for whatever treasure may be hiding amid the dross. Personally, I think what lurks there is just more dross. No one has touched it for the past fifteen years—not since Gracie pulled the clean-up crew from the job. It's not going to be pleasant.

"I hate to shock you and run, but unless you have any questions about the property, I'll leave you to it," Juliette announced, noticeably eager to withdraw. "I'm available should you need anything concerning Gracie, and I trust you'll be arranging visits without me from now on, but as for Gold Farm," she nodded to them, "Kent, Lucy, I think we're done here. If you need a lawyer, Mr. Gillespie, please keep Garner & Garner in mind. It's been a pleasure."

"But we also need to discuss the L'Orté properties with you sometime, and I must say I'm feeling rushed here, and I really don't understand why, Juliette. If not now, then when?" Lucy could feel the hairs on the back of her neck begin to prickle like a cat's.

"I'm sorry, Lucy, Kent, I scheduled this meeting quickly for you because I knew that it was important to you. I have facilitated a rapid transfer in the ownership of the property from Gracie to Lucy. Based on the reason for our meeting, the matters have been concluded. I must now complete the filing of these documents back at the office and arrange to have your copies couriered to you. I will clear my schedule if necessary to accommodate whatever date and time you want to discuss the L'Orté properties—you name the place, just let me know."

Kent and Lucy broke from their stunned silence. They said their cordial goodbyes to Juliette and then returned to their vehicle as Juliette pulled away in her car.

"Well, that was odd," Lucy commented.

"To say the least," Kent replied. "I've never experienced anything close to that. And you said you actually *like* this woman!"

"Perhaps she's right. I mean, Gold Farm is mine now, free and clear. What are you planning to offer me for it? There may be other interested parties, you know," Lucy teased. "We'll eventually get around to the L'Orté properties, but for now we do have enough on our plate, so to speak."

"Okay, let's go with that."

Lucy dangled the keys in front of Kent and suggested that all three of them take a look inside.

Albin changed his footwear and grabbed a flashlight. The windows of the house were boarded securely; there would be little natural light. Then he looked down at Kent's shoes and shook his head. "Missus, I'd prefer to see sturdier shoes on your feet, but you, sir, are hopeless. Unless you consider those disposable, that is." Clearly, Albin was in his element. The Cheshire cat look on his face confirmed that for both of them.

After Lucy's unsuccessful attempt to open the front door, Albin was given the keys. A short time later, and with a bit of jiggling, the door was unlocked. As he opened the door, the stale and foul air wafted toward them, assailing their olfactory senses. "Ooh, I think this is a hazmat job."

Lucy and Kent both agreed with his assessment. Albin shone the flashlight around the room very slowly, and it was apparent that with the boxes stacked as they were, little light would have penetrated the gloom even in the absence of the boards. Albin tried moving forward through a path set among the towers of plastic and cardboard boxes, but was brought to a full stop. There was no way to determine what lay beyond. Lucy suggested they should secure the door again and take a look into the garage.

The garage door was particularly sturdy, and, though it wasn't new, it showed little wear from use. Although the locking mechanism was a bit corroded, Albin worked his magic once again and opened the large door, sliding it up and parallel to the ceiling. As in the house, the entire garage was packed full of an assortment of boxes, and in some cases their contents were strewn about. The building was insulated, but whereas there was sheetrock covering the interior walls, the ceiling remained largely unfinished. A bulkhead covered with sheetrock had been constructed on the ceiling, forming a U-shape surrounding the raised garage door. The floor was poured concrete, and there was a good slope leading downward to the level of the yard. All three acknowledged that they didn't detect any dampness in the garage, so they were optimistic that none of the boxes would have water damage.

"I can't tell yet about the house itself, but the garage will serve you well during construction," Albin surmised. "Hmm-m. Whatever was in those storage vehicles ended up shoved into the house and in here when they got rid of the vehicles. Mould spores, maybe hantavirus if there's mice. Fun stuff! I wouldn't go further without proper hazmat gear." Neither Kent nor Lucy disagreed with him.

They stepped back beyond the garage foundation, and Albin swung the garage door downward in its tracks and locked it. Then he presented the key to Lucy.

"See, my shoes were just fine," Kent said, directing his comment to Albin.

As they climbed back into their vehicle, Lucy asked, "Care to pop by L'Orté Park to see Gracie for a short visit?"

"That sounds good. She did just give you—excuse me—*sell* you this huge property. You're going to make a sizeable chunk of cash out of it when you sell it to that property developer who hangs around with you," Kent opined, winking at Lucy. "But on a more serious note, you'll need to get this formally assessed and—"

"And would you please handle everything?" Lucy interjected. "I know nothing about such things. This is your area of expertise, not mine. Besides, I can't begin to express just how burdened I'm becoming. It's as if I'm drowning, suddenly submerged in this terrible family history and all this *stuff*. The property is, for all practical purposes, yours, so do what it is you do, Mr. Gillespie."

Albin reset the GPS and they followed the driveway to the main road and turned toward Simcoe.

CHAPTER 16

He had a small bouquet of spring flowers in hand and had just signed the guest register. He was planning to affix his signature a second time to correct for the blank he had been forced to leave the previous day, when a senior employee, who was unfamiliar to him, whisked it away. Ashley was otherwise occupied, so he made his way quickly to the elevator, sharing it with two employees.

"Oh, Ashley says to tell you that you should let Ms. Hogan know to expect guests shortly and ask if she wants tea and shortbread brought to her room," an employee whose tag identified her as 'Jessica P' said to one whose tag read 'Jessica R'.

"Okay. Heh, did ya' see? Dragon Lady's in one of her moods again. I think she's gonna tear a strip off Ashley—somethin' to do with the register, I think," said one of the pair to which the other sniffled, "Poor Ash!" The first nodded her head solemnly.

He heaved a sigh of irritation. *Three trips to this place so far and little to show for it.* The photographs from the first trip had revealed next to nothing useful for him. He wasn't certain what he had expected to find in Gracie's rooms, but he had hoped that seeing those things she treasured from the past might give him an idea. *Time is running out.* He would need to be more assertive. He needed a new tactic. *And now Dragon Lady was giving Ashley trouble.*

L'Orté Point

"But of course! A name that sounds French—I should have guessed the place would have a mansard roof. By the way, any idea what 'L'Orté' means or is?" Kent was on a bit of a roll; predictable architecture irked him.

Lucy stifled a chuckle; Albin turned toward her and smiled. She chided Kent impishly. "Kent, dear," she said, getting his attention, "You know you're a snob, right?"

"Yep, just like you when it comes to fine art. And, just like you, I can keep my opinions to myself when required. Have no fear, I only rant in private."

The parking lot was nearly full. Albin parked the luxury sedan in a space that had just become available near the tulip tree. He decided to stay with the vehicle, and Lucy suspected he was going to grab a bite to eat from the provisions Helen had packed.

In his usual gentlemanly fashion, Kent held the door for Lucy as they entered, and she immediately went to the reception desk where she was greeted by Ashley. Lucy would have made small talk with her, but Ashley's supervisor had come to speak with her, so Lucy availed herself of the ballpoint pen on the desk, and entered their names in the guest register. There had been many visitors in the facility that day, but Lucy happened to spot that a signator from the previous day—who hadn't signed out—was the same as one who had just signed in prior to their arrival. *Perhaps that was the topic of discussion between Ashley and her supervisor*, she considered.

Rather than chance encountering Gracie's visitors, he continued farther along the hallway and took a turn toward the far wing of the residence, retreating into the garden where he sat and gave thought to what he might now do. It had been necessary to park his vehicle rather near to the industrial waste bin at one end of the parking lot when he arrived. He planned to dispose of the bouquet. He had no further use for it. *A well-dressed man attracts attention, especially when carrying a bouquet of flowers.* As he lowered the bin's lid back into position, a man of his general age dressed in black trousers and a white polo shirt, and sporting aviator sunglasses rounded the corner, surprising him. Although they didn't speak, on some level there had been more communication than he had wanted, which was none. He wasted no time getting into his car and driving out of the lot, away from Gracie and Albin and Lucy and Kent.

Gracie's door was wide open; she was waiting. Lucy was glad she had phoned ahead to let Gracie know she and Kent would be visiting. "I'm delighted you called, Lucy. Otherwise, I might have been in the swimming pool or doing chair yoga, and I don't even like chair yoga," Gracie said in a conspiratorial tone.

"Grandaunt Gracie, this is my husband, Kent."

Kent extended his hand toward Gracie in greeting, afraid he might hurt the fragile-looking elderly woman, but Gracie grabbed ahold of him and pulled him in close for a hug. "Don't worry, I won't break!" A surprised Kent survived Gracie's hug attack and smiled broadly at the welcome. "Come and sit yourself down over here," she directed him.

They followed Gracie and took their seats in the living room. Gracie had arranged for tea and shortbread, which were waiting with cups and the other necessary items on a tray on the coffee table. While Gracie poured the tea, Lucy began to thank her for her generosity in transferring ownership of Gold Farm to her, but Gracie waved her off.

"Well, Juliette explained that it just so happened to be a property Kent had enquired about, not knowing I owned it, so I thought—why not? Makes sense. The buildings are ugly as sin. Always have been. Neither Laszlo nor Goldie ever had any taste. I presume the yard looked much as it did when they lived there—tall weeds. However," she said, pausing and making eye-contact with Lucy, "there might be something of value to you hidden in all that garbage. I really don't know. I hope so, for your sake. Nevertheless, it is the only hoard of Szabo stuff that remains—especially fitting because Goldie was a hoarder."

"I understand that you had some of the stuff carted away when it came into your possession," Lucy said.

"Yes, it had to be done. I didn't get rid of anything but absolute rubbish. Not only did Goldie keep everything, but she died there. Her son, Paul, lived elsewhere at the time, and it was quite a while before her body was found. Clearly, he wasn't visiting often. It wasn't a pleasant sight. She'd had some sort of accident in the basement—likely as a result of a heart attack, stroke, or just falling amid all the stuff she had piled up."

Gracie paused for a moment before continuing, "Anyway, he must have gone through those boxes himself. I don't know what he was looking for, but he sure made a mess, scattering things all over the place. What I had removed was stuff that was rotting, such as old food, and things that Paul had scattered about, but only after my workers examined it for anything hidden—money or jewellery. The old cars and vans she'd parked outside were chock-full of stuff as well. If anything was in a good box, it was transferred to the house where there was room, but that ended up closing off some of the pathways. It'll be quite a challenge for you."

Lucy and Kent shook their heads in amazement. Lucy reached for a shortbread and found herself at a loss for words. This was a great opportunity for her to learn about the family in which her father had grown up, but the work involved overwhelmed her.

"I do thank you, Gracie, very much, in fact. The rest is now up to me." Lucy sighed inaudibly, then continued, "By the way, try as I might, I can't remember my mother's maiden name. Do you happen to recall it?"

"Not off-hand, dear, but if it occurs to me, I'll record it for you. I think her people were from the West—perhaps Alberta. I saw them but once, and I don't think they were even at the wedding. I have remembered the name of that girl though, the one I thought was sweet on either your father or Laszlo—the one who died by suicide—it was *Elda*. It's been so long, I can't recall her last name. I promise to work on my recordings, so when you drop by next time, there'll be lots of information for you."

"I have a question if I may," Kent began, "Would I be correct in saying that the relationship between Goldie and her son wasn't particularly good?"

"Oh my, no, it certainly wasn't. Most of the trouble was due to Laszlo, but Goldie went along with everything, so she's equally responsible as far as I'm concerned. When Paul wanted to attend university, his father insisted he hitchhike all the way to and from the Waterloo campus each day. Paul started school but thought he could arrange to stay with friends instead of returning home each night. Laszlo did not approve of that and stopped Paul's allowance. And remember—that allowance was money Paul had earned and put into Laszlo's account, just as your father and Laszlo had into Jozsef's."

"That's a distance one-way of about seventy-five kilometres!" Kent exclaimed. "That's got to have broken the kid."

"Oh, I'm sure it was one of the things because it wasn't long before he dropped out. But definitely not the only thing. With the Szabos, there was always something in the works."

"But Laszlo must have thought well of his wife. I mean, Gold Farm is named after Goldie, right?" Lucy asked.

"I'm not too sure about that, dear. Laszlo renamed it after Jozsef died. It was called something else before I took off for Ireland, though I can't recall that either. Funny, the things you remember and the things you forget."

Lucy wanted to end the visit on a happy note. "Would you care to spend a day at our home, perhaps next week?"

"That would be lovely, dear."

"We'll pick you up in the morning and—" But Gracie didn't let Lucy complete her statement.

"Unfortunately, I think my travelling days are past. I have my funny little habits, and whenever I get tired, I prefer to sleep in my own bed. I thank you, but I must decline your very kind invitation—both of you. But if you have photos, I always love to see photos."

"I do have a few photos, though not of our home. Does the person in this painting remind you of anyone you knew back then?" Lucy asked as she showed Gracie the photos of the previous night's sleep-painting.

"Let me see . . . interesting, a bit scary . . . He does look somewhat familiar, but I can't place him. Then again, at my age and when you've seen so many people over the years, everyone starts to look familiar. I think there's not as much variation among people as some like to think there is."

Lucy switched out the recording device, and conversation diverted from the Szabos and toward more pleasant topics for the balance of their visit. Having finished their tea and shortbread, Lucy and Kent excused themselves and said their goodbyes to Gracie with a promise to visit again soon. Lucy signed the guest register, noting the time of their departure. Having been chastised by her supervisor, Ashley's behaviour was subdued, and she failed to make eye contact with Lucy.

Back in the parking lot, Albin was nowhere to be seen. However, as they approached their car, he arrived, having taken a walk around the park-like setting.

CHAPTER 17

When they arrived home, Albin and Kent hunkered down in Kent's office to devise a plan of attack for the Szabo hoard of boxes. Kent wanted to begin implementation of a plan later that day, or the next at the latest. The sooner Lucy's concerns were addressed, the sooner the site would be available to him and his investors to begin development.

Lucy changed into a comfortable tracksuit, uncertain what she would do for the balance of the day. She didn't want to listen to more of Gracie's audio recording, just in case it triggered another sleep-painting session so soon after the last one. She needed a good night's sleep.

Helen was just finishing the tidying and cleaning of the studio when Lucy arrived, looking forward to enjoying an espresso while seated in her favourite chair. Helen was hovering, clearly concerned that Lucy had spent the previous night painting.

"What's on your mind, Helen?"

Helen sighed and gave Lucy a concerned smile. They each knew what the other would say, so there was no need for words. Then, just before she left the studio, Helen looked at the first of the two sleep-paintings and puzzled aloud, "You always say you know little about plants, yet you've painted these very accurately, you know. This is a pawpaw . . . over here you've got a blue ash . . . and some honey locust," she said, pointing to specific areas of the painting. "I just don't see how you could do that, especially because you were asleep at the time. Very odd indeed."

Lucy was intrigued. She could understand Helen's bewilderment; now she was bewildered, too. "So, which is which?" Helen pointed to those she had named and identified them for Lucy. "And what might these three have in common with one another, Helen?"

Helen thought about it for a moment. "Well, all three are distinctly Carolinian species, so would be found in a region very near Lake Erie. The pawpaw thrives in moist soil, so you find it near rivers. The honey locust is planted a lot now as an ornamental, but it would occur naturally on some of the Erie islands, and the blue ash as well. It's quite rare here, so generally just on the Erie islands."

"When you say Erie islands, that includes L'Orté Island, doesn't it?" Helen nodded her head. "Thanks, I appreciate the information. I've been amazed by your ability to keep the orchids in my bedroom so beautiful, but I'm particularly impressed by your keen eye in noticing the specific types of trees in that painting. You're the only person to have picked up on that."

Helen was noticeably pleased with the praise Lucy had given her for her botanical knowledge and left the studio happier than Lucy had found her.

Lucy thought about it awhile, but there were so many thoughts competing for her attention that she couldn't come to any conclusion based on Helen's information. She decided to send Donald Gallagher whatever additional family information she had obtained since she last updated him, in the hope that he might have something significant for her in return. Shortly after sending off her email, she received a reply from Donald.

Have located some information on a Peter Szabo (d.1933) who lived in what is now Simcoe. Likely born before 1870. Still trying to determine when/how/from where he came to Canada. Name turns up as that of a Klondike gold miner and business owner in 1896-1899, mentioned in Dawson City records—photo available but of poor quality. Also mentioned in development of oil fields of Petrolia, Ontario, 1899-1927—photo available but of poor quality. Occupation listed as a farmer from 1928 until his death. Considerable property purchased in Ontario, some of it used for tobacco, logging . . . I haven't done a detailed search of property records, thus the general statement. No marriage information located.

Jozsef Szabo, D.O.B. 1910.01.27, (d.1979), father listed as Peter Szabo, mother's information unreadable. Born in Petrolia, Ontario. Married Gracie Hogan in 1959. Could find no other marriage listed.

Erzsebet Szabo, D.O.B. 1910.01.27, (d.1958), father listed as Peter Szabo, mother's information unreadable. Born in Petrolia, Ontario.

Note: Jozsef and Erzsebet Szabo were twins—brother/sister, not husband/wife. Will continue to dig in case we can clarify further.

Laszlo Szabo, D.O.B. 1933.11.21, (d.1993), mother listed as Erzsebet Szabo, father listed as Jozsef Szabo.

Hope things are going well for you. Thanks for additional information. Will continue.

Donald

Lucy read Donald's email several times. *Twins. He might have led with that bit. They lied about being married; what other lies might there be?* Lucy wondered what Gracie's reaction might be to this information. Might it cause her to re-interpret some of the things she thought she knew? *Maybe I shouldn't tell her, it might be too shocking.*

Lucy, espresso in hand, stood in front of her first sleep-painting, the one Helen had found so interesting. She wasn't sure how long a time she spent staring at the jumble of rock and vegetation, but eventually she came to a decision. *Clearly, there's more to this painting, more than meets the eye.* She called Yoichi.

"Hi, I won't keep you long. I was wondering if the photographer you mentioned could enhance a photo of that first sleep-painting as well. I don't want to be a bother, but it might be very helpful."

"Oh, Lucy, I was just going to give you a call about that. The photographer's name is James Gregory, and I've told him a bit about the paintings. He's here right now, actually. I suggest you speak with him directly; it might be best." And with that, Yoichi was gone.

Lucy exchanged pleasantries with James Gregory, and they discussed the reason for her call. "I looked at the files Yoichi has—the photographs of what she says is the second of two paintings," the photographer began. "I would certainly be able to do what she has suggested, which is to enhance and clarify the detail, and then convert the face, specifically the eyes—into more of a photo of a person rather than a photo of the painting of a person. I've got all the software. However, I'd prefer to take my own photos and work on them rather than use these."

Lucy was thrilled. "Sure, that's not a problem for me. The reason I was phoning Yoichi was to see if you might also work on the details of the first painting. It wouldn't require increasing the human element, if I might call it that. It's a matter of clarifying the detail. I'm finding it difficult to assess what's depicted because I keep getting lost in the brushstrokes. I don't know how else to describe it."

"I think I understand. And sure, I'll work on the other one as well; it's quite interesting. Again, I'd need to take my own photos. When may I drop by? There's no concern about time of day to catch the light. I'll have all of my equipment with me."

As it happened, James Gregory lived in Niagara Falls, and it was decided that as his business at the Song Gallery was nearly concluded, he would arrive at the Gillespie residence that same day, inside of a couple of hours.

True to his word, James Gregory had come, taken his photos, and gone as promptly as he had arrived. After his departure, Lucy was more energized and keen to continue working on her family's mysteries. Chancing yet another sleep-painting episode and the resulting loss of sleep, she decided to listen to the second of Gracie's recordings.

Again, there were long intervals of housekeeping sounds that had been recorded before Gracie began to reminisce.

> *"I'm hoping this will be easier for me than having you here and trying to tell you in person, Lucy. It's hard to be honest with yourself sometimes, especially when the matters are so personal.*
> *"I've been wondering why I married Jozsef, and I guess you might be wondering too."*

There was a long pause before she continued.

> "I guess there are several reasons. I wasn't the same person back then, and it wasn't the same world. Things have changed—I know I have, presumably as a result of me being on my own in Ireland all those years."

There was a deep sigh, and she continued.

> "I was brought into the Szabo household at the age of ten and had no further schooling. My only learning was at home, watching the people around me. Annie died when I was fourteen, and I was alone except for the Szabos. By staying, I was able to be with my nephew, your father, and to raise him to some extent, especially when he was just a small child. Then again, if I'm honest with myself, it's because I was afraid. The devil you know, I guess.
>
> "When Erzsebet died in 1958, I was already thirty-nine years old. Other than the work I'd done at the Szabos, I'd never held a job. I had no money—Jozsef was miserly. While there was food and shelter, I received barely enough spending money to clothe myself and buy some personal items. I know, it sounds as if I'm making excuses, and maybe I am. But you do what you can with the opportunities that present themselves, and Erzsebet's death was such an opportunity, I admit. It sounds very cold of me, I know. But she was dead, and I was still alive. And so was Janos. He was in his mid-twenties and the only way I was going to be able to see him was to stay in that family somehow.
>
> "There were no prospects for me as an unmarried, uneducated, thirty-nine-year-old woman in 1958, so I convinced Jozsef that he needed me. I was familiar

with the household and could cook and clean. He couldn't. He was fifty-three and in 1958 that seemed older than being fifty-three today. I think he was frightened of aging, of dying alone, and being without someone to take care of him.

"Anyway, I didn't trust him, so I thought I should secure our arrangement by marrying. He didn't care one way or the other about that, but it was important to me. He was business-minded, and I'd picked up some ideas by listening to what he told the boys and how he dealt with other men who were in business. So, I set about negotiating an allowance for myself, and insisted it be done through a lawyer. I was very nervous that he would get mad and remove me from the house. But I don't think he wanted to deal with a new person to do those chores. As a result, we were married.

"Jozsef was mean, but not at all in the way his father, Peter, had been. Jozsef was really stingy and did a lot of shouting and threatening and throwing things, but I learned how to ignore it, or deal with it if needed. He drank too much—something called slivovitz, a very strong Hungarian plum brandy. But even then he never touched me. Jozsef never came to my bed, and for that I am grateful.

"I really don't know what I would have done had I even suspected he'd been involved in Gianni's death. I really can't . . ."

Lucy could hear Gracie weeping softly and her own heart broke. Later sounds were the housekeeping variety, but Lucy continued to listen. If Gracie could record such personal information for her, she felt the least she could do was to listen to the entire recording.

Toward the end of the recording, the doctor and nurse were heard, and Lucy could detect when the trio entered Gracie's bedroom. Shortly after, the door could be heard opening. Lucy thought it must be picking up her arrival with Juliette for the second visit, but it was something else. Nothing was said clearly or loudly, though Lucy thought she could detect a mumble—a sound consistent with someone speaking in a very low register, quietly reading the sign aloud—the same sign that Juliette and Lucy had read on the bedroom door. There were sounds of movement in the room and the hall door being opened and then closed.

A short time after that, Lucy heard the hall door open once again and it was clear that the recorder was picking up her and Juliette's arrival. *What had been those earlier sounds?* Although Lucy was curious, she determined to put the matter out of her mind, at least for the time being.

CHAPTER 18

The scent of morning lingered in the air. Kent found Lucy relaxing in the small hot-tub on their shared patio.

They greeted each other as he lowered himself into the hot, churning water. "Ah-h, this is so good!" With his head tilted back and his eyes closed, he savoured the moment and sighed. Somewhere nearby, a mourning dove cooed.

Twenty minutes later, the timer clicked and the water stilled. Neither Lucy nor Kent moved from their positions. Neither spoke. Finally, they made eye contact, emerged from the hot-tub, and donned their terry cloth robes, taking care to preserve the peace they had enjoyed together over those twenty precious minutes.

A short time later, they were seated at the kitchen island, sharing breakfast. The air was heavy with the aroma of coffee.

"Albin and I considered several ideas, and this is what we've come up with. See what you think. We'll get a nice motor coach set up for you at Gold Farm, something that will accommodate a friend if you want someone to visit with you periodically while you're there. There'll be a car at the site, so you can drive into Simcoe to visit Gracie. Albin will stay at Gold Farm with you. And of course, I'll visit. He'll use the motor coach we've had at other sites and be there to provide some security for you, as well as some muscle. There'll be a temporary shelter into which you can have him move the boxes, so that you can rummage through them at your own pace and in comfort. We also located some locking storage containers for any items you decide to keep. The rest can be tossed into industrial waste bins that will be on-site. Albin is rounding up four sets of hazmat gear, along with shovels and other items he thinks would be useful. Much of it is stuff we'll need at the site after you're finished with it—it's just a matter of not cluttering the area with things you don't actually require for your work. I'm trying to get the electrical service assessed, but we may need to provide a generator if the lines have been damaged. Don't want to take a chance with anyone's health, so we won't rely on the existing septic system or the well water. The property has never accessed the municipal water supply, so we can't just tap into it." He paused to take a deep breath. "What do you think?"

"Sounds really good. I think that between the two of you, you've addressed everything. I'll ask Helen to put together some groceries, and whatever else she thinks may be necessary. I guess I'd only need my personal items. I also need a whiteboard, the kind on a rolling stand. Will there be room for it in my motor coach?"

"No problem. By when do you think you could be ready?"

"I can be ready in a couple of days if the site can be ready by then. And thanks, I really appreciate all your work in organizing this."

They worked toward their self-imposed deadline as a team. However, their original timelines had been somewhat optimistic, and it was four days before Lucy and Albin were finally ready to take up temporary residence at Gold Farm.

They drove to Harkness early in the morning, their Escalade packed with provisions and personal items. The drive felt longer than before because Lucy was eager to start her search of the Szabo boxes. *Are we there yet?* At last, the GPS announced that they had arrived at their destination.

The site was more than Lucy had dared to hope. A coverall building had been erected in front of the garage and positioned so that air flow didn't channel foul air directly into it. Kent pointed out the large table and heavy-duty locking cabinets on wheels inside the temporary structure. A large motor coach was parked to one side of the coverall building, and a smaller motor coach was parked at the other side. At that same side, but closer to the roadway, there were several industrial dumpsters, the largest one with a ramp.

Kent was eager to show Lucy the inside of her luxury accommodations. Her motor coach lacked nothing in its nearly fourteen-metre length. "This is great, Kent! And you remembered the whiteboard."

Kent continued with his guided tour, pointing out all of the features, including the guest bed, video screens, USB ports, washer and dryer, dishwasher, air-conditioner, and the emergency exit available from the master bathroom. "I thought you could use some luxury after a day spent digging through all the stuff in those boxes. There's auxiliary lighting in the coverall building and some portable systems as well that Albin can set up in the house itself, but I think that once it gets dark you'll likely be ready to call it quits and recharge here."

"You said there'd be a car."

"Yes, I'm not surprised you missed it—right there," he said, pointing toward a small Smart Car parked beside the motor coach. It was painted black and red, and reminded Lucy of a ladybird beetle—Kent humour. "While I'd love to stay and chat, I've got my work to do, so I'll leave you to yours. Let me know about all the treasures you find, okay?"

After unloading the black Escalade, they unpacked and Lucy and Albin organized their motor coaches, returning their empty bags and suitcases to the SUV rather than leaving them to be stored at the site. They said their goodbyes, and watched Kent drive down the long driveway toward the highway and turn homeward.

Having discussed the relevant pros and cons, they decided to begin work on the boxes from inside the house. Albin helped Lucy don her hazmat gear, then began to bring boxes to her in the coverall building. There, she assessed the contents quickly but thoroughly. Trash was placed in a bin, which Albin emptied into the appropriate dumpster as needed. Initially, the work went quickly and Lucy was pleased. Then things slowed down.

"I think my brain is turning to mush. Are you ready for a break, Albin?"

"I wouldn't say no, ma'am. I'll just grab myself a protein bar and a smoothie from my coach. I've a couple chairs and a table set up under my awning if you'd care to join me."

"What gear should I remove while I take a break? It's presumably not smart to wear the same stuff while we eat—not after rummaging through that junk. I sure don't want to chance bringing any wee beasties into my coach."

As advised by Albin, Lucy decided that if they were going to take a break, the hazmat gear in its entirety must be removed. That itself took time. *This project is going to take longer than I thought.* She grabbed a sandwich, an apple, and a bottle of water from her coach, then returned to find Albin seated under his awning.

During their lunch, they discussed the items Albin had removed from the house. "I thought it might be easier for you if we started on those stacks of newspapers. They don't strike me as being anything other than bundled stacks of old newspaper—not like there's currency being pressed between the pages."

"I think you're right, Albin. I snipped the twine holding the bundles and selected random papers to examine more carefully, but there was nothing hidden. Mice had gotten into some of the bundles, so those went into the trash right away. I think we can rip through a bunch of them this afternoon, don't you? Are there many?"

"Enough." Albin had a way with words. "The bundles are easy to identify, so I'll keep grabbing them. At the very least, we'll be making room to move in there. It's pretty tight right now. The entire house is packed floor to ceiling, with only little pathways from one room into another. And some of those have been filled as well."

After their short break, they geared up again and returned to the task. The day dragged on, but Lucy experienced a sense of accomplishment when Albin announced that there were no more bundles of newspaper within his reach. The feeling was short-lived, however. She checked out the house with him, and her sense of accomplishment was diminished when she saw the little impact their day's work had brought upon its contents. *Oh boy!*

When her eye caught a group of matching blue plastic boxes, she decided to tackle those next. Albin began to bring them to her table in the coverall building. Dolls, doll parts, and doll clothing in various states of disrepair—none of any great interest or value. Box after box of dolls was tossed into the waiting dumpster. Fortunately, the task was completed easily.

Lucy suggested that Albin pick the next grouping, so he selected some smaller boxes, the size of boot boxes, which were impeding access to one of the back rooms. "Rats!" Albin exclaimed, disgusted.

Assuming he'd been disappointed by the contents of the boxes he'd selected, she asked, "What's wrong?"

"Rats!"

"Oh, you literally mean *rats,* don't you?" Lucy shuddered. "Do you think it would help if we picked up a cat or two?"

"No, then you'd just hear me hollering out: cats! Besides, they'd just be homeless once Kent moves onto the property and deals with the buildings. The beasties just took me by surprise. I wasn't battle ready. Shouldn't let my guard down." Albin had served with the Canadian Armed Forces. He had been sent to Rwanda with UN peacekeepers in the 1990s and sometimes, such as now, that experience was closer to the surface for him.

Lucy opened the boxes one by one and found that each and every one contained party balloons. *Party balloons.* Some were stuck together, forming a large sticky latex gum-ball, while others had dried to a powder. After celebrating the end of the party balloon cache, Albin found a collection of old suitcases.

All the suitcases were locked, so in addition to bringing them out, Albin pried them open, breaking the locks. While most of the suitcases were filled with old cameras, some of which showed damage, others contained photographs. Lucy was delighted. She quickly sorted through the camera equipment and decided to put some of it aside in case James Gregory collected old cameras. Then she began to sort through the various snapshots and portraits.

Based upon the notes written on the back of some of the photos, many of them were old photos of Goldie's family before she married Laszlo. In most of the photos, there was no one familiar to Lucy, and even the very few photographs of Goldie and Laszlo didn't trigger any memories for her. She put a few photos aside to show Gracie, then disposed of the rest in the dumpster.

It had been a good first day. As the sun hung low on the horizon, Albin locked the house and garage, leaving Lucy to lock the cabinet containing the few items she'd saved.

"I think I'll give my sister a call. Is there any message you want me to pass along?" Albin asked.

"Nothing I can think of at the moment, Albin, just say 'hi' to Helen for me. I'll see you in the morning. Good night." And like that, their first day came to a close.

Lucy found the shower to be much better than she had expected. Although she was tempted to linger, she thought better of it and fought the urge. Bundled in a terry cloth robe with a towel wrapped around her head, she popped one of the meals prepared by Helen into the microwave then connected with Kent via Skype.

When there wasn't much of note to report concerning their treasure hunt, conversation shifted to Albin and the rats. "He truly hates rats, but he'd deal with a room full of them in order to protect you," Kent informed her. "We've had some security concerns around here for the past while, Lucy, so I'm happy that Albin is with you." Kent went on to outline the odd things that Albin had reported were occurring on the Gillespie estate. "One of the solar panels was found damaged the day before I arrived home from my trip in March and another the night of the Monroth party. Albin said it wasn't damaged due to natural causes: not weather, not squirrels–or rats—or nearby vegetation. It looked to him as if someone had fallen against it, bending a portion and cracking the housing. He's been on the lookout for someone on our property, but I didn't want to worry you about it. Now that you're away, especially with Albin there, I'll keep a lookout here with Helen. Albin installed some motion-activated cameras in the periphery. Both Albin and Helen have seen footprints and the odd item that may have dropped from someone's pocket or perhaps was just dropped by a bird or carried by the wind. Today, Helen found an empty liquor bottle when she was gardening; clearly, it didn't find its way here as a result of a bird or the wind."

Lucy had been tired, but Kent's news put her on edge and unable to sleep. She decided to listen to the third of Gracie's recordings, expecting that the white noise of household sounds would put her to sleep. *It should be a short recording—just a single day's worth.*

Unlike previous recordings, there were no household sounds. Gracie had heeded Lucy's suggestion and had set the audio recorder to the *off* position. The recording began shortly after the arrival of Juliette in Gracie's suite. Gracie must have wanted the conversation recorded. *I wonder if Juliette knew she was being recorded?* It was interesting from the onset.

> "I do not want this recorded, Gracie. This stays between us."
>
> "Juliette dear, you saw me flick the little switch on it, didn't you? Now, what do you have to say that you don't want Lucy to hear?"
>
> "There are two items I need to discuss with you. The first is a minor one. Kent Gillespie, Lucy's husband, has repeatedly shown an interest in purchasing Gold Farm. I've been thwarting his attempts at contact because it was just an unwelcome complication, but because you've arranged for Lucy to inherit everything anyway, I think you should just sign the property over to her now, and she can deal with his subsequent purchase of it. I know you want her to be able to search through the stuff stored there. Well, she

can do that while her husband gets things together on his end. There's no need to wait."

"Alright. I guess that's a good idea. Do you have any papers for me to sign? Let's take care of that."

There was the sound of a document folder being opened, papers being shuffled, and a pen scratching on paper, then the document folder being closed.

"Now, Juliette, you implied there was a second item, one of greater significance. What might that be?"
"John Taylor."
"Do you mean Janos?"

Gracie's tone suggested she was toying with Juliette.

"No, I'm referring to the John Taylor alias created by B Garner."
"What about it?"
"I don't want that mentioned to Lucy, or anyone for that matter!"
"Juliette, dear, you've really got yourself worked up about this. What's the problem? Gianni Sarto did business on his own, using a number of names, but the name John Taylor was only for certain dealings for which he acted as an agent for B. I've known that for many, many years. He was dealing with people more dangerous than he could have possibly imagined and he ended up dead. That's the short of it."

There was a lull in the conversation, as if Juliette wanted to say something, yet was so frustrated that she couldn't find the words. But soon thereafter, she once again she became coherent.

> "Garner & Garner is my family, and I'm going to protect its reputation. There is no proof whatsoever that B was involved in Gianni's death, but if there's even the slightest connection—opportunistic gossip can be pernicious. The firm must be protected. It doesn't matter that B is long dead—he's the foundation of our firm. If you mention it to Lucy and she starts digging—I'm asking you, Gracie, please don't. Just that one little omission. Don't mention the John Taylor identity that Gianni used."
>
> "I promise, Juliette. I won't utter a word to Lucy about the John Taylor identity that Gianni used when doing work for your forebears. You have my word."
>
> "Thank you, Gracie. Now I must get myself to Harkness—I'm meeting Lucy and Kent at Gold Farm."

There were the usual cordial goodbyes and the door to the hallway could be heard, opening and closing. Then Gracie was alone again in her room. She continued to talk.

> "Yes, recorder, I'm talking to you now. B Garner was doing work with the mob in the States. I think that's why he came here from Montreal in the first place. That's how Gianni found out about the Point that Peter owned. B's idea was, I think, to arrange for the transport of alcohol from Canada into the States. The Point is only twenty-five kilometres from American waters. Prohibition in the States made the production and sale of illegal alcohol very lucrative. You've heard the name Al Capone, well, that's the sort of gangster we're talking about. I'm certain that Gianni wanted only to develop the Point, that's why

he built the lodge there and the manor house on the island . . ."

At this point, there was a knock at the door, and the recorder was shut off.

Lucy was stunned. *Well now, that explains why Juliette was so agitated when we met her at Gold Farm. She really didn't want to discuss the L'Orté properties after her time with Gracie,* she reflected.

CHAPTER 19

He parked his car in the alleyway behind the shop. Angrily, he ripped off the note that he found tucked into the doorframe of his unit, then unlocked the door, and mounted the stairs to his small apartment. *Another wasted day.*

One by one, each idea he had formed to advance his plan had gone sideways. The delivery of a magnificent floral arrangement in which he had secreted a listening device—a bug—had been redirected to the lobby when Gracie had judged it too large for her rooms. He had entered her rooms once while she was asleep but had barely managed to take a few photos before she began to stir. And the photos had been useless—nothing significant to his purpose had been revealed. Then there was the day the doctor visited and another time when Kent and Lucy decided to visit at the time he had selected. *It was just so unfair!*

He opened the cupboard and removed one of his liquor bottles, pouring a generous quantity of the potent liquid into one of the mismatched drinking glasses. He couldn't say that he actually *enjoyed* the plum brandy—it was merely a deeply-ingrained habit. Like other habits he had, they were all *very manly.*

He had been carefully developing a valuable relationship with a skinny blonde employee, with plans for how she might be of use to him, but now it looked as if Ashley had gotten herself sacked by the Dragon Lady. He had waited for Ashley to join him once her shift was over. He had finished a pack of cigarettes while waiting in the car for her. He had waited and waited, until he was forced to ask another employee—one of the Jessicas. (He didn't know which and he didn't care.) So today, there was time lost and more money wasted on the flashy rental car. *Damn Ashley.*

He thought about how exciting his life had been when he had been younger. Opportunities of various types were presented before him, and he had merely to select among them. *Should he have been grateful? Had he been wasteful? No, there should have been more opportunities. They should not have dried up. He knew he deserved better and more. Life's unfair. None of this is my fault,* he lamented.

He hated Kent, though Kent was his best customer. The more he drank, the more he hated him. Kent was younger by fifteen years and had achieved so much more success. *Kent probably had it easy,* he decided. He'd take all of that away from him. He'd take Lucy from him. That's what he'd do.

He had tried to gain access to the Gillespie house to take a look around—pick up the odd thing to cover the rent—but Kent had rejected his offer to deliver goods right to his door. *Who does that? And the handyman and the woman were always lurking around somewhere.* One or the other nearly interrupted him each time he had gone to case the estate.

Then there was all that time spent on the neighbour, the tall Swede. That had been especially costly. *It should have worked.* He didn't understand what had happened to make his plan fail. *A waste of time and money.* He wondered what Kent had done to cause this.

It was through Jozsef that he had come to know those who required his services. The lawyer, Clarence Garner, had clients who paid handsomely. When he needed to get out of town, it would be arranged. With the proper paperwork, he'd been able to continue working in Europe. He'd enjoyed Naples in particular and maintained good friendships among the locals, even now. And he had developed his interest in tailoring there. He thought it ironic that he should have become a tailor. Laszlo wouldn't acknowledge him, so he was never to be a Szabo, but he was a tailor nevertheless.

He wouldn't have made the connection except for Janos. For a long time before he died, Janos considered breaking away from the family and changing his name. Janos had explained to him that szabo wasn't just a surname, but that it was the Hungarian word for tailor, so Janos was planning to change his surname from Szabo to Taylor. He hadn't discovered until later, when he was in Italy, that Janos had gone through with the name change.

He poured what remained of the brandy into his glass and tossed the empty bottle in the general direction of the waste container in the corner of the drab room. He missed, and it rolled on the warped floorboards. He always drank slivovitz. Despite his time in Italy, he had not developed a taste for grappa.

He opened the mail that had been delivered into his mailbox and disposed of the numerous flyers. Bills were marked 'Past Due'. There were a few letters threatening legal action. He decided that they could—and would—be ignored. The note from his landlord angered him. He did not want to have an order posted on his door. It still mattered to him. He concluded that he would need to make the right noises and promise to pay his landlord in short order. He simply needed a bit more time.

He checked the results on the race sheet he had acquired earlier in the day. He was a betting man, but more recently people like Kent had stolen his *mojo,* so he wasn't raking in the winnings he expected. *Damn Kent.*

He considered opening another bottle.

CHAPTER 20

Days later, the only change noticeable at Gold Farm was that the big dumpster required emptying. The locking metal cabinet remained largely empty. Lucy and Albin had settled into a sustainable pattern and pace of working through the Szabo hoard, and several rooms of the house were now empty. Albin seemed to have made peace with the rats he encountered, and Lucy with the odd nest of mice in the boxes he brought to her in the coverall building.

Each day, Lucy had a brief telephone conversation with Gracie, but she had not made the drive to Simcoe to visit. However, today she and Albin decided to break from their pattern. While Albin relaxed and did some laundry, Lucy drove to Simcoe, planning to arrive after Gracie's breakfast but before her nap.

The drive from Harkness to Simcoe was a pleasant one and Lucy enjoyed her little ladybird. Now that the leaves were out in full on the trees, the park-like setting of L'Orté Park was more apparent. Residents, some alone and others accompanied by their visitors or staff, walked under the leafy green canopy, taking in the fresh morning air. Benches had been set out beneath the trees and there were clusters of people visiting in family groups. It was a lovely day.

As Lucy opened the door of the car, she noticed waste strewn on the asphalt beneath. *Disgusting. And there's a waste container right over there.* Either someone had cleaned out a car at that very spot, sweeping debris onto the asphalt, or an impatient driver waited in the car, snacking and smoking while his passengers visited a resident.

Ashley was not at reception today. Instead, the supervisor, whose name was Mrs. Drogan, greeted Lucy and chatted with her briefly. She signed the register, Mrs. Drogan smiled and nodded, and Lucy continued to Gracie's room.

Always welcoming, Gracie greeted her with a hug, followed by tea and shortbread. Unfortunately, many of the photos Lucy had brought with her meant nothing to Gracie, as most of them concerned Goldie's family and likely had come into her possession upon the death of her own parents.

However, there were a few to which Gracie gave extra attention. She identified Laszlo, Goldie, and Paul as a young boy. A few photos included an older boy who Gracie said resembled a young Laszlo. "That's Elda's son." Gracie tapped her chin with her forefinger and closed her eyes, "For the life of me, I can't think of his name. I've not even been able to remember Elda's last name, would you believe. I still have a mind like a steel trap; it's the resetting of the trap that's become increasingly difficult. These photos might jar something loose—not too loose mind you—else, I'll be losing my marbles," Gracie chuckled, quite pleased with herself. "Well, it's unfortunate you've not found anything more significant, Lucy. With all of the work you're doing out there, it'd be nice to find something of note. Oh well, from what you've said, there's still plenty more to examine."

"I was wondering what business interests the Szabos had over the years. Do you happen to know?" Having heard *the recording that wasn't*, Lucy thought this information might be significant.

"Well, I did pick up bits and pieces of information over the years. Jozsef's businesses were different from Peter's and Laszlo's a bit different again. By the time I met him, Peter wasn't particularly active as a businessman. He sat on his laurels, I guess you could say. I'd heard that he'd spent some time out West—in the Yukon, I think. But that would have been years before I was even born, so I really can't say for certain. I just remember that every so often, he'd tell rather rough stories of his time there. He also had stories about oil wells. He used to talk about accidents that the—What did he call them?—roughnecks had and they sounded terrible, but I got the impression that he enjoyed it.

"By the time I lived with them in 1930, Peter wasn't actually working. I guess he owned a lot of land by then—at one point, much of what is now L'Orté Point. And there was a lot of land in and around Harkness as well.

"Old man Peter argued with Jozsef about the land quite often. After Peter died, more of the land was used for growing tobacco and Jozsef managed the farms. Gold Farm, where you now are, is the only remaining parcel. His son, Laszlo, gradually increased his involvement and then he and Jozsef would argue. Jozsef and Laszlo used some of the smaller parcels for junk-yards, or scrap-metal yards, both in Norfolk County and in the Niagara Peninsula.

"Jozsef treated Laszlo as his trainee and his adopted son, Janos, as his employee. See the difference? Jozsef and Laszlo would argue, but with Janos, Jozsef was more 'my way or the highway'. Janos wanted to build or buy some buildings and rent them out, but it wasn't until Laszlo presented the same idea that Jozsef went along with it.

"After Jozsef died, I heard that Janos—or I guess he was John then—and Laszlo did acquire some buildings. Some were rented out commercially, others were apartment houses. They also had some warehousing that your father developed, where old factories had closed down, including the conversion of a large tannery in Hamilton.

"So that's that—quite a range! See, my mind works just fine for that sort of thing. Names are the challenge—Smith!" Gracie suddenly declared, her eyes bright. "Your mother's maiden name was Smith, Betty Smith."

Gracie was energized and talkative. Lucy didn't need to prime her with questions.

"Did you remember anything about 1983?" Gracie wanted to know. Lucy had just taken a bite of shortbread, so she merely shook her head. "Well, perhaps this will help, perhaps not—when Betty wrote me that she was going to have another baby, I sent a gift for you from Ireland. You must have been seven years old then, I guess, and I thought that with all the fuss over the new baby, you could use some special attention. It was a white gold *Claddagh* ring set with a small heart-shaped emerald."

"I *do* remember it! I didn't know that it was a Claddagh ring, just that it was very pretty. That was from you? I'm sorry; I hadn't realized. I don't know what became of it, but I do remember considering myself to be very special whenever I wore it. My father wouldn't let me wear it as much as I wanted because it was a bit loose and he thought it would slip off my finger."

"Perhaps it did," Gracie suggested. She smiled sadly at the loss of her well-intentioned gift. And with that, energy appeared to drain from her body. Clearly, she was tired and in need of a nap before lunch.

They said their goodbyes and Lucy signed herself out at reception, but before she began her drive back to Gold Farm, she phoned Yoichi.

"So, have you decided whether or not you're coming to visit me at the farm, Yoichi?"

"Yes—I'll be on my way shortly. I was just speaking with James Gregory. He was planning to place your files in a Dropbox account for you to access, but because I'm heading out to see you, he's given me a thumb drive with the files. Donald has a conference at Western in London. He's the keynote speaker at the gala dinner tonight and plans to stay tomorrow as well. You're kind of on the way, so he'll drop me off, and then pick me up tomorrow."

"Wouldn't you prefer to go with him, seeing as he's the keynote speaker?"

"Definitely not. It's just not my crowd. You remember me at uni; I couldn't wait to get out!"

Lucy arrived back at Gold Farm to find that Albin had been busy during her absence rather than relaxing—or his idea of relaxation merely differed from her own. He had begun the transfer of items from the basement to the main floor of the house. He had also taken some of the items and placed them directly in the coverall building, explaining that, although the quantity was significant, he considered the entire lot to be deserving of the dumpster. Rusty, mouldy, and otherwise visibly deteriorated—they provided certain justification of the need for hazmat suits.

She let Albin know that Yoichi was expected and would be visiting—and possibly working with them—the following day as well. Rather than continue with the more disgusting items from the basement, they would return to emptying rooms in the house, or would take items from the garage for a while where things looked to be in better condition.

Eventually, Yoichi arrived, but as soon as she removed her overnight bag from Donald's silver Prius and exchanged goodbyes with him, he made his way back up the driveway and turned toward the highway, heading for London. Due to traffic, they had fallen behind in their schedule, so he had no time to linger.

Yoichi was impressed with the organization of the site and especially the luxury of Lucy's home away from home: the motor coach. Albin continued in his attempt to bring order to the chaos of the basement, while Lucy and Yoichi enjoyed the amenities of her motor coach.

"Donald sent you an email just before we left to come here; you've presumably not taken the time to read it yet. I just thought I'd point it out to you. What I'm more interested in are the files that James Gregory prepared for you. Can we see them?" Yoichi had been drawn to Gold Farm by her curiosity.

"You pour the wine—raid the pantry and fridge if you're hungry—and I'll set this up so we can view everything on the monitor. It's hi-def and should catch all the detail there is."

By the time Yoichi had poured the wine and found some cheese and crackers to her liking, Lucy had adjusted the lighting, positioned the television, and arranged two chairs.

The first painting was presented in incredible detail, and Lucy could enlarge specific areas for an even closer look. In the photo, the detail of the scene was sharpened, making it display as a natural setting rather than as the photo of a painting—Lucy's style converted to hyper-realism. On a copy of that photo, James Gregory had circled a total of seven awen—many more than they had located on the original painting in the studio. Lucy wondered if she'd recognize the spot if she were to come upon it in real life. Most definitely, this was not a photo of any part of Gold Farm.

The final photo of the painting shocked Lucy. It was a Claddagh ring set with a heart-shaped emerald. Lucy googled 'Claddagh' and showed it to Yoichi. The article she found explained the symbolism: the two hands represent friendship, the heart symbolizes love, and the crown on top, loyalty. Yoichi had not grasped the significance of the ring, but had been impressed that Lucy recognized it as a Claddagh.

"Gracie gave me such a ring when I was seven years old, but I lost it many years ago. I'd forgotten about it until Gracie reminded me during one of our visits," Lucy explained. Yoichi was flabbergasted. "This calls for another glass of wine," Lucy said, "I'm getting used to such weirdness, Yoichi, but this is rather new for you."

"True, but this is personal for you, so even though it certainly is weird, it's *out there* for me yet it's *in here,*" Yoichi said, pointing to her heart, "for you. I'm just glad I can be here for you."

There was nothing to suggest that more could be learned from the first painting, so Lucy selected the first file for the second painting. As before, the file provided incredible detail that could be selected readily and enlarged further. A second file made the face look more natural, as if it hadn't been painted. Yoichi excused herself and when she returned, envelope in hand, she gave Lucy a photograph, which James Gregory had printed from that file. Immediately, Lucy felt that she knew this person, but it was just an impression. She would show it to Gracie.

The final file for the second painting concentrated on the eyes of the figure. Both women found the results disturbing. The reflection was that of a toddler, a girl. A hand was reaching down toward the child, but whose hand it was remained a mystery. The child was looking toward the person in whose eyes she was reflected. The child was Lucy.

"Caesar!" Lucy exclaimed.

At that moment, it was as if she had seized a key and unlocked a door. It was opening gradually, allowing memories to pass through from beyond. Things that she thought she knew were now seen with a greater clarity. At first an unsettling jumble, they quickly began to take their rightful place in her memory.

Lucy was teary-eyed, but the arrival of long-lost memories gave her a strength she had not known before. She experienced anger, though she wasn't certain at whom it was directed. For all that, she smiled, content in the knowledge that she was now more than she had been just moments earlier.

"Who's Caesar?" Yoichi asked, trying to help but not knowing what to do or where to begin.

"I don't think I know. I just know that he was called Caesar. This must be what Gracie has been encouraging me to remember. In 1983, she was already in Ireland, so this is what my mother must have written to her about. I'm still not sure I know what happened, except that it was traumatic for me."

"What do you remember of your early childhood, Lucy, from the beginning?"

"Things are bound to come back to me more now, but I remember just the things of a normal childhood. I recall climbing out of my crib while the household was still asleep and going into the living room. I recall sitting in the morning sun and playing with the rainbows that my mother's favourite crystal vase would make on the wall. I recall playing with my favourite stuffed toys and looking at the pictures in my books.

"Then I remember that something happened that made me feel ashamed. My parents were angry; everyone was angry. There was shouting. I didn't understand what I'd done wrong. I remember being taken to doctors and they'd talk to me . . . and a strange memory of a room with padding, and of another with a trampoline, I think.

"And then at some point, my mother looked even more beautiful to me than she had previously. She dressed differently and I was told I was going to have a baby brother or a baby sister and we were all excited. And then she died and so did my baby brother.

"Then it was just me and my dad. But I was in school, so I didn't see him much— just on holidays and some weekends. He sent me to a boarding school. When high school was done and I was preparing to go to Queen's, he died and that was that."

CHAPTER 21

Lucy awakened to the sounds of breakfast being assembled. She rolled out of bed, tied her robe about herself, and ambled half-asleep toward the aroma of coffee. The cobwebs of sleep persisted.

"Sleep well?" Yoichi asked cheerily. But it was an act and they both knew it. She was concerned for Lucy's well-being. She had already returned her bed to its daytime position and the area was again a living room.

"Actually, yes, thanks. You?"

Yoichi smiled and bobbed her head in response, her mouth full.

"I phoned Kent with an update. I haven't looked at Donald's email yet though I will–soon. I see you've found breakfast. Some host, I am leaving you to your own devices out here."

"No problem," Yoichi answered before taking another bite of her bagel with cream cheese. "I'll check in with Albin first and get dressed in my gear, so I'm ready for you, okay? I think I've already heard him moving stuff around out there."

"I'm starting to think that's his way of signalling to me that it's time I got myself together and started work. I'll just grab my usual and be out shortly."

Work continued in the coverall building and Yoichi and Lucy were able to chat nonstop—or so it seemed to Albin. Box after box was investigated and then discarded into the dumpsters.

Eventually, Albin transferred a sturdy metal box from a cart onto the sorting table. It looked promising. Again, it was necessary for Albin to force open the lock. The box contained a variety of smaller boxes of similar quality. Many were empty, but a few contained jewellery, and others contained coins, including rolls of 1948 Canada silver dollars. These smaller boxes were stored in the locking cabinet. Lucy was pleased that they had found something worth putting into it, especially while Yoichi was visiting. Wading through garbage is disgusting; sorting through treasure is fun.

The last of the smaller boxes contained documents. A quick scan of them indicated these were more significant than the earlier document finds. Those had consisted of instruction manuals and warranties for long-defunct small appliances. But rather than taking the time then and there to inspect them any further, Lucy placed them in the locking cabinet for closer inspection at a later time. Albin had obtained a fumigant to which the items would be exposed before leaving the confines of the coverall building.

The rest of the day passed uneventfully. Although they had churned through many boxes, as evidenced by the new accumulation in the dumpsters, they were far from finished. It would take another week. At least.

When Yoichi received a telephone call from Donald to say that he would be leaving London shortly, they brought their workday to a close. They were relieved to separate themselves from the grubbiness of the boxes.

Lucy and Yoichi were clean and refreshed well before Donald arrived, and Lucy found sufficient time to read his most recent email. Rather than the expected genealogical information, his email contained historical information and concerned the Point.

When they heard Donald's vehicle approaching and went out to greet him, Lucy saw that Albin was continuing work in his hazmat gear. He had exposed the contents of the locking metal cabinet to the fumigant, and was now organizing the house and identifying those boxes which might be rendered an easy decision.

Lucy hadn't realized how much she missed social interaction. She had invited Albin to join them, but he had declined. *The strong, silent type,* she thought. So the three friends enjoyed companionable conversation, including a brief discussion of Donald's recent speaking engagement. However, Donald was more interested in continuing with Lucy's story, as were both Lucy and Yoichi.

"The information I obtained on L'Orté Point came as quite a surprise to me. One of my colleagues is an historian who has been researching the cross-border activities that occurred with Americans and Canadians between the two world wars, so from 1918 to 1939. His research is quality academic work, seeking out a variety of original documents. He's a stickler for detail, so I trust his findings." Donald turned to the notes he had on his smartphone.

"To recap: you already know that the Point consisted of various parcels, the largest owned by Peter Szabo. Some properties were bought by Johannes Schneider, others by Jean Couture. Eventually, they all ended up owned by Giovanni Sarto. However, there's another name that keeps cropping up: John Taylor. Now, this can't be your father because he only became John Taylor in early 1980, just before you were born."

"I just recently learned that my grandfather, Gianni, *may* have used that name as one of his aliases. Or, the identity may have been created for him and then used by someone else. The information wasn't clear, and I didn't want to prejudice your research and get you started down the wrong path. Because you've come across the name independently, it might be worth investigating more thoroughly. As you said, it's definitely not my father because he wasn't born until 1934."

"I guess you've not realized this—how could you—but 'John Taylor' is the English version of 'Janos Szabo'. What is particularly interesting is that 'John Taylor' is 'Johannes Schneider' in German. In French it's 'Jean Couture' and in Italian it's 'Giovanni Sarto'. I don't think the pattern is entirely by chance, do you?"

Lucy shook her head. "But you said that the name 'John Taylor' isn't used in the real estate transactions. So, with what *was* it associated?"

"The name gets mentioned in connection with mob activity."

"You mean, Al Capone?" Lucy realized that this was verification of what she had learned from Gracie. It also explained a bit more of why Juliette had been so vehemently opposed to any mention being made of the John Taylor alias. That alias had been used when Gianni did work on behalf of Bennett Garner. Mob-related work.

"Yes, but not Capone per se, rather his peers or his competition. It looks as if liquor was being smuggled through L'Orté Point, so money flowed north in that transaction. But that came to a grinding halt about the time Gianni died because prohibition ended in 1933. With an established mob connection, my friend tells me that it is reasonable to assume that the relationship went beyond liquor sales." Donald poured himself another glass of water, took a sip, and continued, "I'm told that the mob became increasingly sophisticated and sought to appear legitimate, which is why the role of consigliere was eventually filled by those with a law degree, preferably a family member. The mob tended to think in terms of continuity; they respected family connections. So, such a lawyer in the States would deal with a similarly-inclined lawyer in Canada to arrange for quasi-legal deals to secure and launder mob money."

"And just perhaps, with such respect for family as you've said, they might tend to prefer dealing with a family firm," Lucy considered. However, she had no intention of relating any part of the private conversation between Juliette and Gracie.

"Sounds more than plausible," Donald agreed. "Another point I nearly forgot to mention—these other lawyers were often referred to as a Janus."

"Janus?" Lucy tried to recall where she'd heard the term before. "Yes, that's the two-faced god of the ancient Romans, a god of beginnings and transitions. He's commonly associated with doorways, isn't he? So, I guess that's appropriate."

During this time, Yoichi had been silent. "Guess what I just discovered," she suddenly declared. "You've been talking about all the weird name connections, their translations and so on—well, I know nothing about that sort of thing. I was thinking of homonyms and being creative with names in other ways, other than translations: L'Orté has two syllables. Switch them around and you go from L'Or-té to té-L'Or. Anglicize the spelling and you get: Tay-lor—*Taylor*! Do you think these are in some way breadcrumbs being dropped by Gianni?"

"Hmm-m, there's a little town in Florida called El Jobean. It sounds Spanish, but it isn't," Donald offered. "It was a planned town and built about the same time as Gianni was planning things at the Point. The developer was a chap by the name of Joel Bean, a lawyer out of Boston, if I recall correctly. So, it's not without precedent that's for certain. And I think the mob was big there, too, at one time in connection with rum running out of Cuba.

"I see you've got a whiteboard. Are the markings on it to remain, or may I erase them?" Donald enquired.

"Erase away. That was just me thinking, but not getting anywhere."

"Let's put aside the history of the point for awhile, okay?" Donald said, as he cleaned the marks from the whiteboard and began to apply his own notes. "What do we know specifically about the Szabo bloodline? Peter—we'll put him at the top—is registered as the birth father of twins, a boy and a girl, Jozsef and Erzsebet. They, in turn, are registered as the birth parents of Laszlo. Laszlo marries Goldie, and they are registered as the birth parents of Paul. Based upon what you've told me about the people behind these names, I propose that Laszlo was the product of an incestuous relationship between Erzsebet and Peter, rather than Jozsef. I care about the documentation, but the truth can be manipulated; an error or some false information entered because a government employee is paid off and doesn't recognize the seriousness of their act. I think it's time to factor in the characters, their personalities, and interactions. What do you think, Lucy?"

"I think you've made a good point. I tend to want to reject it because it's just so twisted, but I think you could be right. Based on comments from Gracie, it is more likely to be as you've suggested. There was likely incest between father and daughter, rather than brother and sister.

"At the same time, I'm stuck with a bunch of questions whirling about in my head and I can't catch any of them to put them into words. Does that make any sense to you? It's as if I'm missing something," Lucy stated in frustration.

"Perhaps there's a lack of players," Yoichi suggested as she made her way to the refrigerator. "I'm famished."

"Oh, let me get something for you—" Lucy said, but she was interrupted by Yoichi.

"No, continue with this. I need sustenance, but I know how to raid a fridge. If Donald is hungry, I'm certain he can do the same. We're not here for fine dining, Lucy. Let's make some headway, and solve this crazy puzzle." Lucy was relieved and agreed.

Donald continued, "I think that's an excellent observation, Yoichi. It's a puzzle. I think we've placed some of the pieces appropriately, but we may be missing some of them. And we all know how frustrating a jigsaw puzzle can be when you don't have all the pieces. In this case, it's always possible that certain pieces are from someone else's puzzle and don't have anything to do with solving yours. Some of your pieces might be missing permanently. Are there any people who keep cropping up when you talk to Gracie yet who are not on the board here?"

"Well, there's a minor player, a woman by the name of Elda. I have no surname for her yet. She was a farm labourer but quite a bit older than my mother. Gracie says Elda had her sights set on either Laszlo or my father. She had a son, but I have no name for him. She died by suicide the same year my parents got married, which is why Gracie mentioned her to me. Now that I think of it, the son is in one of the photos I found. I've shown it to Gracie, and she thinks that the boy resembles Laszlo at the same age." Lucy went off to locate the photo.

When she returned, Donald and Yoichi were assembling subs from the cheeses, cold cuts, and salad fixings they'd found in the refrigerator. *I'm a bad host*, Lucy chastised herself.

"When paired with the right wine, a sub is a beautiful thing," Yoichi extolled, laughing. "And this white is excellent—a Chevalier-Montrachet from the Côte de Beaune region."

"Good, I'm glad you're enjoying it," Lucy said, somewhat relieved. Then she picked up the thread of the discussion once again. "Okay, let's assume, at least for a moment, that this teenager is the elder son of Laszlo Szabo. Clearly, he's been cut out of everything."

Donald suggested a scenario. "He too might be dead. People are dropping like flies at various times. I mean, there's a cluster in 1933 when Gianni and Peter die. In 1979, you've got the death of Jozsef and while there's not another death, there certainly is a lot of significant change occurring with your father changing his name and starting to break from the Szabos. Then, of course, you're born. And finally, between 1993 and 1998, there's the death of Laszlo, then Goldie, Paul, and then your father. One after the other."

"I guess I need Elda's surname and then the name of her son. Otherwise, we're pretty much scuppered, aren't we? Too many missing pieces."

"Once you get those names, Lucy, I suggest you try to find out *how* they died. We now know that the mob was involved. I'm not suggesting that these were actual mob hits, but there were some pretty unsavoury characters associated with Gianni and, through him, Jozsef and the entire Szabo family. Digging *might* get you *some* answers, that's all I'm saying." With that, Donald took a big bite of his sub, squeezing mustard out the other side.

"Lucy, did you look through the jewellery we found today?"

"You mean, *did I find my ring*, don't you? No, it wasn't there, I checked. Maybe Paul found it and sold it. Or maybe it's elsewhere, and I'll never find it."

Donald looked mystified, so Yoichi told him about Lucy's emerald ring, and Lucy showed him the detail in the first set of photographs James Gregory had prepared. She did not show the second set of photographs to him, though she assumed that Yoichi would tell him all about the eyes, during their return trip to Toronto.

The remainder of the evening passed pleasantly. Lucy remembered to give Yoichi the camera equipment she had put aside for James Gregory. The items had been fumigated and placed in a clean box. Soon, Yoichi was ready to transfer her overnight bag to Donald's car, and in short order, she and Donald were reduced to a set of red lights heading down the long driveway and toward the highway.

Lucy phoned Kent to give him an update regarding both the progress at the site and the additional insight that was developing regarding her family history. After she wished him good night, she considered whether she might visit Gracie again in the morning.

CHAPTER 22

Work was progressing at Gold Farm, but beyond that nothing more could be said. Lucy had postponed a visit with Gracie in the hope that she might find something significant hidden within the hoard, but that had not happened. She remembered Juliette predicting that amid the dross, there would be only more dross.

There was a single document, which Lucy considered a great find. It had been put aside in the metal box containing coins, jewellery, and documents. She now had in her possession the adoption papers identifying Baby Boy Hogan *hereby* adopted by Jozsef Szabo and Erzsebet Szabo and *henceforth* to be named Janos Szabo.

Someone really dropped the ball on this one, Lucy thought. In 1934, there would have been no way for a brother and sister, or an unmarried couple, to have adopted a child legally. Yet that is precisely what had occurred. Lucy recalled Donald's comment about mistakes occurring in records and she wondered if this mistake had been truly accidental or if a bureaucrat had been paid to look the other way. *Could such a thing have been facilitated by a lawyer?*

Contrary to Gracie's assumption that she and Erzsebet had successfully kept details of the baby's parentage from Jozsef, it was clear that he would have known. His signature was written directly beneath the adoption details, as was Erzsebet's. Given her state of mind, it was likely that the significance of this was lost on her. Lucy wondered how this information had influenced Jozsef's treatment of Janos.

Although she had been hoping for more, here was at least one treasured document she would share with Gracie. Once again, the big dumpster was full, and Albin called the disposal company for it to be emptied. This presented the perfect opportunity for a rest day and a visit with Gracie.

Lucy drove to Simcoe the next morning, timing her visit to occur much as she had on previous trips—after Gracie's breakfast but before her nap. A young woman, Sarah, was sitting at reception, pleasant and alert to Lucy's arrival. In a manner which was both warm and business-like, she requested identification and checked the named guest's list of approved visitors for a match before having Lucy sign the register, reminding Lucy to sign again before leaving. The heightened attention to security pleased Lucy.

Gracie was in fine form as usual. She shared a few humorous anecdotes concerning things which had occurred within the group of residents and staff at L'Orté Park since Lucy's last visit. There was a knock at the door, and Jessica P entered, carrying a tray with tea and shortbread. She apologized to Gracie for her tardiness.

As the door closed again upon Jessica's departure, Gracie asked if Lucy had discovered anything interesting at Gold Farm since they last spoke.

"Unfortunately, not a lot. A few rolls of old coins and a bit of jewellery . . . but not the emerald ring. There were some documents though, and you might find this one particularly interesting." Lucy presented Gracie with the adoption papers.

Gracie examined the document and, as she handed it back to Lucy, she sighed. "So, Jozsef knew how I was related to Janos . . . sorry, I mean John. Interesting. He never said.

Perhaps that's why he was so different with how he treated him compared with how he treated his natural son, Laszlo."

"It's more complicated than that, Gracie. Jozsef and Erzsebet weren't husband and wife. There is no record of their marriage being registered. However, there are birth certificates for each of them on file. They shared the same last name, Szabo, and the same date of birth: January 27, 1910. They were brother and sister—twins—and Peter was their father."

"Well, I'll be . . . I didn't know. One just assumes, I guess, and doesn't give it any thought." Gracie paused and gave the matter additional consideration. "That actually makes some sense now that I think about it. I mean, Jozsef wasn't interested in me in that way. Perhaps he wasn't interested in Erzsebet in that way, either. Peter had been the dirty old man, not Jozsef. Do you think Peter had taken his own daughter?"

Lucy raised her eyebrows and made eye contact with Gracie in a gesture, which was an affirmation. Gracie shook her head and shuddered in disgust, then continued, "That would explain why she was so upset when she became pregnant, wouldn't it? And it might also explain her response to Peter's death."

"Do you think Erzsebet had anything to do with Peter's death? Give it a moment and see if you can go back in your mind to that time."

There was a long pause. "You know, now that you mention it, it makes perfect sense. I mean, I don't condone violence, not usually, but this situation with Erzsebet . . ." Gracie paused, reflecting upon the situation. "I feel it was completely justified for her to have had a violent response, even patricide. And she got away with it—good for her! You know, back in 1933, Peter would likely have gotten away with what he did, but she would have been ruined, no matter. He was a man with considerable wealth. He might not have favoured spending on household niceties but to cover up his crime—most definitely. Disgusting!"

"So, Laszlo is a half-brother to Jozsef through Peter and also his nephew through Erzsebet. That's how it works out, I think. This would have complicated any inheritance, wouldn't it?"

"I guess it might have, except that Peter had established that trust, guaranteeing that Jozsef would inherit and treating Erzsebet as Jozsef's spouse, not Peter's daughter. When Laszlo was born, Jozsef modified it, made it even more unfair by specifically excluding your father, even though he was adopted and in every respect, should have been treated as a natural son. All those legal contortions to cover-up past crimes, or just to be plain mean. Typical."

While Gracie munched her shortbread, Lucy took the opportunity to remove a photo from her purse. "This is a computer-generated image, Gracie. Can you tell me if it reminds you of anyone in particular?"

Gracie took one look at it and said, "Caesar." Lucy took the photo from her and returned it to the envelope and her purse. "You know," Gracie continued, "Caesar wasn't his real name. We just called him that because he was such a little emperor, strutting about and making demands. He was about five years older than Paul."

"Gracie, you had described Elda's son as a little emperor."

"Yes, that's him, the one who looked like Laszlo."

"So Paul was Laszlo's son by his wife, Goldie, and Caesar was Laszlo's son by Elda, or at least we're pretty sure. We just don't have Elda's last name, nor the real first name of her son."

"I find you can't force memories. You can encourage them but not force them. It'll come to me and I'll tell you or get a recording of it for you—I promise. But right now, I don't know." Gracie was annoyed and frustrated with herself.

"I've remembered something about 1983, Gracie. Caesar was at the doorway to my bedroom and I was lying on the bed. There was a hand near me that I don't think was Caesar's.

And I recall there was lots of turmoil as a result of this, but the memories are those of a child and I don't know how to interpret them. Did my mother write details about it to you when you were in Ireland?"

"Yes, dear, you're quite right. Somehow, both Caesar and Paul were involved. You were the victim. Paul would have been 18 at the time and that means Caesar was 23—both old enough to know better. Unfortunately, both of them were sons of Laszlo and we now know—or think we know—that Laszlo was the product of incest. I think something got really messed up with him. Caesar had been away for a few years, Betty said, and John had invited him to stay with them until he got himself settled again. When he returned, this occurred, and then he went travelling again, I guess, because she never mentioned him again."

"What about Paul?"

"Paul was an odd one, alright. I always thought he was more of a follower than a leader. He looked up to Caesar as a big brother, you could say. Of course, that was more correct than he knew. The whole matter caused the final break between your father and the Szabos, according to Betty. He broke all ties with them—until Laszlo died and he went to see Goldie and ended up with Gianni's watch."

"Quite a complicated pathway to follow, isn't it?" Lucy observed. Gracie agreed, and both women went quiet as they sipped their tea.

CHAPTER 23

Two full weeks had come and gone. Two huge dumpsters full of refuse had been removed from Gold Farm, yet most of the locking cabinet remained empty. Little of value— either monetary, documentary, or sentimental—had been found. Albin remained task-oriented, which Lucy appreciated, but her spirits were sorely sagging, and a burdensome oppression stalked her. Kent had visited for a short time and while that had lifted her spirits, it did little to advance the task at hand.

The house was now empty; both the attic and basement had been cleared. The garage was their current focus. Lucy chided herself for wanting to just dump the remaining boxes, sight unseen, into the dumpster and consider the job finished.

It was then that Albin announced a breakthrough, "Look what I've discovered!"

Eager to see what he'd found, Lucy abandoned the box with which she'd been occupied and quickly made her way to him. "What have you got?"

"Look . . ." One by one, Albin lifted the lids and revealed—nothing. The boxes were empty. "Now, I'm not saying that all of these are likely to be empty, but a good many are. That'll shorten the timeline for the work here to be done," he said, sensing that Lucy's enthusiasm for the task was waning.

Lucy's expression revealed her relief at the news. Granted, nothing much of note had been discovered, but there had been a few things worth keeping. It was nearly time to walk away from all of this. They quickly assessed the situation and determined that they could finish the task the following day—Tuesday—and be home Wednesday. Re-energized and optimistic, she returned to the coverall building and the task awaiting her there, while Albin disposed of the empty boxes into one of the recycling bins.

Mid-day, she received a text message from Eve, who had been planning to visit with her but hadn't gotten around to doing so yet. Eve planned to arrive late the following day. She had no way of knowing that it would be the final workday at the site, and Lucy decided not to mention that fact to her. Eve had one request—she asked Lucy not to tell Albin that she was coming. *Ah, she's missing Albin, not me,* Lucy chuckled to herself.

According to Kent, Eve and Helen were once again on friendly terms. Helen had been upset with Eve for her brief dalliance with David Tremblay, which Helen had interpreted as disloyalty to her brother, Albin. But the matter was now settled, creating the impression that things were back to normal.

The rest of the day unfolded without incident, and the dumpster was half-filled by the day's end.

Recently, it had been a trying time for Julius, but he'd succeeded in keeping his landlord at bay and the shop open. Fortunately, with a luxury store such as Roman's, sparse offerings being on display were a common occurrence. Therefore, it wasn't apparent to his customers that the few items available in the shop also represented the total of what he had in stock.

His mood was tolerable at best. He could do solicitous when required, perhaps even obsequious should the situation warrant it. The slivovitz he kept handy under the counter helped. He poured himself a drink and welcomed the burn of alcohol down his throat.

It was merely Tuesday, but already the week seemed long. To make matters worse, random thoughts bounced around in his head, all concerning the things he hated about Kent Gillespie. Julius was formulating a plan to deal with that, but he couldn't decide what precisely would give him the greatest satisfaction.

Then, just as he decided he had quite enough for the day, Kent Gillespie himself walked into Roman's. "And how might I assist you today, Mr. Gillespie?" Julius smiled, faking sincerity.

Kent was in a particularly upbeat mood, verging on jovial. Julius found him particularly offensive today. "I'm looking for a very light-weight suit. I was thinking something Neapolitan in styling, perhaps in linen," Kent declared.

"Please permit me to lock up first, so we're not disturbed, and then I'll locate my special fabric samples in the back for you. May I offer you a beverage?" Julius said. Kent declined the beverage. "As long as you're sure," Julius responded. "Please take a seat—I'll return in a moment." With that, Julius entered the stockroom and unlocked the rear door, located his car keys, and reinforced himself with a swig of the slivovitz he kept tucked under a workbench.

The rest of the procedure went smoothly. With the blinds already drawn in the showroom as part of his closing routine and Kent intent on examining the fabric samples Julius had quickly grabbed from the stockroom, Julius immobilized him with a taser. Julius' attack went smoothly—taking Kent completely unaware. Julius found it enjoyable to watch Kent writhe in pain on the floor in response to the muscular contractions triggered by the electrical charge. He had often suggested such a private consultation for Kent with this very scene in mind. Finally, Kent had taken him up on the idea.

Julius had not yet worked out the details of his plan concerning Kent—just that he would ultimately die. Julius enjoyed the sweet metallic scent of blood so much that it sometimes distracted him when it became abundant earlier on in his process. He had learned that by using a taser, he could efficiently secure a victim and take his time with them in some appropriate setting. Now that this business had begun, everything else would fall into place. Suddenly, he relished doing business with Kent. Such an undertaking came easily to Julius; it was his second nature.

"What did you expect, coglione? You come to the tailor, you get stitched up," Julius said to his unresponsive customer.

He secured Kent's cellphone and identification then dragged him into the depleted stockroom. There, he secured Kent's feet using a couple turns of duct tape and a large quantity of black electrical tape. He found the combination of tapes superior to either on its own for such jobs. He shoved the fabric samples into Kent's mouth and used a single piece of duct tape to cover his mouth before securing it further with electrical tape, which he wrapped around Kent's head several times. Then Julius sedated him with a little concoction he had found useful over the years for such occasions. Kent was heavier than he had expected, but he was able to haul him into the open trunk of his maroon 2001 Chevy Malibu; the dumpsters in the dirty alley provided adequate cover. Once he had positioned Kent in the trunk, he secured Kent's wrists with a pair of handcuffs that he looped around a metal frame, which he had specially welded to the inside of the trunk. Julius was pleased with the result; Kent was now secure.

Although Julius was undecided about which of his many great plans he would follow—in all of them, this had been the first step. He felt his excitement growing; he felt young again, virile. He closed the trunk, placed the bag containing Kent's identification and cellphone on the passenger's seat for later disposal, and locked the back door to his shop. As he approached the driver's car door, Julius took note of his bag of gear already on the floor behind the driver's seat. There would be time during the drive to decide what to use first. As he opened the door and slid into position behind the steering wheel, a bottle of slivovitz rolled from under the seat. He grabbed it, took a quick swig, and tucked it between the seat-back and the passenger seat, under the bag containing Kent's things.

Let's get this done! Without having had an opportunity to ply his trade for quite a while, he found it exhilarating to be involved once again. *Much better than retail.*

As a result of late afternoon traffic, it took a little while to get out of the downtown core, but he found himself making up for lost time once he cleared the suburbs. He could hear Kent in the trunk begin to stir. *Good, he's not dead—yet.*

He wanted to look the old lady in the eye and tell her exactly what he thought of her. *If she had been more of a woman, her pig of a husband wouldn't have gone looking elsewhere for satisfaction. It was her fault.*

He reached over and found the bottle of slivovitz, opened it, glanced around at the other cars travelling alongside, and enjoyed another swallow. A moment later, a light-blue Bentley Continental GT, driven by a blonde woman, scorched past him on the left. He imagined seeing her crash and burn. Anger and jealousy raged within him.

Eve followed the instructions provided by her GPS. She couldn't recall ever having been in Harkness. The sun hung low on the horizon as she turned into the driveway, stopped her vehicle, and made a quick phone call to Lucy. A short time later, Eve's phone rang in return and Lucy gave her the all-clear. She steered the car down the long driveway, taking it slowly so as to make as little noise as possible, and positioned her light-blue Bentley Continental GT along the far-side of Lucy's motor coach.

Lucy was waiting for her. The emergency door to the motor coach was open, and she was beckoning Eve to enter quickly. Eve grabbed her overnight bag and a second bag from the passenger's side, carefully closed the car door, and entered the master bathroom of the motor coach.

"Well, so much for a grand entrance!" Eve said when she noticed where she was. "How are you, Lucy dear?" Lucy reached up as Eve bent down, and they hugged in greeting, laughing at the absurdity of arriving in this manner. "I want to surprise him."

"Yes, I figured that out. He's checking something in the basement. He mentioned it earlier today, and I managed to put him off the job until now. Let me give you the grand tour." Lucy secured the door once again and then pointed out the various features of the motor coach, but Eve's favourite remained the emergency door in the master bathroom.

"That's a great safety feature. This thing must be over thirteen metres in length, so it's a long way to the front door should you have a fire in the kitchen. Smart design. Speaking of the kitchen, I brought some goodies." Eve pulled out a variety of items that Lucy identified as Albin's favourites. "Luxury take-out!"

As Lucy cleared her laptop from the table to begin preparing for dinner, Eve asked, "What are these?" She was pointing toward a small box and the audio recorder.

"I've been exchanging audio recorders with Gracie. She records her memories as they occur to her. When I visit, I give her another recorder in exchange for the one she's used, download the audio file, and exchange it again the next time I see her. I received this one just a few hours ago. Kent found it online from a site called Spy Shop." As she opened the box, she continued to explain, "Gracie's been putting her recorder in the pocket of her cardigan and sometimes the sound's been a bit muffled. This new one is a pendant necklace—quite pretty. As with the other one, once she turns it *on*, it's sound-activated to record. If she likes it, I'll pick up a second and exchange those instead of the two we've been using." Lucy placed the necklace over her head, admiring it in the mirror. "I think she will. I'm so glad the courier was able to deliver it promptly. I'll turn it *on* and test it with our dinner conversation, unless you mind, Eve." Eve dismissively shook her head.

Julius was familiar with the drive to L'Orté Park. Although his car lacked a GPS, he made all the correct turns and wasted no time. He planned to enter the residence by the rear door near the dumpster and was confident there would be no problem—even if the rear door were already locked. He had the passcode. He had been very successful in manipulating Ashley—not that the task had been difficult. He'd been well-groomed and stylish in his choice of apparel; he had used a bit of cologne and charmed her as only he knew how—another skill he had picked up in Naples. She assumed he was a man of means. It worked to his benefit that she was desperate for male companionship. The stories he had used to gain Ashley's trust had been simply ludicrous, but Ashley had wanted to impress him. When he complained to her that sometimes he was forced to park far from the front door and found the side door near the dumpster locked on occasion, she gladly shared the passcode for the door with him. It changed monthly, but he even knew where to find it written down in reception, if need be. It shouldn't have changed yet: one, nine, seven, nine. It was a sign that things were destined to go his way— 1979 was the year of his first kill.

He turned his maroon sedan into the driveway of L'Orté Park and took the spot nearest the dumpster. After yet another swig of slivovitz, he got out of the parked car. Then he entered through the rear door, just as he had planned. The residents took an early dinner, and he expected that by now she would be in her suite, likely reading or watching television. His careful surveillance had revealed as much. Residents and employees tended to take the elevator, so he used the stairs to access her floor.

Employees were instructed to keep the door ajar when they were inside the room of a resident. Gracie's door was fully closed. He pressed his ear against it to make certain that no one was with her. Then he entered.

It was clear to him that she had not heard him. He saw that she did not react, but continued to read, reaching into her pocket and withdrawing a tissue. *Old people are always sniffling*, he observed.

"Long time, Gracie."

"Caesar!" Gracie exclaimed, rather loudly. "Elda Roman's son."

"No one calls me Caesar anymore, I use the name Mama gave me, Julius."

"Yes, yes, Julius Roman—now I remember. Why are you here, Julius?"

"I want what's mine as Laszlo's son; that's what I want."

"But that was all up to Laszlo, wasn't it? I mean, *if* you are his son."

"What do you mean *if*? He admitted it to me. I got him drunk on slivovitz and he *admitted* it. Rather than marry Mama after he got her knocked up, he goes and marries that American, Goldie, and then they have that stupid kid, Paul."

With every statement, he had moved closer to Gracie. Agitated, he was now pacing back and forth directly in front of her.

"You were friends with Paul, so Laszlo must have been good to you too."

"Friends? He was my half-brother! Even when I got rid of Laszlo for him and he inherited everything, he wouldn't believe me. I got one of those DNA tests that proved we were kin and he *still* didn't believe me. We spent hours together searching through stuff in that damn house and never found it."

"Found what exactly, Julius? What were you looking for?"

"Gold, old lady, gold. Why the hell do you think the place was named Gold Farm? Jozsef and then Laszlo made a tidy sum working with the mob over the years. You think he'd put that money in the bank?" He wanted her to face his truths—all of them.

"How do you know this, Julius?"

"For years, I did work for the same people and word gets out. They thought I already knew—me being Laszlo's kid and all."

"What do you mean when you say that you *got rid* of Laszlo for Paul?" Gracie's tone was very calm; she was controlled and showed no fear of her uninvited guest.

"What do you think? Paul spent whatever he had on drugs. Like I said, *stupid boy*. I hated Laszlo for not saying I was his son, and Paul was pissed at him too for some reason. We gave him one last chance, and, when he was still acting like a prick, we got him stinking drunk on bad booze. Enough alcohol and he was a goner. I even injected some 'tween his toes." With that, he bent his head close to Gracie, and she could smell alcohol and acrid cigarette smoke on his breath.

"I went to see Goldie a while after that. She said Janos had been by as well and claimed that neither of us was getting anything—it'd all gone to Paul. That place was disgusting! I figured there had to have been something there—I mean, the woman had been married to Laszlo—so I thought I'd shake her up a bit. She goes and trips on some trash. Fell down the basement stairs. Bump, bump, bump . . ."

Clearly, Julius was deranged. "You *killed* her?" Gracie was incredulous. She hadn't thought well of Julius, but it had never occurred to her that he was a murderer.

"No, she wasn't dead. Probably just broke something. She couldn't get up on her own. I just ditched her there to work it out for herself. Paul certainly wasn't going to be visiting her. He hated her for not standing up to Laszlo for him. But *stupid boy* wouldn't share. I did all the work, and I could see that he'd come into some serious money, but it was all going to drugs. He would have died eventually. I didn't have time to wait."

"How did you kill Paul? You *are* saying you killed him, right?"

"Hell, yes! He bought a sport-fishing boat . . . about six metres long. We went fishing out on the bay, toward L'Orté Island. Then he tells me that he paid *eighty grand* for the damn boat. I coulda killed him with my bare hands, then and there. Instead, I got *him* drunk and tipped him into the water. *Glug, glug, glug,* and he was fish food." Julius chuckled to himself and even his laughter sounded vicious.

Gracie was horrified, yet she managed to maintain her composure. She continued to speak to Julius in a soothing tone, but she herself was tense. Her blood pressure was up, her ears were ringing, and her head was pounding. "Then what happened?" she asked, urging Julius to continue.

"Oh, Janos happened, but that story is for dear Lucy, not for you, Gracie. I want to talk to *you* about Jozsef."

"I don't understand, Julius. Truly, I don't. What has Jozsef to do with this?"

"He was my first, you know. Jozsef was a pig, but if you'd been a better wife, I bet he wouldn't have gone elsewhere to satisfy himself . . ." Increasingly, what Julius mumbled was incoherent.

"I don't understand, Julius. Jozsef didn't make your mother pregnant with you— that was Laszlo. Jozsef wasn't like that." Gracie realized she was losing whatever little control she thought she might have established in the situation.

He sat in the chair opposite her own. "No, he wasn't *like that,*" Julius said, mocking her. "Didn't you ever wonder why, after my mother's death, he would have me spend so much time at your house? Why your husband was drinking slivovitz with a kid, barely a teenager? You're just as bad as that pig husband of yours!"

Gracie could see that there was little point in trying to direct the conversation. Ultimately, it would go in whichever direction Julius' mind wandered. She kept silent as he continued his rant.

"The mob guys figured out that I'd bumped him off, but when I explained what kind of pig he'd been, they gave me a job instead of a bullet. They figured I had talent, so after I did Jozsef, they sent me to Italy. Worked there for a few years. Learned a lot. Got even better. Very well paid too. Came back in '83, but I didn't stay long."

"What you did to little Lucy," Gracie hissed, finding it increasingly difficult to control her emotions.

"Ah, yes, *poor Lucy.*" Julius replied, taunting her. "That wasn't me—well, not completely. I had questions. I wanted to find out more about Paul, in case I needed someone else on a job. Paul had questions too. Laszlo was controlling every part of his life, including girls. Paul didn't have any sisters; he'd never even seen a naked one. So Paul went for Lucy. I had questions, so Paul; he had questions, so Lucy. See? He just messed around a bit with her before Janos found us and all hell broke loose. I took off like a bat outta hell and went back to Italy for ten more years. Sure didn't need that shit!" Then he added, "But this time, *I'll* be taking care of Lucy. Already got ol' Kent in the trunk."

Gracie exploded out of her chair toward him. She couldn't bear to listen to Julius say these things, especially not about her Lucy. But as feisty and motivated as Gracie was, with adrenaline coursing through her veins, she was nevertheless a tiny and frail ninety-six-year-old woman. Julius swung a haymaker, making easy contact with her jaw, breaking it, and knocking her backward. She crashed to the floor, her head hitting the corner of the end table beside the chair in which she had been sitting.

Julius knew she was dead. His concern now was to achieve a quick escape. He closed the outside door behind himself and returned to his car. His only regret was that he had not been able to tell her *how* he had killed Jozsef. *Lucy will pay for denying me that pleasure,* he thought.

CHAPTER 24

Julius kept his speed at the limit for the drive to Gold Farm; he didn't want to attract the attention of the police. Having surveilled the site periodically over the past couple of weeks, he was aware that work at the farm was coming to an end. If they had found the gold, he was planning to take it. If not, he would take whatever they *had* found. Somewhere there would be a clue about the location of the gold.

He lit another cigarette, and the image of Gracie's crumpled body lying on the floor popped back into his mind. He shook it off, only to find that the image returned. He was troubled by it—but not by guilt—by something else. Then it occurred to him: *she was smiling.* Faces sometimes contorted in death, especially given the death experience he provided his victims, but he could not recall seeing one with such a smile. It hadn't been a big smile, just a small one. *Then again, maybe not. What had she to smile about?*

He cut his lights and pulled into his usual spot. *Cazzo!* He had forgotten to dispose of Kent's things in Simcoe. *Too late.* He would take care of it later. He reached into the large bag behind the driver's seat and withdrew two syringes—each filled with his favourite drug cocktail—some duct tape, a fully-charged taser, and a telescoping police baton. He put on the hunting vest he'd kept at the bottom of the bag and stashed the items in the pockets of the vest. A short walk over a small knoll brought him to Gold Farm.

From the summit, he could see that the garage door remained up and that the interior of the garage remained well-lit. A man emerged from the house and was now occupied with removing boxes from the garage and disposing of them into a dumpster. By the time Julius reached the dumpster, the man was busy inside the coverall building erected in front of the garage. *Lucy must be in the big motor coach. Maybe she's already gone home. No, the little car is still here.*

Julius crept from behind the dumpster and toward the coverall building, its two open ends facing the motor coaches. He found the man in the hazmat suit now occupied with a canister from which he was directing gas into a metal cabinet. Julius paused, trying to determine what the gas might be. He decided it was best to wait. A short time later, the man closed the valve on the canister, disconnected the hose, and began to remove his hazmat gear. *The handyman!*

Albin had become distracted. He had suspected something was afoot when Lucy insisted he postpone checking the sump-pump pit and then, a short time ago, insist that he do it. He had picked up on Eve's welcome arrival and the care she had taken in hiding her car. He was glad they had overcome their little problem of late. Life was too short to hold tight to hurt feelings. He had tried to explain that to Helen, but his sister had not experienced the same challenges in her life.

His final task for the day was nearly done—fumigating the few items Lucy had recently uncovered. As he was removing his hazmat gear, he detected an odd smell—faint but unlike the various foul scents that he had encountered periodically at the site. Just as he identified it as stale cigarette smoke, Albin experienced a shooting pain up his back, rattling his body. He became disoriented as 1,200-volts of electricity jolted his body. Without muscle control, he lost his balance and fell to the ground.

From four metres away, Julius hit him with a second discharge, just to be sure. According to the supporting literature, his taser produced an arc of 50,000-volts and he could fire it three times without recharging. He decided to save the final one for later.

Another one bites the dust. Julius sat on him and used duct tape to secure Albin's mouth and hands. Then he injected him with the contents of one of the syringes. A moment later, Albin lay unconscious. Julius gave him a kick—then a second one—just to be certain.

Julius grabbed him by the ankles and dragged him toward the largest of the dumpsters. He planned to secure his feet with duct tape, throw him into the dumpster and tend to him later, when he had more time available to enjoy himself. The night was still young. It was too soon to kill him.

It was at that moment he heard Lucy calling out for Albin from the door of the large motor coach. Given the placement of things in the yard, she wouldn't be able to see them, but it was just a matter of time before a new vantage point might cause him to be discovered. Rushed, Julius dragged Albin up a ramp placed by the dumpster, and, as he tipped him in, he realized that he had failed to secure the feet, breaking from his plan yet again. He grabbed for him, but it was too late; Albin tumbled down and disappeared amid the debris. *Cazzo.*

Again, Lucy called out to Albin. She heard the sound of something being dumped. She could see into the coverall building and noticed that he hadn't returned there. Whatever he was doing, he would need time to get cleaned up before eating, and she was already hungry. As she crossed the yard, she called out to Albin a third time. She was rounding the corner on her way to check for Albin in the garage when she was struck by the taser.

As she awakened, disoriented and in pain, she found herself secured by tape and fixed to a chair centred inside the garage. Although there was light in the garage, anyone driving by would assume that work was being continued. No one would see what was actually happening because the view of the interior was blocked by the closed sides of the coverall building. Lucy began calling out, "Albin, *call the cops!*" She called out again and again, "Albin, *don't come* get me, just *call the cops!*"

Eve heard Lucy call out—again and again. It confused her that Lucy should call out in such a manner, emphasizing *call the cops* instead of simply screaming out for help. She grabbed her phone and hurriedly called the police. She wasn't able to provide much of the information the officer requested. She knew the name of Gold Farm, but not the address, as it had been programmed into her GPS. Her car was hidden from view on the far side of the motor coach, but she feared she couldn't safely return to it, so she couldn't check the history on her GPS without attracting attention. She tried to describe her location. When asked what the problem was, all she could say was that Lucy had called out several times in distress and stressed *call the cops*. The officer assured her that they would send a car as soon as they determined her location. She promised to call them again as soon as she could get more information safely, then disconnected.

Eve phoned Kent's number. The phone rang, but went to messages. She left a quick message and then phoned Helen on the Gillespie house line. "Helen, Eve here. Don't speak; just listen to me. Call the police and get help out here. There's some sort of trouble, I think. Lucy's in the garage and I get the impression she's talking to someone. She was just screaming, *call the cops.* I can't see Albin. I don't think the person she's talking to is Albin. I called Kent, but it went to messages. I left one. I've called the police, but they can't figure out where I am because I can't describe the location accurately. Call the police, and get help. I'll call again when I know something more. I'm going to check it out now. Please, hurry!"

Eve grabbed a knife from the kitchen, vacated the motor coach by way of the emergency exit, and sneaked between the little car and the tail end of the motor coach. Then she executed a perfect ballet move, a grand allegro, leaping into the yard, her long and graceful strides being few but bringing her to the coverall building in complete silence. She hoped that Lucy, but no one else, had seen her. Carefully, she rolled back one of the vents on the side of the coverall building facing the garage and peered out.

"Oh, your friend, the handyman, won't be helping you. I've already taken care of him," Julius said, looking toward the large dumpster. "No one will hear us way back here with all these boxes, Lucy, so save your breath." He walked behind her and stroked her throat, menacingly. "All that hollering for nothing, just irritating your throat. Tell me where it is and I'll let you go."

Though Lucy was staring at him, her eyes now focussed on the blank wall of the coverall building, where she detected that a side vent was slightly opened. "What do you want? Who are you? What have you done to Albin?" Lucy said, loudly, tense but ready for this to play out.

"I want the gold, Lucy, the gold."

"What gold? What on earth are you even talking about? Who are you? What have you done to Albin?"

"Just tell me what you've found here—here at Gold Farm," he said, gesturing grandiosely to emphasize the latter part of his statement.

"Nothing, or nothing much at all. A few trinkets, a few coins, some papers."

"What papers?"

"I'm not telling you anything more until you tell me who you are."

He bent toward her, his back to the coverall building, and met her eye-to-eye. "I'm the man who killed Janos." He spat the words toward her.

Lucy gasped when she heard he had killed her father and again when she realized who he was. *Those eyes—Caesar!*

"Oh, you didn't know. You thought he'd actually overdosed, a suicide. Nah, my mama was the only one who committed suicide. Janos married your mother instead of her. She thought he might make a good father for me. Was he? Just think, we might have been brother and sister. Yummy."

Lucy shuddered, trying to awaken from this bad dream. Needing to hear his last name, she asked, "Who *are* you?" But it remained unspoken.

"Let's just say I'm well-acquainted with Kent. And no, he won't be joining us either."

"But why did you kill my father?" Lucy cried, disbelieving anything that Caesar implied about Kent. He was at home in his library finalizing plans for Gold Farm. She *knew* this.

"After I took care of Paul—"

"You mean you killed him too?"

"Now, don't interrupt. I tried to find the gold, but no luck. *Never any luck.* Janos wouldn't help me get what was rightfully mine—outright refused—all because Paul and I had some fun with you when you were a kid. Don't even remember it, I bet. Anyway, he made a big deal about it. But I figured he was doing alright for himself, sending you to boarding school and everything, so I figured he must have gotten the gold after Laszlo and Paul were out of the way." Julius was pacing the garage now, ranting. "I told him what I'd done for him, that I'd benefitted him. He owed me. But he didn't believe me, I guess, or maybe he was just greedy. It was unfair, and when things are unfair they gotta be made right."

"How can this be made right? There is no gold. The only interesting documents we found were my father's adoption papers. That's all—I swear!"

"I've seen those. Paul and I found them when we were going through this stuff after Goldie died. Well, I guess we'll just need to convince Kent that you're worth something then, won't we?"

There was a noise from the direction of the dumpsters, as if the contents were shifting. Julius cagily moved to check out the source of the noise, providing Eve with the opportunity to approach Lucy and cut her restraints. But before they could escape, Julius returned; in his hand, he held a police baton.

Eve focussed on the baton, then she looked at the face of the man holding it. "David Tremblay!" Eve exclaimed. Immediately he swung the telescoping baton, but Eve nimbly executed a grand plié, gracefully dropping out of reach. Lucy scrambled out of the way just as Eve followed with a series of fouettés en tournant, taking Julius by surprise and hitting him in the head as she whipped her leg around while spinning. Eve wasn't wearing pointe ballet slippers, but sturdy pale pink Mary-Janes that increased the weight and power behind each connection she made with Julius.

Just as Eve was beginning to tire, a hulking figure emerged from the direction of the dumpsters. "Rats! You threw me in there with rats!" Albin was somewhat disoriented from the drug cocktail, but it wasn't having the effect Julius had relied upon. When Julius turned toward the dumpster escapee, he was met by Albin's powerful right uppercut. Under normal circumstances, Albin's uppercut would have taken Julius down, especially after Julius' pummelling by Eve. However, Albin wasn't fully recovered from the drug cocktail and his punch had not been well-placed. Julius came back at him with a vengeance.

Eve picked up the small chair to which Lucy had been secured, and, in a series of ballet moves, crossed the length of the garage with it, hollering, "Not my Albin, you don't!" Before Julius' raised baton could be lowered upon the disoriented Albin, Eve struck Julius across the back while completing an impressive stretch étendre, knocking the baton from his hand in the process.

Cazzo! He had failed to secure the baton with a wrist strap. He then turned toward Eve.

Eve and Albin struggled with the ill-effects of their encounters with Julius, but Julius was also dazed and hurt. Lucy had stayed out of the way when the others were better able to deal with Julius, but when he turned away from Albin and faced Eve, she realized she had to join the fight. Suddenly, she didn't feel small.

Lucy thought of Caesar and what he had done to her father and to her—and the rage within her swelled. She raced toward Julius with fury sparking from every fibre of her being. He looked at her in condescension, aware of her coming at him, her arms extended. Suddenly his body encountered the full force of her contact. He had expected her arms to flail against him with her hands outstretched while she tried to scratch at his eyes. He had been ready for that. Instead, he experienced a shockwave of pain radiating upward and throughout his entire body. He had been unprepared for the impact of her improvised two-legged flying kick to his groin as Lucy hurled herself at him with all the power she could muster. All breath escaped his body; he collapsed in excruciating pain, barely conscious and aware only of his agony.

Disoriented as he was, Albin lumbered over to Julius and sat, straddling him as he lay on the floor of the garage. Albin kept Julius immobilized, using his weight and strength. Eve, fuelled by adrenaline, grabbed a shovel she found nearby, and raised it above her head. "If you move, I swear I'll kill you!" she shrieked. Julius complied.

In landing on the cement floor of the garage, Lucy had bruised her tailbone but was otherwise unharmed. She picked herself up off the cement floor and hobbled over to retrieve whatever items Julius had in his vest pockets. The tape that she found was used to bind Julius' hands and feet together.

Eve tossed the shovel aside, and phoned the police to provide them with an update on the situation.

CHAPTER 25

Lucy repeatedly tried to contact Kent. Her anxiety rapidly mounted when she failed to connect with him. Although numbed by concern, she nevertheless had the presence of mind to transfer the audio file from the pendant to her computer, then rejoined Eve and Albin in the garage to watch Julius and wait for the police.

Albin phoned Helen, who explained to him what actions she had taken upon receiving Eve's call. She confirmed that she too had been unable to reach Kent. Helen assured him that the police would be arriving at Gold Farm very soon. By the time the call ended, police sirens could be heard as several cars and emergency vehicles sped down the driveway toward them.

Julius was taken into custody by the police. His physical injuries were evaluated by a paramedic, and he was rushed by ambulance to the regional hospital in Simcoe where he would remain under guard. It was apparent that Lucy's kick had caused a severe rupture—he required surgery.

Lucy was becoming frantic. *Where was Kent? Was he okay?* Police officers began to question Eve and Albin, but when an officer tried to question Lucy, she refused to answer until they took immediate action to determine Kent's whereabouts and safety. The officer in charge, Detective Sergeant Kovacs, was informed about her refusal to cooperate and so assumed Lucy's questioning. She saw him approaching. He conveyed the impression of being irritated, but not as irritated as Lucy was.

The detective was average height, with thick, unruly dark hair and bushy eyebrows that were even more unruly. "Evening ma'am, I'm DS Kovacs," he said, handing his card to Lucy. "Ma'am, I understand you're refusing to answer questions. Why is that?"

"Caesar said that he's well-acquainted with Kent—that's my husband—and that he—meaning Kent—won't be joining us. I've tried, and others have tried to contact Kent, but we can't and I'm worried. I want you to look for him, then I'll tell you everything I know. But first, please find Kent!" It was apparent to Lucy that DS Kovacs was genuinely listening to her, so she breathed deeply and relaxed just a bit.

"Your name?"

"Lucy Gillespie. Kent should be at home or his Toronto office, but he's not. I'm worried. You have no idea how worried I am. You've got to find him!" Clearly, Lucy was frantic.

Using a calming tone, DS Kovacs resumed his questioning, "Okay, is there any other place he might be? Any friend he might visit, an errand he might need to take care of, an appointment?"

"I can't think of anything, and certainly if there was something, he'd be home by now anyway."

"Ma'am, when did you first notice the intruder?"

"Caesar?"

"That's his name?"

"I think it's more a nickname. I don't know his real name. But, please, first find my husband."

"We've already got constables looking. Shall we go into your motor coach? You might be more comfortable."

Lucy agreed, and DS Kovacs followed her. He displayed skill in his questioning, and his manner did not cause Lucy to become further agitated. While Lucy, Albin, and Eve were being questioned separately, constables fanned out. Eventually, they located the maroon sedan with Kent stored uncomfortably in the trunk. Although he was experiencing the side effects of his confinement, as well as the tasing and the drugs he had received, it appeared he was otherwise unharmed.

In the middle of questioning Lucy, DS Kovacs took a telephone call. When the call concluded, he looked at her and smiled reassuringly. "Your husband has been found alive and well. He's just over the knoll," DS Kovacs explained, nodding his head to indicate the direction. "He'll be taken to hospital in Simcoe as a precautionary measure, and you can see him there shortly. I just need to get a bit more information from you first if you don't mind."

"Oh, you'll presumably want this," Lucy said as she removed the pendant necklace with the audio recorder and handed it to DS Kovacs. His eyes widened when he recognized the device. "It just so happens I was wearing it the whole time," she added.

Eve insisted that Albin go to the hospital for emergency treatment as well because he was experiencing the lingering effects of his ordeal. The paramedic agreed. Once Kent was loaded into the second ambulance, it stopped to collect Albin, and both men were transported to the regional hospital in Simcoe. DS Kovacs informed Lucy that one of the constables would remain on the property, securing the site until evidence was obtained, at which time it would be released back to her.

Shortly after DS Kovacs left them, Eve pulled her light-blue Bentley onto the roadway and the two women left Gold Farm, and headed for the hospital in Simcoe. A bank of fog rolled in and made the drive even more depressing. Lucy and Eve didn't speak, keeping their eyes intently focussed on the road ahead while Eve heeded the instructions of her GPS.

After they arrived at the hospital and Lucy confirmed that Kent was with an ER physician, she was once again located by a police officer who wanted to question her. She was confused at first and disbelieving that his questions concerned a separate matter. He explained that Juliette had been contacted regarding Gracie's death and had identified Lucy as the victim's sole family. So, while Kent was receiving medical treatment in the ER, Lucy was learning about Gracie's violent death at L'Orté Park that was also being investigated.

When the questioning was completed, Lucy joined Kent at his bedside. She was overwhelmed and numbed by the news of Gracie's tragic death, and the events of the evening at Gold Farm.

"He must have hit me with a taser. It felt as if my brain were being shaken inside my head," Kent informed her. "What a horrible sensation that was!"

"Yes, I know precisely how it feels."

"He got you too? Should have the doctor look at you while you're here." Concern etched on his face, he then turned to the doctor, "Shouldn't she, doctor? Would you please take a look at my wife's injuries."

"They think you were drugged as well, Kent. I wasn't, and I'm fine now." *Fine* was an overstatement. Lucy perceived that the experiences of the past twenty-four hours were surreal. She was detached, flat.

"It's possible to develop an infection in response to the taser darts," the doctor explained. "Are you currently experiencing any pain, shortness of breath, or headaches? Did you vomit at any time since you were hit by the taser?" When Lucy answered *no* to all the doctor's questions and the nurse had tended the small wounds left by the taser, Kent was visibly relieved.

"How soon before I'm released?" Kent enquired. Neither he nor Albin was inclined to malinger, so Lucy assumed a similar query was being made by Albin elsewhere in the department. Now that he was out of danger, Kent needed to reconnect with some part of his normal life.

"We're going to keep you here for another day—at least—in order to monitor how well your body is clearing the drugs you were given," the doctor advised. Kent looked at Lucy, his eyes communicating dismay at the news. "At this point, we're uncertain what all the injection contained. Your electrolytes are off a bit and we're concerned about possible kidney damage. We'll re-evaluate again in the morning once we've received all the lab results," the doctor informed him.

"You've talked with the police already, haven't you?" Lucy enquired, addressing Kent.

"Yeah, I told them that Julius got me at Roman's but that I have no idea why."

"So, that's your tailor, Julius Roman? I knew him as Caesar, and Eve called him David Tremblay. Remember the woman, Elda—the one I said died by suicide when my parents married?" Kent nodded. "Well, we're pretty sure he was her son by Laszlo. He admitted to murdering my father, Kent. He actually admitted it." Kent took her hand, squeezing it in his. Lucy then spoke slowly and softly, "Kent, I was just told that Gracie was killed tonight at L'Orté Park."

"We're going to move the patient upstairs now. I suggest you get some sleep as well, Mrs. Gillespie. An ordeal such as yours can take more out of you than you might imagine." And with that the doctor made it clear it was time for Lucy to leave. She kissed Kent goodnight and watched as his bed was wheeled to the elevator. She knew he had heard what she'd said about Gracie, but the look on his face told her that he had failed to process the information. She understood.

By the time Lucy returned to the waiting room, Eve was already there, waiting patiently. Albin—who had suffered a cracked rib as well as the effects of tasing and the drug cocktail—had been sent upstairs for observation and given the same conditions and timelines as Kent.

Lucy and Eve departed, returning to Gold Farm in the fog. During the drive, Lucy told Eve about Gracie's death earlier that same evening. While the police had taped off the garage, dumpsters, and coverall building, Lucy was advised that she could use her motor coach. Relieved to hear the news, she invited Eve to join her, and the women locked themselves inside for the night.

Though the hour was late, they were wide awake, somewhat agitated, and definitely hungry. Eve set about organizing a meal for them, using some of the take-out she had brought for Albin, and Lucy set up her laptop to access the audio file from the recorder pendant she had worn during the ordeal. While they ate leftovers, they listened to the replay of their experience earlier in the evening. Neither one paid any particular attention to the food; it was merely an intake of much-needed nutrients. Given the experience they'd shared, their priorities were somewhat shifted.

"That should clarify things for them regarding what happened here tonight. I didn't want to share it with them before getting a download for myself, just in case they wouldn't let me get one before they took control of the audio recorder pendant."

"Well, shouldn't Gracie have had her audio recorder as well, Lucy?" Eve asked.

"I hope so," Lucy said, beginning to regret having suggested to Gracie that she turn off the recorder when she wasn't reminiscing, "but I'll just wait until I can claim whatever she was wearing, or gain access to her room. Hopefully, they'll have recognized it for what it is and already have the information—but I want a copy of it as well. I'll take my laptop with me so I can download it right there when I find it. The police will get it as quickly as possible after that."

Eve had brought a bottle of Arrack Punsch with her from home. Trying to distance herself from the events of the day, she explained to Lucy that if they were going to have pea soup, she would have heated the spiced liqueur, but because they weren't, it was best to enjoy it chilled. Eve was babbling. Lucy had never tasted Punsch, but after a day such as they'd had, the strong drink was very appealing. *And it might help us sleep*.

The day that dawned was less bright; a portent of a world without Gracie. Lucy rolled over in bed and groaned, then arose and readied herself for the day. She found that as long as she was busy, she could pretend to be doing well, but whenever she thought of Gracie dying violently and alone but for her attacker—that's when she would break down, overtaken by emotion.

Eve was already having breakfast as Lucy left the bedroom. "Find everything you need, Eve?" Lucy called out.

"Yes. I'm doing just fine. And you? You look rough. Is that due to the Punsch or last night's ordeal?"

"Hard to say, but that Punsch packed a punch. Try to say that really fast: Punsch packed a punch, Punsch packed a punch, Punsch . . ." and then Lucy started to sob. Her tears flowed, and Eve held her until they ran dry.

"You have what in Swedish is 'Is i magen' translates to 'ice in the stomach'. It means that you remain calm in the midst of chaos. Now the ice is melting a bit. It's understandable. And I think it's good sometimes to let it all out when you can, like now," Eve said, soothingly.

It wasn't long before Lucy was doing somewhat better. She assumed it was due to the combination of food and a good cry. The fact that she had a good friend in Eve helped as well.

The fog had given way to a fine drizzle. When she realized how very late in the morning it was, Lucy made a quick telephone call to L'Orté Park and spoke briefly with Mrs. Drogan. She learned that the investigation was continuing and Gracie's suite remained unavailable.

Lucy and Eve decided to purchase a change of clothing for each of the men on their way to visit them in the hospital. Albin needed clean clothes, but neither of them was prepared to search through his private possessions. Moreover, Kent's suit had been completely destroyed, and he had not kept a change of clothes in the motor coach.

As they prepared to return to Simcoe, DS Kovacs arrived. He had already listened to the audio recording provided by Lucy and had additional questions. Lucy answered them and provided him with a quick summary of the Szabo family history to help him put things into perspective. She shared with him her suspicion that Gracie's death would most likely have been at the hands of Julius Roman, aka Caesar, aka David Tremblay. He appeared to agree, though he said that the outer doors at L'Orté Park used passcodes and there was no evidence of forced entry into the home itself. Clearly, further investigation was required.

By the time the detective departed, the drizzle had subsided, and the two women were ready to visit Kent and Albin. Unthinking, Lucy approached her little car and then realized that they would need to take Eve's Bentley. There was no way Eve would fit into the smaller vehicle. She turned to see Eve opening the door of her own car, shaking her head at Lucy. "You are distracted," Eve observed, "I'm not surprised, but it's probably good that I'm driving."

The men were sharing a semi-private room and had finished their lunch by the time Lucy and Eve arrived. While they were thankful for their visitors and the gifts of clean clothes, they were disappointed not to be leaving the hospital.

"Have you located my wallet and cellphone by any chance?" Kent asked.

"I'll look into that. The police presumably have both by now. Do you know if your phone and wallet were in the car with you, or were they left back at Roman's?"

"I actually don't know," he answered. "If the police don't have them, then we'll need to assume they're lost—"

"I'll phone DS Kovacs and take care of it. Don't worry." Lucy said, interrupting him. She went on to summarize the visit they had received from the detective just prior to leaving for the hospital. "There's little to be done by us until you're released from the hospital, and the police let us have access to Gracie's suite and all of Gold Farm," she stated in conclusion.

"Albin tells me you and he had expected to be leaving Gold Farm and returning home today. Hopefully that will happen tomorrow. There's still a problem with our test results, but they say that they're improving. I think we're altogether exhausted."

The fine rain stopped during the night, and Thursday morning looked promising. After a good night's sleep and a hearty breakfast, both women were ready to begin the day. Lucy phoned the hospital and confirmed that both Kent and Albin were due to be released later that morning. Her call to the detective also produced some good news—Kent's wallet and cellphone had been located. They would be brought to Gold Farm by the officer coming on-duty there.

There was a new thought taking form in Lucy's mind, though it remained amorphous. She brushed it aside for the moment to greet the young officer, who had just arrived at the door of the motor coach with a bag containing Kent's items. Soon after, they were back in Eve's Bentley, heading once again toward the hospital.

While waiting for Kent and Albin to dress and receive medical instructions regarding their follow-ups, Lucy phoned the detective. She asked when Gracie's jewellery and clothing would be released to her and was told that Gracie wore no jewellery. Whatever clothing had been worn by Gracie was being retained as evidence until her case was closed. However, the police had concluded their collection of evidence from her suite so anything there was available to Lucy.

It wasn't long before the four of them were ensconced in Eve's Bentley, leaving the hospital. "I'm sorry, but unless anyone objects, I need to visit L'Orté Park. It'll take just a short time," Lucy promised. Of course, no one objected, so Lucy provided Eve with directions to their destination. Although they each offered to accompany her, she thought it best that they remain in comfort in the car while she alone carried out her mission.

Mrs. Drogan approached Lucy as she entered through the front door and offered her condolences. Lucy could see that Mrs. Drogan was visibly shaken by what had happened to Gracie. As the Supervisor of the residence, the security of its residents was one of her most sacred responsibilities. She seemed nervous and unusually talkative as they made their way to Gracie's suite. "As you instructed, no one has entered since the police released it."

Lucy thanked her and explained the reason for her visit. "I'm looking for a small audio recording device that Gracie used to record her thoughts. Sometimes she kept it in her pocket, but other times it was just left out, usually on this end table. I wouldn't want to lose her last recording—her final words. The police said it wasn't with her when she was brought in." The sitting room was in disarray as a result of the emergency personnel who had attended Gracie. They took a moment to orient themselves and then began their search.

They moved every knick-knack on the shelves and tables and shoved their hands into the crux of each seat-back but found nothing. On her hands and knees, Lucy searched near Gracie's favourite chair. When she raised her head, Lucy saw blood—Gracie's blood—on the corner of the end table. The shock of seeing evidence of Gracie's violent encounter startled Lucy. As she fell back on her haunches and pain radiated from her tailbone as it hit the floor, her hand happened to touch a facial tissue that had fallen and become lodged behind the leg of the sofa. In it, Lucy could feel the audio recorder. She grabbed it, thanked Mrs. Drogan, and went to rejoin Kent and her friends in the parking lot.

As Eve turned the Bentley toward Gold Farm, Lucy enquired, "What kind of equipment is needed to dig a hole in the garage floor? And follow-up question: Is that equipment available at the site now?"

"The floor is poured concrete, so no, currently the equipment necessary to dig a hole in the garage floor is not on the site. However, I can certainly get the equipment in short order if you need it. Why do you ask?"

"I noticed something about the garage that night. I may be wrong of course, but I've got to check it out. We've been working out there and doing a very thorough job of it, but we've really not found anything significant. Julius was very insistent that there was gold to be found. He even implied that was the reason for the name of Gold Farm. Please make that call for me. I need to look under the floor—it's the only place left."

Kent completed his call and announced, "The equipment needed will be on-site by mid-afternoon today. Will the police permit it?" He received no reply.

Lucy was focussed on downloading Gracie's final recording. Once she confirmed that she had secured a copy of the file, she phoned DS Kovacs and asked him about the release of the site. "I have something that may answer any questions you still have regarding Gracie Hogan's murder, detective. It's a recording Gracie made last night and contains some very interesting admissions by Julius Roman. Shall I give it to the officer on-duty at the property, or will you be by to pick it up?" She was relieved to learn that the site was being released to them, and the police officer currently on duty would withdraw upon their return to Gold Farm. Detective Kovacs promised to drop by later in the day to secure the recording.

Once they returned to Gold Farm, Eve set about making lunch while Kent and Albin returned to the garage with Lucy. They were eager to hear her reasoning for the dig, which would be occurring soon in the garage. Kent swung the garage door up and it slid along the tracks until it was parallel to the ceiling. The trio stepped inside and Albin turned on the auxiliary lighting.

"I was sitting back there in a chair," Lucy explained, indicating a location far back in the garage. "I was trying to calm myself, so I ended up staring at the ceiling a lot and then out at the coverall building—any boring surface, actually. Getting tasered left me somewhat confused and I was trying to focus, to think. I didn't realize it right away— probably because we had far more important things happening—but after it was all over, for some reason one little thing kept niggling me."

Lucy took a deep breath before continuing. "Look at the ceiling. When the garage door is up, as it is now and as it was that night, it completes a box on the ceiling. Why? I've never seen any garage—not that I've seen a lot, but nevertheless—why bother to build a bulkhead around three sides? I don't think it's to cover pipes or wiring or for any aesthetic reason certainly. In other garages, the metal track for the garage door is the only thing you see all the time, and the garage door obscures a portion of the ceiling when it's up, but you can still see the ceiling above the door when you look at an angle. Here, you can't see the ceiling at all when the door is up, no matter your angle—all because of that bulkhead. Please pull down the door; I need to see the ceiling up there."

The door was slid back along the track, revealing the ceiling, and the opening to the garage was again closed. There, on the ceiling, just inside the bulkhead perimeter, was an awen seared into the wooden beam, as if by branding. "I say we dig here." Lucy pointed to a spot on the floor directly beneath the awen. Kent and Albin remained in stunned silence.

Leaving Kent and Albin to discuss the practicalities, Lucy went to join Eve in the motor coach. She had just entered when she heard a car approaching. DS Kovacs was eager to receive the audio recorder from Lucy, though curious about why Gracie had such a device. Never had he investigated a case that went so quickly from having very little evidence to such significant evidence. It certainly looked as if there were many deaths attributable to Julius. He thanked Lucy and soon was gone, keen to hear the new recording.

Kent and Albin returned to the motor coach, hungry for lunch. They were both frisk, according to Eve. Lucy was appreciative of her friend's help, and discovered that she, too, had more of an appetite than she expected. Kent explained that they thought it best if the remaining boxes were transferred to the coverall building, emptying the garage completely. Kent had already moved them, though there had been much grumbling from Albin who was sidelined as a result of his cracked rib. They were certain that there was enough room available for a small front-end loader to access the garage without first having to dismantle the coverall building.

Kent suggested that during the removal of that portion of the concrete floor, Lucy should deal with the remaining boxes in whatever manner she thought best. She was tempted to throw all of them directly into the dumpster but thought better of it. Having spent many days painstakingly sorting through the dross, she would complete the task.

As they finished lunch, they heard a loud crunching noise—the sound of a large vehicle being driven down the gravel driveway. Mike and Bill, workers contracted by Kent on a regular basis, were arriving with the equipment Kent had requested.

Eve, Albin, and Lucy worked in the coverall building, sorting through the last of the boxes. Although Eve and Lucy wore hazmat gear, Albin did not. He declared his invincibility, pointing out that he had already survived a dumpster full of this same garbage, plus rats. The task went quickly. By the time the front-end loader had removed the cement slab from the floor beneath the awen, Eve and Lucy had already discarded their hazmat gear. No boxes remained in the coverall building. Nothing more of significance had been found.

Kent instructed the operator of the front-end loader, Mike, to be especially careful once they had removed the concrete and reached soil level. After a few scrapes of the underlying soil, they hit a metal plate. With the shovel from the front-end loader raising a corner of the metal plate, Kent and Bill were able to tip the plate off and away from the hole. Beneath lay a vault topped by a piece of plywood.

Kent pulled his men off the job and sent them home without the front-end loader. Then he made a quick telephone call. Once Mike and Bill were gone from the property, it was time to investigate the vault. Kent removed the piece of plywood. It was as though a small submarine had been buried, with only a piece of plywood covering the hatch. A ladder could be seen affixed to the side of the opening. Albin's flashlight revealed a small chamber less than two metres deep and extending lengthwise toward the back of the garage. Kent thought it might be too dangerous for Lucy and that he should enter the vault.

"Don't worry," Lucy assured him, appreciative of Kent's concern, "I'll be just fine." She climbed down the ladder and into the vault. "I just need to crouch down a bit in here. Hand me the flashlight, please."

A moment later, Lucy handed up the first of nearly one hundred, one-kilogram gold bars and several locked metal boxes. Kent, Albin, and Eve all watched in amazement. When Lucy had offered up the final item, she emerged from the underground vault, intact but dirty. The plywood was returned to its original placement and Kent positioned the front-loader over it.

Eve disappeared into Lucy's motor coach and soon reappeared with glasses and champagne, which she had brought with the intention of enjoying with Lucy and Albin Tuesday night. "I think it's time for a toast, don't you?" she said, looking at Lucy as she proffered a glass of bubbly.

"To Gracie," and they all joined in.

The sudden rumble of a second heavy vehicle on the gravel driveway caught their attention. "Earlier, I phoned for an armoured truck, just on a hunch," Kent announced. "We live in a world where a guy can't even trust his tailor, so why take any chances? If I'd been wrong about it, no harm done. Let's document this with plenty of photos and videos, okay?"

The gold bars were transferred to the armoured truck; all paperwork was completed; photographs and videos were taken. Kent had arranged for the storage of the Gold Farm treasure in a bank vault. It wasn't long before the precious cargo was on its way.

"Now what?" Lucy said, watching the armoured truck as it returned to the highway. "Who's staying the night and who's leaving?"

It was agreed that they would secure the site and return home in Eve's Bentley. Each needed time amid familiar surroundings to fully relax and heal. As Eve explained, "We are frisk, but we are not completely healthy."

CHAPTER 26

It had been a very intense couple of months for Lucy since the events at Gold Farm. Julius Roman had been held in police custody at various secure locations in Ontario as the legal system evaluated the range and magnitude of his numerous crimes, many of which had involved gruesome deaths of his victims. The police services in several other countries were also investigating his possible involvement in unsolved murders within their respective jurisdictions. The wheels of justice may turn slowly, but progress was apparent.

Focus shifted to his mental capacity. After a substantial number of hours spent with mental health professionals, Julius was deemed fit to stand trial. He was merely a nasty, avaricious man with few prospects, but with a taste for slivovitz and a penchant—but little skill or luck—for gambling. It was expected that the recordings of his confessions, both to Gracie and to Lucy, would result, ultimately, in the speedy disposition of the case.

Lucy had concluded the sale of Gold Farm to Kent's investor group, Aureus. The house and garage, including the vault, had already been demolished, and the entire site was in the process of being graded. Once developed, it would be known as either Aureus Park or Aureus Gardens. A marketing study to resolve this had been commissioned at the insistence of a few large investors. After his experiences there, Kent was unimpressed with the kerfuffle over such a minor point. In the meantime, it was the Aureus project—a self-contained green community located near the junction of several major highways.

In accordance with Gracie Hogan's final instructions to her lawyer, Juliette Garner, Gracie's remains were cremated and her ashes interred within the gravesite of her sister, Annie, in Simcoe. Lucy had tried to locate the grave of Giovanni Sarto, but without any success to date. She and Kent had been present at Annie Hogan's gravesite, as had Juliette and Mrs. Drogan.

Because they were all together, it was decided that they would complete the transfer of Gracie's remaining assets to Lucy and discuss the matter of L'Orté Point and L'Orté Island. Juliette had arranged for the three of them to use a private meeting room at L'Orté Park. Lucy's first surprise was to discover that she now owned the facility. *That might explain the abundance of shortbread.* She hadn't realized that Gracie had been responsible for its construction. The second surprise was the impressive extent of Gracie's more liquid assets. There were no additional properties. She had organized and simplified her estate as much as possible many years prior to her death.

"Next, you have the trust set up by Gianni. Essentially, this was just a way of putting all of Gianni's assets into one basket and then managing them for the benefit of named beneficiaries: first Annie, then through her, to Gracie, and now to Lucy. The beneficiary can take full control at any time by dissolving the trust. It contains L'Orté Point and L'Orté Island and some more liquid assets that have been managed to ensure growth and the ability to pay any costs associated with the properties."

"So, I could dissolve that trust today and take full responsibility for both properties?"

"Yes, indeed. I have the necessary documents, which would require your signature releasing Garner & Garner from any future involvement. However, I first need to disclose to you a few important details about the properties."

Juliette collected her thoughts and began, "L'Orté Point, as you know, is a massive piece of real estate. Gracie wasn't planning to use it, and the firm didn't want to see the liquid assets depleted in paying for property taxes and liability insurance, so we signed an agreement with the province of Ontario, which renewed repeatedly over the years. L'Orté Point is owned by the trust, but, under the agreement with the province, the trust has no costs or legal responsibility for it. The Province of Ontario assumes those responsibilities in exchange for it being designated a nature preserve."

"I wasn't aware they did that sort of thing so many years ago," Lucy admitted.

"Oh yes, since about 1893 actually, with the establishment of Algonquin Park. Moreover, the Point is now considered ecologically sensitive, and it is doubtful that any building project would be permitted under current environmental guidelines. The relationship, however, can be re-negotiated every twenty years—previously it had been every thirty years—and the next deadline is 2017. If there is no agreement, you will be presented with a property tax bill on L'Orté Point for 2018. Even though it is posted to warn against trespassing, you would require liability insurance because the remnants of the old lodge are extensive and could present a danger to anyone wandering about there."

Lucy and Kent listened attentively.

"Now, L'Orté Island is a bit of a different issue. Currently, it is included in the agreement with the Province of Ontario with regard to the province assuming all costs and responsibilities. They've also agreed that—other than signage to minimize trespass—they will not utilize the property in any regard: no camping, no temporary buildings or structures such as docks—nothing. However, you and anyone you designate have full access at all times, even while the agreement with the province is in place. So, you're not paying property tax on it—yet—but you could go camping there or apply for a building permit. You might decide to rebuild the manor house. I understand it was so well-constructed that much of it is still standing."

"I assume this stack of documents is for me then," Lucy concluded.

"Actually take the entire briefcase. I packed it with everything you need. Think about it. You might choose to see another lawyer. But decide promptly. You need to be ready to make your proposal next year in order to have everything ready for 2017."

Kent interjected, "There's a lot to consider, but tell me, given your familiarity with all this, is there any question Lucy should be asking that she isn't?"

Juliette reached for a shortbread, "I wouldn't presume . . . Okay, in Lucy's shoes I guess I'd be asking what it is I truly want. How might all this fit—or not fit—into your life?" Then she sat back in her chair and nibbled her shortbread.

CHAPTER 27

Her business concluded, Juliette paused at the front desk and caught the eye of Mrs. Drogan. After a brief and cordial goodbye, the lawyer walked beneath the old tulip tree and looked back at L'Orté Park for the last time.

Having spent so much of her career acting on behalf of Gracie Hogan, Juliette now had a void rapidly developing in her life; her sense of purpose was diminished. She was upset at how things had ended for Gracie; the old woman had not deserved to die under such circumstances—though it was facile to think that no one did.

As she merged her Mercedes into traffic heading for Toronto on the controlled-access highway, her mind wandered back to the one unpleasant discussion she had with Gracie—the day Gold Farm was turned over to Lucy. She hadn't intended to be so truculent with the woman, but fear had overtaken her. She had to protect the firm, her family, her heritage—just as Gracie had protected her nephew and later, Lucy.

While doing research for Lucy, Juliette had been devastated to learn that C Garner had been a Janus. While Bennett had created the John Taylor alias and directed Gianni Sarto in its use, he had sought merely to profit from those shady dealings with the mob. Clarence had gone much deeper into the muck. On one hand, the lawyer reflected all that was good in Garner & Garner, while on the other hand he worked for the mob when their known consiglieri was thought unsuitable for a particular matter. Clarence must have been excellent. No one at the firm would have thought the conservative lawyer had such socially destructive proclivities. He had been dead these past fifteen years and Juliette had never heard mention of such things. None of the surviving partners who would have worked with Clarence ever breathed a word of such a distasteful association. She couldn't help but wonder if there were a Janus among them as well.

She had returned to the retirement home the day after the unpleasant conversation, leaving her own audio recorder secreted in one of Gracie's knick-knacks, unbeknownst to her. Unlike the device used by Lucy, this one relayed a signal to a device Juliette placed elsewhere in the home. She merely convinced Mrs. Drogan that she required a secure place—a small office—at the home. Mrs. Drogan was compliant because, as Gracie's lawyer, Juliette was effectively her boss. Juliette had been able to confirm that Gracie had kept her word and said nothing about the John Taylor alias to Lucy.

While searching the archives for information on Gianni Sarto, she had noticed that Andrew and Bennett Garner had created the identity, along with several others, but they had not been used in the same manner. It was apparent that the other aliases were all used by Gianni when he purchased parcels of land on the Point. He would buy under an alias, securing a low purchase price, then sell at a significantly inflated price to himself under his own name. While highly unethical today, this was merely creative business practise at the time. As he collected investors for his L'Orté Lodge project, they would assume that the property was far more valuable than it really was, and invest accordingly. After the fire, no investors came forth to lodge a claim, which was rather odd yet fortunate. It was possible that many of the investors had money that was not above scrutiny, so they couldn't avail themselves of a justice system that required them to have 'clean hands'.

Juliette had recognized something else in the archives. Bennett Garner's son, Clarence, who had been considered a legal prodigy, did a considerable amount of work for the Szabos over the years and Caesar's name had been mentioned in notes and memos toward the end of Clarence's career. She had learned that in his later years, he helped a nineteen-year-old Caesar escape to Italy after killing Jozsef. The notes were highly cryptic, but she was sufficiently familiar with the names mentioned to know that this was not the sort of business in which Garner & Garner should have been engaged. She wondered who had helped Caesar return in 1983 and then leave again later that same year. And more importantly, did someone help him return in 1993 and if so—Who? *Caesar would know and that meant Julius Roman would know.*

As soon as she arrived back at her office, Juliette returned to the dusty files in the firm's archives. What she needed was there, somewhere. A missing piece for this jigsaw puzzle. She just needed to find it—and soon. Julius Roman would be getting desperate, and desperate people do desperate things. She had to protect the firm.

CHAPTER 28

Everyone recognized that Lucy's spirit was flagging after news leaked that the Crown might *do a deal* with Julius Roman, aka Caesar, aka David Tremblay. Whether it was true, or not, it was logical to think that he would try to secure a shorter sentence for himself by providing names and giving testimony against the upper-echelon criminals he had come to know over the course of his lengthy career. The Crown was also discussing his extradition and whether or not it would supersede his trial in Ontario. While she didn't care where he was incarcerated, anything other than a full life sentence with no chance of parole struck her as inconceivable, especially with the evidence against him—evidence she and Gracie had secured.

In the hope of cheering her up, Kent organized the getaway they had been discussing since their final meeting with Juliette at L'Orté Park. Yoichi, Donald, Eve, Albin, and Helen would be joining them. Kent's planning was painstakingly detailed, yet his purpose was straightforward: he hoped it would take Lucy's mind off Julius.

A Sikorsky S-92 helicopter provided a new experience for Yoichi and Donald. Although the others had flown in helicopters on previous occasions, Albin and Helen's experience had been in military, not executive, aircraft. The flight attendant provided snacks and drinks in the spacious and well-appointed cabin as the helicopter flew southwest toward L'Orté Point.

Although Donald was visibly nervous at first, he quickly took delight in his new favourite mode of transportation. It took Yoichi a while longer to relax.

"This is my hello and goodbye to L'Orté Point," Lucy said. "We've told the provincial authorities that we want to speak with them."

"I doubt they'll turn down such a generous gift," Eve declared, sipping her mimosa. "Are you certain you don't want to walk the land before it's no longer yours?"

"Yes, I'm sure. I know it sounds a bit odd, but I really *don't* want to."

"After everything that has gone on out here over the years, it's good to think that nature can just be left to heal on her own. You're doing a good thing, Lucy," affirmed Donald.

L'Orté Point jutted out into Lake Erie from the mainland. Kent had determined where Lucy's property began and was able to point it out to the other passengers. It was obvious from the air—no paved roads entered that portion of the Point. There were a few stands of what Helen said were likely black maple or black walnut, the trees sought by the loggers of the early twentieth century. Now, most of the trees were cottonwood, their heart-shaped leaves fluttering silvery in the breeze. Near the end of the Point, there was evidence of a cluster of dwellings, some substantial in size. From the air, the site gave the impression of an archaeological dig with evidence of buildings obscured by vegetation. They concluded that this must be the lodge that had burned in 1933. Somewhere down there, Lucy's grandfather, Giovanni Sarto, had died a violent death.

The relationship between the Point and the curve of the coastline resulted in the formation of a bay in which L'Orté Island was positioned. As soon as Kent was assured that Lucy had seen as much as she wanted of the Point, he informed the pilot and they made the short hop to the island.

The 101-hectare island was nearly tear-shaped, and no sand beach was visible from the air. On one side, small waves rolled against rocks along the shoreline, while the other side was reedy and quiet.

"Oh, there's a boat of some kind," Yoichi noted, happy at the thought of getting her feet back on the ground very soon.

"That's a river barge such as they use in Europe," Kent clarified. "A friend owns it, and it'll be our accommodation during this visit. The luggage is already aboard. We'll be landing near the centre of the island, in that glade. As you can see, there really isn't a beach. Other than that, you know as much as we do.

"Lucy, if you decide to keep the island, we'll need to construct a floating dock on each side," Kent advised her. Then, informing everyone, he added, "I was told the fishing should be good. They said there's smallmouth bass, yellow perch, pike, sunfish, . . . but what do I know about such things? Donald, what about you?"

"Me? My maternal grandfather used to fish off the dock at his cottage, but I don't recall ever seeing him catch anything. That's the extent of my experience. Anyone?" In response, everyone shook their head and shrugged their shoulders. "At that rate, there won't be any fresh fish, I guess."

Abruptly, Yoichi pointed toward the island and asked, "Is that a house?"

"You mean in the centre of the island? That would be our yurt for daytime cover, relaxing, and eating," Kent answered, reaching for a small wedge of brie.

"No, not the yurt. Over there, in that bunch of trees over on the rocky side. I think we're looping over there again. Check it out."

Everyone was interested in seeing the structure Yoichi had spotted, aware that it must be the manor house built by

Gianni. It was well-hidden amid the foliage, but they took note of its location.

Lucy was particularly interested. "I think that after we get settled in and grab a bite to eat, I'll walk over and take a closer look at that. You're all welcome to join me, but really, please spend your time exploring or fishing or just relaxing. Kent arranged for gear and there's a small motor boat."

Once again, Kent signalled the pilot. Soon the helicopter was setting down at one end of the glade.

It was a perfect September day. The air was dry, the sky clear and blue, and a gentle breeze blew in from the south, across the lake. During the day, it was comfortably warm, while nights were getting longer and colder with the approach of winter. Kent spoke briefly with the pilot, then the helicopter returned to the sky. Their little party made its way toward the yurt located on the far side of the small meadow

"We'll be eating dinner this evening on the barge, but there's food and drink available here in the yurt during the day, so if you get thirsty or feel peckish, you know where it is. If you have a question about the barge or the yurt, just ask Elinor," Kent announced, introducing them to the woman who greeted them at the yurt. Elinor wore a casual uniform, not unlike what Helen wore when on the job. "She is the person to ask. I know nothing." He urged everyone to do their own thing. It was to be a simple and rustic experience, he claimed. "There are wash-up facilities at the yurt, or you can try to find the barge. That reminds me—I have GPS tags for each of you. Just use your cellphone to register your GPS. We'll register the entire group so that each of you knows where everyone else is, within a few metres at least."

Lucy was eager to explore the island. She had come dressed in her hiking gear in anticipation and had encouraged others to do the same. Eve was an outdoorsy person, so she already had the requisite clothing, as was also the case with Helen.

Yoichi, however, was more familiar with the paved and highly urban world. Lucy was relieved that she had been present to intercede when Yoichi had considered the purchase of unsuitable footwear, favouring a pair she thought more à la mode. *The term à la mode does not pertain to hiking shoes!* thought Lucy, remembering that day.

Donald and Albin wanted to try their hand at fishing while everyone else decided to wander toward the ruins of the manor. By default, Eve led the way—her long strides making it impossible for her to do anything else. No one had realized that she was an avid birder until she became excited upon hearing *dick-dick-ceessa-ceessa.* "A dickcissel," she enthused. "It's rather late in the season for him to be here. He looks similar to a sparrow, except he's got vivid yellow markings on his head and breast." No one saw the bird, and a moment later she was pointing out a little grey bird with big black eyes, a small round bill, and brushy crest, which she identified as a tufted titmouse. Just then, a red-headed bird flew by, and then another. "You have a family of red-headed woodpeckers! If you've got oak trees on the island, they'll stay all year long and gorge on acorns. I'm off to get some photos." With that and a little wave, she was gone.

Helen lagged behind the group, enjoying herself amid the lush plant growth. Already, she found herself hoping to return late in the spring, when the flowering dogwood would be at its best. She pointed out a green dragon plant to Yoichi, who was also taking a bit longer, though not for the same reason. Then she introduced her to a Shumard oak and later a pin oak, but detected that Yoichi wasn't impressed. "Botanical knowledge is essential for survival," Helen declared. "You'd starve to death or die from exposure out here on your own."

"I'd *rather* die than live out here!" There was no further immediate comment from Yoichi. She had become entangled within a spider's web suspended among the low branches of the pin oak. "Ugh," Yoichi exclaimed as she stomped her feet and flapped her hands about, and glared at Helen, warning: "Don't you dare laugh!"

Muffled laughter emanated from Helen.

Lucy and Kent ambled side-by-side where possible, stopping periodically to consider the view and condition of the terrain on their little island, and wondering how long it would take before they knew each rock and tree.

Suddenly, Yoichi found herself enveloped in a dense cluster of hackberry. The trees had been severely damaged at some point in the past and had regrown more shrub-like. Additionally, an abundance of flowering dogwood sealed her inside the thicket. "Helen!" she called out. But Helen's eye had caught something of interest to her, and she had gone off in the opposite direction to investigate. It took but a moment before Lucy received a telephone call from Yoichi asking for help. A short time later, with the aid of the GPS, they were all circling back to locate Yoichi.

"If I had a Samurai sword I could hack my way through, but that's not the case so I'm afraid you're going to need to find your own way out. We're out here, just move toward my voice," Kent called out to her. "Helen says I'm now standing where she last saw you, before you were devoured by the thicket."

"Thanks, I'll just keep going toward your voice. Ouch! Something in here has thorns, yuck!"

"How are you doing now, Yoichi? At least with the right clothing, you're somewhat protected and shouldn't get all scratched up." Lucy felt sorry for her, but it had been such a struggle to get her to select the more rugged apparel.

The branches rustled as Yoichi moved cautiously through the thicket, then *thud!* Lucy was just going to call out when she heard Yoichi's voice call to her. "Lucy! Lucy! You've got to get down here. Everyone, I've found it!"

L'Orté Point

Upon hearing Yoichi's call, they all hustled through the undergrowth and down the side of the knoll, each person picking their way carefully and creating their own pathway through the dense undergrowth. They met again at the bottom of the knoll, but Yoichi wasn't among them. "We're here, where are you?" Kent called out. "Yoichi?"

"Follow my voice. You've got to come to me."

"But we're at the house already. Where are you?" Lucy shouted.

"Follow my voice . . ." she responded. Yoichi continued to speak. Much of what she said was gibberish, complaining about bugs and branches, and such. They heard her squeal in panic when a garter snake crossed her path.

They broke branches and created a new pathway toward Yoichi's voice, finally arriving where she stood. The space was adequate to allow for all five of them to gather near a portion of the house that was obscured from other angles. Lucy, Helen, and Kent noticed the cause of Yoichi's excitement immediately. The scene before them resembled Lucy's first dream painting. The house was more dilapidated and the vegetation more overgrown, but it was definitely the same place. Helen confirmed it when she identified a number of pawpaw trees and honey locust in the same general area as she remembered them in the painting, though the honey locust was considerably larger. The blue ash was the clincher, located precisely as depicted in the painting. It, too, was larger in actuality, but its lower branches formed the same pattern as those in the painting.

"What do you want us to do, Lucy?" Kent asked. "I don't want to mess anything up for you by scavenging around here."

Lucy thought about it for a moment and then asked, "Is there a shovel available?"

"Not at this location, but I'll soon get one here." In short order, Kent was on the phone with Albin. While the five of them waited, they broke small, low-hanging branches and removed debris from the area, increasing the size of the clearing and providing a greater ease of access.

"Well, I must admit that I was expecting something quite different for a manor house," Lucy acknowledged. "This is more a very large stone cottage, wouldn't you say?"

"Though large, it's definitely a stone cottage—similar to the kind you might find in Ireland. However, parts of it suggested Tudor features given the use of timber, even though the exposed beams have clearly had a hard time dealing with the elements. There's even a bit of French Norman, given the pitch of the roof—or what's left of it. It's an odd mix that's for certain. For all your grandfather's apparent talents, architectural styling definitely wasn't one," Kent said, assessing the structure. "You've got a real mishmash here."

By the time Albin arrived with Donald, the two men were spared the ordeal of forcing their way through the thicket. Albin came well-equipped to slash his way happily through the remaining underbrush, while Donald followed at a safe distance.

"Welcome to MishMash Manor, gentlemen," Lucy chuckled. "Why on earth is this referred to as a manor? That implies something quite grand—clearly, this isn't."

"Strictly speaking, by referring to it as a manor house, they were merely acknowledging that it's the house of a significant landowner, which your grandfather was most definitely, Lucy," Donald explained. "It might have been that he was a practical man and preferred function over style."

Kent and Albin agreed that the structure appeared to be surprisingly sturdy—it posed no danger to them in the course of their poking around outside. Yoichi sent everyone the photograph of Lucy's painting with the numerous awen located by James Gregory. They studied the photo on their cellphones, then set about looking for awen markings while Lucy moved to the spot most likely represented in the painting by the emerald ring.

A branch had fallen and become entangled in the hackberry. It required all three men to dislodge and remove it. When they finally did, Eve was the first to see the awen. One was seared into a large beam, exactly as in the painting. Another was carved more crudely into a large flat rock abutting the building and beneath the carving on the beam.

With the equipment they now had, they were able to remove the rock from its resting place and dig beneath it. Their excitement was palpable when the shovel hit a metal box buried there. The box, wrapped in layers of plastic, was about the size of a ream of letter-sized paper. It was locked. Lucy decided to take it back to the barge, unopened.

"How about looking around inside the house itself, do you think it's safe?" Donald asked Kent.

"I'm confident enough for myself, Donald, but I'm not going to decide for others. I can't say for certain that it's safe. That's the situation as it applies to each of you. Enter at your own risk."

As he was considering Kent's statements and whether or not he would go where his curiosity was urging him, Donald kicked the toe of his hiking boot into the dirt, dislodging something. It looked different from the other debris, so it caught his eye. He bent and picked it up, cleaned it off a bit, and presented it to Lucy.

"My ring!" Lucy exclaimed. "Thank you, Donald. This means I've been here before. And if I have, then my father had been here too. My guess is that my father, and not Gianni, buried that box sometime after 1987. I guess the plastic wrapping is a dead giveaway that Gianni didn't wrap it—I don't think they had plastic during his lifetime. I want to go inside and look around, but not today. Tomorrow. For now, I think I'd prefer to go back and get cleaned up for dinner, open the box, and just enjoy the evening."

The idea appealed to everyone, so they placed the shovels inside the house and out of the elements, even though the sky was predicted to remain clear. The walk back to the yurt didn't take as long as the walk outbound had been. Being more familiar with the path from the yurt to the barge, Donald and Albin led the way with Eve.

Lucy was silent during the walk to the barge, distracted by all the unanswered questions swirling about in her head. She knew so much more now than she had before receiving that fateful telephone call back in March, yet there seemed to be even more questions. She remembered one of her favourite professors who years before pointed out that the accumulation of knowledge merely gave one the means to ask better questions. No matter what was in the metal box, she knew it would raise more questions for her than it answered. *Stephen Hawking, Albert Einstein, and Lucy Gillespie—all wishing we could travel in time. At least to the past, as an observer,* Lucy mused.

PART II

CHAPTER 29
1917-1918

Gianni had been learning and working for as long as he could remember, planning his life. Before he was even ten years old, he had already taught himself how to repair damaged tubes from discarded tires. He collected, repaired, then sold the repaired tubes to neighbours and those who owned automotive garages. Even earlier, he had earned a bit working for bars, delivering pails of beer to people in their homes, as long as they were within a reasonable walking distance of his father's grocery store. His parents operated a small farm with help from a few immigrant labourers and sold their own produce in the city. He wasn't paid for the work he did there, so he preferred to work elsewhere and pay his parents for the room he occupied above their store. However, there were times they still needed him. They had no other surviving children and preferred to keep him close. The arrangement worked rather well.

Gianni shoved his hands deep into his pockets. Although the day held the promise of spring, a chilling breeze hit him in the face no matter which direction his nose was pointed. He stood near the water, a sheltered enclave of the mighty St. Lawrence River, and admired the mahogany motor launch berthed at the port where he worked. He was so deep into his reverie that he failed to spot the middle-aged gentleman approaching along the quayside.

"Something you're looking for, young man?" The officious-sounding voice broke the spell, and Gianni was a bit disappointed to find himself back in Montreal in 1917. He had been imagining a time in the future, a time by which—he promised himself—he would have made his fortune and become successful and well-established. He would have a launch such as this and the lifestyle to match. Thirty-five was the age he decided upon.

"I'm talking to you, young man!" The gentleman wasn't at all pleased with being ignored.

"Oh, sorry, sir. I was just admiring this lovely launch. She's truly a beauty." As Gianni spoke, he cast his eyes toward the craft yet again, then touched his cap, nodded toward the man, and began to walk past him.

"So, you fancy my Ditchburn, do you? She's the last boat to leave the Ditchburn boathouse before the Gravenhurst Wharf fire in Muskoka back in 1915."

"Ditchburn, sir?" Gianni collected information as a sponge does water.

"An ancestor, one William Ditchburn, was naval advisor to Queen Elizabeth I back when the English faced the Spanish Armada." He expected the young man to have some questions; a smart man would ask those questions.

"So Ditchburn is the company then, rather than a new type of boat I've not yet heard about. And about the Armada—that didn't end too well for them, did it, sir? Significant victory for England and one of those things that changes the course of history."

The gentleman took an instant liking to the young man; he had a wealth of charisma. He had noticed him about the Port of Montreal on a regular basis over the past year or more and learned that his name was Giovanni Sarto. Those in management had mentioned that Gianni was employed in various capacities at the port, given that he was a quick study and highly adaptable. This Italian—his name alone gave that away—had characteristics which were hard to discern: a je ne sais quoi.

"Giovanni, I believe. Correct?" He expected a surprised response but received none, merely a nod. "Your English is excellent—do you still speak Italian? In fact, you don't look very Italian."

Hearing those words, Gianni bristled but kept his emotions in check. "I speak Italian and French as well as English, and I'm working on German. My grandparents immigrated from Latte, a town near the border with France, and I was born here in Montreal, or, more accurately, in Latte, just downriver from here. Once they learned of Latte in Quebec, they decided that fate had brought them here." It didn't concern him that the gentleman knew his name; he remembered having seen him in the executive offices from time to time when work required Gianni's presence there. And he had already known that the gentleman was the very proud owner of the mahogany launch, though he hadn't known it was a Ditchburn.

"You work here at the port and also on the family farm?"

"Not quite, sir. The family grocery store and elsewhere, such as here at the port. I don't work on the family farm, though there is one."

"Are you looking to change jobs, perhaps?"

"I am open to the idea, sir."

"Come to my office tomorrow evening, I think I might have something for you." Gianni took the card the gentleman proffered and read that the man's name was Bennett Garner, a lawyer. He tucked the card into an inside pocket of his jacket for safekeeping, agreeing to meet with him at six o'clock the following evening. Their chance encounter had gone just as Gianni had hoped; the odds had been in Gianni's favour.

By this time, Gianni had been working at Garner & Garner for over a year, doing for Bennett Garner what he had learned through his parents in dealing with immigrant labourers. The Garners had given him two new names—Jean Couture and John Taylor—which he used upon occasion. They'd explained that sometimes people made decisions or took attitudes based on nothing more than the ethnicity apparent in the name of the new person they were dealing with. So, when he thought that Giovanni Sarto might not be welcomed, he became Jean Couture or John Taylor, matching his language with the name. He thought of himself as a chameleon, even adjusting his appearance to suit the situation whenever necessary.

Gianni's desk was located in the outer office, in the same room as the receptionist's desk and the chairs provided for clients who arrived too early for their appointment. There were three doors, which opened onto the outer office: the one on the left was Andrew Garner's office, on the right was Bennett Garner's office, and behind Gianni's desk was the door to the file room, with Andrew's files on the left side and Bennett's on the right. There was a door in the file room through which there was access to the firm's law library. While the outer office was grand—an opulent space of high ceilings, dark oak panelling, and richly coloured fabrics—the Garners' offices were even more luxuriously appointed.

It was late in the day. No more clients were expected, and the receptionist-secretary had already gone home. Gianni was in the law library, browsing.

"There's another group arriving here from Halifax shortly, Gianni. They're originally from Sicily. Some will be moving on to Toronto and then Hamilton. Make sure all the paperwork is up to snuff," Bennett Garner barked as he was preparing to withdraw from the office for an extended trip to the USA. He would be attending a legal conference in New York City and then visiting his eldest son, Clarence, at the University of Buffalo.

"When you check the arrival time for their train, arrange for my trip as well."

"Already done, sir, and I'll finalize your booking today. It'll be a nine-hour trip on the New York Express from Montreal-Windsor Station. After the conference, you'll take the Buffalonian to Buffalo. From Buffalo to Toronto, there's the Canadian. You mentioned spending some time in Toronto, so there's either the Dominion or the Imperial Limited to get you back to Montreal. The Montreal Express isn't available. Many of the routes haven't been reactivated due to the war, at least not yet. I'll put together a package for you with all the details."

Gianni had made himself virtually indispensable to the Garners, and Bennett in particular was impressed by Gianni's ability to recall information, such as the train travel details he'd just provided. But that was just how his brain worked. Gianni hoped he wasn't filling his head completely with the legal information he was accumulating by reading in the law library—there was other information he wanted to collect as well.

He'd overheard the brothers—in his head, he referred to them as A and B—discussing the possibility of opening an office of Garner & Garner in Toronto. There were some challenges in the regulations, but Bennett was certain he could satisfy the authorities and was prepared to write whatever qualifying exams they required. As Andrew was senior to Bennett, Gianni thought there was a good chance he might soon be asked to move to Ontario and new opportunities in Toronto, but he worried about his parents.

Gianni provided Bennett with the documents, tickets, and information he required for his trip to the States.

"Close the door and take a seat for a moment, Gianni," Bennett said from behind the grand desk in his office. Gianni sat, filled with anticipation. "I'll be leaving Montreal shortly after I return from the States, Gianni. I'm moving to Toronto to open our new office there. So while I'm away, Mr. A,"—that was how the brothers referred to one another when speaking with others—"will give you directions about packing up my things here in the office. I'm certain that he'll have much to keep you on your toes, so you'll continue to earn a pay cheque." Gianni was disappointed, yet he remained hopeful.

The week passed uneventfully. Gianni was busy at work in the back office, organizing files to combine Andrew's existing files with Bennett's because they would no longer be handled by him once he moved to Toronto. While he continued his work in silence, Bennett arrived in Andrew's office and plopped himself into one of the comfortable leather client chairs on the opposite side of Andrew's desk, unaware of Gianni's presence in the file room. "Well, Andrew, I'm back," he announced.

"I see that, dear brother. I thought you might have gone home first; you must have some interesting news from New York. Or Buffalo perhaps? Do tell." He relaxed in his chair, tilting it back.

"I'll give you the short version, and you can mull it over. Prohibition is coming to the States, and there is strong evidence that it will be enforced more stringently there than anything we've seen in Canada. Furthermore, even when it is enforced in Ontario, there is no prohibition against manufacture, only sale. There's a spit of land in Lake Erie that is merely fifteen miles from American waters. You see where I'm going with this, don't you? I'd have Gianni use the John Taylor alias so we never confuse the activity with any other business. There's a fortune to be made, I'm telling you, and it's *technically* legal for us." Andrew was deep in thought, so Bennett continued, "Ditchburn Sr., before he died back in 1912, had a friend in Guelph who owned a brewery, if I recall correctly. And there's a distillery in Waterloo—or perhaps it's Kitchener—as well, so I already have two firms in Ontario to approach. I doubt either one will turn down this additional opportunity."

"Interesting." Clearly, Andrew was intrigued. "You're certainly right about the profit potential, but you've focussed on production and transport to the States. How do you propose to find connections in the States—the chaps prepared to purchase the product from our John Taylor? They'll need to have distribution capability on that side of the border and be prepared to work under threat of legal penalty. Have any ideas there?"

"As a matter of fact, I do. I've got Clarence looking into it. He spends more time than I approve attending parties, it seems, but perhaps that will put him in the right place at the right time to make a serious connection. I've suggested he begin quietly. My boy is quite the whiz, you know, and pretty much the top of his class, even though, as I understand, he has a hectic social life. I would never have been able to do that, I admit. Don't know who he gets it from—clearly not my dear wife, heaven help me!" Bennett chortled.

"Well, I'm sure Clarence is a bright young man, but isn't this rather a serious business requiring, one might say, a sober approach?"

"Clarence is about the same age as Gianni. I think we underestimate that generation, Andrew. Clarence might not have Gianni's charisma, grant you—I mean, Gianni can be a regular pied piper—but my boy has made inroads socially in Buffalo, and that takes a certain skill that is outside our sphere of expertise, dear brother."

"Granted. I'll give the matter some serious consideration. What sort of timeline do you sense we have?"

"I expect—and everyone I met at the conference would agree—that they'll ratify the Eighteenth Amendment next year and prohibition will be in effect the following year."

"Hm-m, so we have some time yet none to waste," Andrew said before redirecting the conversation. "Well, clearly you had an interesting time in Gotham. Did you encounter that chap from Boston, the one who attended Swarthmore? I can't remember his name, but he always had a real estate scheme in the works. Very creative, if I remember correctly."

"Oh, you must be thinking of Bean. Yes, on all counts. He's been seeing a lot of real estate deals on Florida's east coast, but he's got his eye on the west coast instead, where he claims there's a greater chance for profitability. The east coast is rapidly pricing itself out of the market, according to Joel."

"He always tries to do something a little different; what is it with his Florida plan?"

"I don't think he's finalized the purchase as yet, but what he wants is land near the mouth of a river. He refers to it as 'The City of Destiny'. I don't think he's settled on a name yet. It's to be a planned city based on the number six for some reason, so with six wards, six main thoroughfares, hexagonal squares—you know what I mean—all using Mediterranean architecture."

"Probably make a fortune. There's a lot of money floating around now that the war is over. As long as the labour cost can be kept low enough—and that's not difficult to achieve in Florida—he should do well. He'll get people from the north buying a winter place for fishing, boating, and golfing."

"The first major building will be a hotel, which is a smart idea. That'll provide the client a place to stay while he's being enticed to purchase an individual lot and—the client pays for the accommodation."

"How large a parcel of land is he aiming to acquire?"

"I believe he said 1,100 acres. He's looking into an old turpentine camp."

Gianni quietly continued to work on the files. He waited until the brothers walked out of Andrew's office before returning to his own desk. His move to Toronto appeared promising once again.

CHAPTER 30
1919

Since Bennett's move to Toronto, Gianni had continued to work for Andrew Garner on a regular basis. A new associate lawyer had taken Bennett's old office, and the new furnishings were not quite as opulent.

Andrew was much quieter than Bennett, who one might have described as bombastic at times, but he continued to encourage Gianni in his search for knowledge. The two men frequently spent extended periods of time in Andrew's office as teacher and pupil. Andrew had no family other than his wife, having lost his sons in the latter years of the Great War and his only daughter in the Spanish Flu pandemic which followed. He spoke of siblings, but there were no lawyers among them save for Bennett.

"Now, I understand that you make yourself available to your parents when they need you, but I'd like you to consider joining Mr. B in our Toronto office. The work you'd be doing would be similar to what you've been doing here, but I'm certain it will have its own challenges for you. You've probably not considered such a move, having been born here, and then there's your parents to consider. So, think about it and give me your answer, shall we say, within the week?"

"Actually, sir, there's no longer a need for me to consider my parents in such a decision."

Normally, the lawyer would not have pried into such private matters, but there was something in Gianni's manner that drew him to request clarification, "No longer?"

"As of a couple months ago, January the fifteenth, to be precise. They were visiting relatives in north Boston when a molasses tank ruptured, and they were killed in the flood of molasses."

Andrew could hear his brother's voice in his head commenting that it must have been a sticky situation, but effectively suppressed a smile at the thought. He had read the stories carried in 'The Gazette', and the event described was truly devastating, resulting in twenty-one deaths. "I had been told it was probably the result of terrorists—a bomb of some sort," he offered instead. "Of course you have my condolences," he added, as an after-thought.

"Thank you, sir. I've made contact with certain people in Boston who have been very generous in providing me with information, and although that story is being spread, the authorities are convinced otherwise. I'm inclined to agree with them. It's more likely due to defective steel, changes in air temperature, and something they call the principles of fluid dynamics," Gianni explained, adding, "I've not been able to read much about fluid dynamics yet, but I intend to."

Andrew had every confidence Gianni would do just that, and that he would presumably understand fluid dynamics as well.

After his parents died in Boston, Gianni had considered continuing with the farm and the store, but that life had never fit into his plans. He sold whatever he had inherited and, after settling debts, now had a little nest egg waiting to be invested properly for his future. The job at the wharf had provided him with the opportunity to make contact with some very interesting people. He had learned a lot these past few years in Montreal. Now it was time to advance to the next stage.

He agreed to the Garners' offer of continued employment with Garner & Garner in Toronto, but requested a favour from Andrew: the creation of another alias, this one in the name of Johannes Schneider. Andrew agreed that Gianni's fluency in German warranted this additional identity.

Gianni's move to Toronto was both significant and uneventful. While Bennett remained in Toronto, for the most part tending to the regular matters of the law firm, Gianni was charged with establishing a working relationship with the man Bennett had identified as owning property near the border with the States. Gianni's job was to facilitate the temporary storage of liquor and arrange for its transport to a spot twenty-five kilometres out on the water, where the American—to be found by Clarence—would acquire the shipment. Bennett Garner assumed responsibility for any legal documents and for contacting manufacturers in the region.

Gianni's research into the titles of the properties revealed that there were about a dozen parcels of various sizes, forming a Point of 3,278 hectares jutting out into Lake Erie from the mainland. At the very tip of the Point was the largest parcel, 1,052 hectares, owned by Peter Szabo of Petrolia, the man Gianni needed to approach on behalf of the Garners.

Petrolia was located nearly three hundred kilometres from Toronto, so Gianni had to be well-organized for the journey. He hoped Peter's English was good because Hungarian was not a language Gianni had acquired. What he had acquired was a bottle of plum brandy from a Hungarian immigrant, Arpad Szucs, who ran a small still at his Hamilton tannery. Arpad assured him that this was an alcoholic beverage enjoyed by most Hungarians and called it slivovitz. Gianni hoped he was right. He had tasted a sample of the brandy and while it burned like grappa, Gianni did not enjoy it. Then again, Gianni didn't enjoy grappa, either. Wine, a nice medium-bodied red, was more to his liking. He took the train from Toronto's Union Station to Sarnia, planning to hire a car to drive him to the Szabo residence in the nearby town of Petrolia.

He phoned the Szabo residence from his hotel in Sarnia and made an appointment to meet with Peter at his home the following day. He thought he detected a slight accent but was uncertain.

No one he met in Sarnia knew the man, and in requesting directions to his home, no one in Petrolia volunteered any opinion of him. Anticipating such an occurrence, Gianni dressed conservatively and frugally—not that he had much choice in the latter. He wanted to look about ten years older than his actual age, so he assumed a subdued demeanour and decided to wear spectacles—not that he needed them. His shoes were in good condition but not highly polished.

The Szabo house was a nondescript two-storey clapboard residence of modest size and in need of a coat of paint. It was situated on a large flat piece of property—an untended field—and was surrounded by drilling rigs and concomitant equipment. The business aspects dominated the property; the house appeared to be an afterthought. There were some wooden outbuildings—but no trees. There was nothing to indicate that the man had a family: no toys in the yard, no flowers, no fresh laundry on the line . . . Gianni thought he saw movement at an upstairs window, but it was so slight, he wasn't certain. Soon he found himself at the door, still without a clear plan.

The man who answered his knock appeared to be at least fifty years old. He had lost hair at the crown and frontal region and what remained was greying extensively, the darkest found in his thick moustache. He was short and stocky, with a muscular physique but a humped back. He was gruff. It was obvious that he enjoyed garlic and that he smoked heavily.

Gianni introduced himself by his real name. After a few niceties of introduction, grudgingly given, Gianni confirmed that the man was Peter Szabo, and presented the slivovitz to him. He now had Peter's attention. The exchange between the two men held the characteristics of a game of cat and mouse, though sometimes the roles reversed.

Peter refrained from sharing information that would have given Gianni an inkling of how to deal with him. But Gianni persevered. He explained that he was the agent for a foreign buyer who was relocating after the war and looking to purchase a large piece of waterfront property, rather isolated, and that Peter's 1,052-hectare property on the Point on Lake Erie was one that met the stated criteria. Was Peter interested in selling this property?

Peter grabbed a couple of small glasses from a cupboard, placed them on the kitchen table, and invited Gianni to sit. As he uncorked the bottle of slivovitz, he answered, "Maybe."

At that moment, Gianni knew he had him. "You've logged the Point thoroughly, I understand, so there's a lot of stumps and old branches and such on the land. What are you planning to do with it now?" Gianni brought the slivovitz to his lips, as if to drink and then kept the glass in his hand, obscuring the level of its contents. Whenever Peter's glass neared empty, Gianni refilled it, then motioned as if he were refilling his own as well.

Peter didn't answer the question. To reduce any tension, Gianni commented on the equipment scattered about Peter's yard. "That's very interesting equipment you have out there, Mr. Szabo, what is it used for?"

Gianni already knew this was equipment used in drilling for oil and maintaining the wells once they were established. Peter brightened somewhat and ran on at great length about his achievements in the Petrolia oil fields. After further refills of slivovitz, he related some of his equally interesting achievements in the Klondike.

"I find it interesting how for a time there's all that gold in the Klondike and then rather suddenly things change. Those like you, who were either smart like you, or just lucky like some people seem to be, manage to get out and reinvest just in time to avoid a downturn in fortune." Gianni refilled the glasses. "When do you think that will happen here in Petrolia?" Peter didn't answer, but Gianni could tell he'd got him thinking.

"There's an increased interest in tobacco farming throughout Norfolk County and some in parts of Elgin County as well. Of course, I'm just seeing the start of it as I travel around, but the post-war demand will fuel a surge for tobacco as well as for jobs and housing." Gianni refilled the glasses. "Too bad about the new income tax. I hear that's going to stay for many years to come, probably forever, though we hope not. There's no tax on what you make when you sell your property, though, so that's good. You could make a fortune selling this property you're on now and there'd be no tax to pay on it. Same with the acreage on the Point." Gianni refilled the glasses.

Suddenly, the screen door swung open, then slapped shut as a boy about ten years of age burst into the kitchen from the outdoors. He was sullen and looked surprised to see Gianni. "Bicycle in shed?" Peter growled at him.

"Yes, Papa. Erzsebet?"

"*Menj föl és manadj ott.*" Peter commanded, and the boy scurried up the stairs.

Gianni wished he had learned Hungarian.

"Why you want my land?" Peter queried.

"I'm just the representative. The buyer is a German, but I'm not at liberty to divulge much more. The family is scattered as a result of the war, and some of his money isn't readily available to him. I was instructed to locate a sizeable property on the water— someplace isolated. He's also looking at properties in Muskoka and elsewhere, but I think the point fits the stated description of what he's hoping to find." Gianni could see Peter thinking, the furrow of his brow deepening, his mouth pursing beneath the thick moustache.

Gianni decided to throw another idea into the mix. "I've been wondering when they'll impose property taxes—either Ottawa for Canadian property taxes, or, more possibly Toronto for Ontario property taxes. Both levels of government need money to reorganize after the war. Some municipalities already have taxes on properties. It's just a matter of unifying such schemes, and we'll have the imposition of property tax, just as we now do with income tax." Gianni wasn't certain how much of what he was saying was factual, but that didn't matter. Gianni filled Peter's glass yet again.

"Well, I shouldn't keep you any longer, Mr. Szabo. It's been very nice speaking with you, especially learning about the oil business and gold mining. I'm heading elsewhere now as I'm under some pressure to find the property the German wants. I think he has another agent working on this in Quebec, so I don't want to lose my opportunity."

"How much?" Peter suddenly asked.

"How much what," countered Gianni, as if he were content in this encounter not resulting in a purchase. "Oh, how much would he pay for 2,600 acres of isolated scrub?"

"Yes," Peter answered, his tone indicating a degree of desperation that Gianni should remain.

Gianni already had an amount in mind. He needed to retain much of his nest-egg to purchase additional properties which abutted Szabo's Point and cover various costs in the near future before he might begin to reap any profits. He knew how much Peter had paid and when he'd purchased the property. He discounted the amount by an additional one-third and declared the offer to Peter.

Peter didn't react by throwing him out the door, but Gianni had caught him flinch. He had offered low, but not insultingly so. He let Peter take his time, giving the grizzled older man the opportunity to think he had regained the upper hand in the proceedings.

Peter countered with an increased amount, though well within Gianni's acceptable range. "Let me just refresh my memory here," Gianni said, as if needing to refer to notes on another pending or possible purchase.

"Is for island. Total with island is 2,850 acres. You pay this; get both Point and island. Just offshore, in bay. Same place."

And the deal was struck. The men shook hands, and Gianni produced a contract outlining the requirements in his Offer to Purchase, pre-signed by Johannes Schneider. The driver, who had been waiting in Gianni's hired car, acted as witness to Peter's signature on the agreement. The method of payment was agreed upon, and the men arranged to meet in the office of a Sarnia notary two days following. There was one final toast with slivovitz.

Gianni could barely contain his joy as he returned to Sarnia. He needed to arrange an appointment with a notary and use a Sarnia bank to secure the funds under the name of Johannes Schneider, making them available to Peter in a timely fashion. His time in the Garners' law library proved well-spent indeed.

Having secured the land, Gianni worked on an agreement that would satisfy the concerns of the Garners for their liquor smuggling venture. His plan was to satisfy the Garners but to utilize the Point in the manner that he had heard Joel Bean was planning in Florida. He had already secured more land than Bean, but he determined that an even greater amount would be better, serving to keep the Point further isolated and secure for the Garners and their venture.

CHAPTER 31

1920-1921

It was the end of January, and Clarence had failed yet again to deliver on his promise to secure buyers for the Garner's distribution of alcohol. Bennett was increasingly agitated, anticipating that the opportunity would slip away.

Bennett himself had not been particularly successful in securing contracts with either the distillery in Waterloo or with the brewery in Guelph. Both enterprises claimed to be content with their current level of profitability resulting from their existing business plans. As usual in such circumstances, Bennett called upon Gianni.

As instructed by Bennett Garner, Gianni became John Taylor for the discussions and soon recognized that an agreement would be relatively easy to secure. Of course, the producers were interested in another profit centre—especially one which required payments to be held offshore. That was the whole point of being in business—profit. The insurmountable problem faced by Bennett was one he faced every morning when he looked in the mirror—himself.

While Gianni was John Taylor in Waterloo and Guelph, he was also Johannes Schneider in the nearby city of Kitchener. Four years earlier, Kitchener had been known as Berlin. There had been a statue, a bust of the German Kaiser, in the city's park. That bust ended up thrown into the park lake, and the city came to an overwhelmingly supported decision to rename the city. Berlin became Kitchener, but that had not changed the ethnic make-up of the city. For a time, Johannes Schneider had a girlfriend there, as Gianni continued to improve his German. He was glad that Gerta spoke high German; otherwise, he might have considered looking elsewhere for female companionship.

Having resolved Bennett's problem in securing a supplier, Gianni used the opportunity to present an agreement he had prepared concerning the Garners' use of the Point. The agreement he struck with the Garners provided them with permission to build small structures on the interior of the Point, well-away from the shoreline, for the temporary storage of stock. The Garners also agreed to build a dock and provide boathouse facilities. The final plans for construction of these facilities required the agreement of both Gianni and the Garners. The Garners would acquire the boats and pay for the construction; Gianni would gather the labourers for the construction project and become legal owner of any such construction. For the right to access the Point and construct their required infrastructure, the Garners agreed to pay a small amount as ongoing rent for whatever length of time they would be involved in this money-making venture. As a result, Gianni was assured a regular source of income, and he no longer considered the work he did in Bennett's office as his primary source of funding.

While he continued to work on his own business plan involving the purchase of additional property on the Point, Gianni's time was occupied in the acquisition of labourers, supplies, and equipment. He also arranged their transport to the Point by boat and barge out of Port Myer, the nearest port and due north of the island and Point, on the far side of the bay.

L'Orté Point

It was early in the morning, and Gianni was at the Toronto office of Garner & Garner, doing research in their law library. He was just finishing before setting out to visit the government offices nearby when Bennett burst into the room, a smile written upon his face.

"Clarence has done it," the lawyer exclaimed. "We're ready to start."

Gianni wasn't certain of the details concerning how or with whom the deal had been struck. Because it wasn't his deal, he refrained from enquiring, thinking that he'd presumably learn more over time, given Bennett's continued reliance upon him. He expected things to change in a few years' time, once Clarence returned to Ontario and passed the bar examination for the province. He was pleased to see Bennett more relaxed and truly excited about his venture.

"I knew my boy could do it, given a bit of time. The Americans operate various entertainment facilities, musical venues, and such, in Buffalo and Cleveland. Prohibition has really taken the shine off their business; we'll take care of that problem for them. Tell me we've taken possession of the Ditchburn Vikings, I ordered."

"That I can do," affirmed Gianni. "They are in their berths in the boathouse." Bennett couldn't resist ordering several of the nine-metre mahogany runabouts from the Muskoka builder. Gianni thought them too pricey and not appropriate for their needs, but these were Bennett's decisions to make and for Gianni to implement. Fortunately, they weren't the sole vessels acquired for the venture.

Bennett was happy and proud that Clarence had come through. His enthusiasm for the new business venture was palpable. Soon he was on the telephone to Andrew in Montreal.

Finally, their smuggling operation was in full swing. Gianni had taken care of the tasks Bennett had set for him, and now the matter was in Bennett's hands. As long as the Garners abided by the signed contract, Gianni was happy, too.

CHAPTER 32

1923-1924

By the end of 1923, Johannes Schneider and Jean Couture had acquired all twelve parcels of land: 3,278 hectares in total. Shortly thereafter, Gianni Sarto registered the sale of those same parcels with the sellers identified as Johannes Schneider and Jean Couture— and the purchaser identified as Giovanni Sarto. The selling prices registered in these transactions were significantly higher than their purchase prices had been. However, neither Johannes Schneider nor Jean Couture would have income tax payable on the sale because it was a capital gain.

Having secured ownership of the land in his real identity, Gianni officially changed the name of the Point and the island. From this time forward, L'Orté Point and L'Orté Island would appear as names on area maps.

It was just a bit of whimsy on Gianni's part, an inspired play on words, converting 'Taylor' to 'Lor-tay' and finally 'L'Orté'. While working in Bennett's office, he had happened upon a letter from the Boston lawyer, Joel Bean. The letter contained a brochure the American lawyer was using in the promotion of his City of Destiny development in Florida. He was trying to interest the Garners, or their clients, in the purchase of property in his city, which he had named El Jobean, a name that sounded Spanish but was a play on the lawyer's name.

The Garners seemed content with the smuggling venture. Gianni continued to work for them as he made plans for a future apart from them. He had become familiar with Hamilton and the Niagara Peninsula down to Welland through his work with immigrant labour on behalf of the Garners. It was here he began to cultivate business contacts.

Gianni had researched extensively and determined that if he built a lodge, just as Joel Bean had built his hotel in El Jobean, he could then arrange to sell lots on the Point to those paying to stay at L'Orté Point Lodge. He planned to take a deposit amount and then take back the mortgage for the balance. The new owner would be under contract to pay an annual tax to the community, meaning L'Orté. Bennett helped him navigate the legalities involved. The purchasers also had to pay interest on the mortgages held by Gianni and were required to build using Gianni's new construction company. He'd written other requirements into the fine print as well.

The lodge was built near the waterfront, and most of the building ran deeper into the Point rather than along the shoreline. The central complex contained a large dining hall and worker accommodations, as well as suites and individual rooms for guests. The building was a two-storey construction, wooden, with a metal roof and a large verandah overlooking the water. A major attractive feature of the lodge was its massive stone fireplace and chimney. Gianni dreamt of replacing the entire structure with stone at some time in the future.

When he could see that construction was going well, Gianni ramped up his advertising, both for stays at L'Orté Point

Lodge and the purchase of lots on exclusive L'Orté Point. He promised the construction of a golf course, though he gave no idea of when it might become available. His advertising focussed on the sand beach located on the Lake Erie side, the fishing available in the bay, and the hunting available at the west end of the Point. Gianni was in the process of applying to have the name of the bay changed to L'Orté Bay, but this was somewhat problematic, as the nearby town of Port Myer preferred the continued use of its current name, Myer Bay. While understandable, Gianni was nevertheless annoyed by this. He resolved to become more involved with the Port Myer community; he might convince them to change their name to Port L'Orté. He began to consider ways to work toward both name changes and decided he should spend more time at the Norfolk County seat in Simcoe.

CHAPTER 33
1927

Gianni identified himself at the door. He wasn't a member at the yacht club, but had been invited to dine with a member, Bennett Garner. He had just as soon have remained in his rooms in Simcoe or in his suite at the lodge, but Bennett was rather insistent that he come to Toronto.

As he approached the table, he saw that Andrew was visiting from Montreal. "Well, it's good to see you both!" Gianni exclaimed. "Mr. A, I'm surprised and delighted to see you again; Mr. B, thank you for the kind invitation to dine with you tonight." The men shook hands and exchanged pleasantries.

"Gianni, have you guessed the reason for our little celebration?" Bennett enquired.

"No, I hadn't given it any thought. Sorry, have I missed something?"

"No, no, B and I are marking the ten years that we've known you, and we've a small token to mark the occasion."

"I was going to wait until C arrived but clearly something has come up so we'll just proceed without him," Bennett announced, presenting Gianni with a velvet jeweller's box. "We want you to have this. I'm surprised you haven't got yourself one already."

Gianni was delighted with the recognition the Garner brothers were bestowing upon him and suitably impressed with the contents of the velvet box. Inside was a gold pocket watch on a gold chain. "Oh no, I couldn't possibly accept this! You're both too generous."

"Nonsense, young man, we've done very well, and you've been highly instrumental in assisting us along the way. Besides, we can't take it back now; the watch bears your initials," Andrew said, chortling until he required a sip of water to soothe the cough he'd triggered.

Gianni couldn't remember seeing the brothers happier. He examined the watch more carefully, noting the elaborately engraved G and S. The engraving was so intricate, he could continue to use the watch even while using one of the other identities. He wondered if they had taken that into account, or if it had occurred through happenstance. All these years he had continued to use his late maternal grandfather's grey metal watch; it had never occurred to him to buy another.

Over a meal of roast beef and Yorkshire pudding, the three men enjoyed a companionable evening. Conversation stayed well away from the activities at L'Orté Point. There was considerable interest shown by both Andrew and Bennett in the activities of Wall Street, and they requested Gianni's opinion of the state of the stock market. Gianni expressed his concerns.

"My opinion is that the market is comparable to a giant bubble, and at some point the bubble is going to burst. When it does, those who have bought on margin are going to be hurt very badly. At the very least, if I were inclined to invest in stocks, I'd not leverage my purchase. It's one thing to lose much of what you have invested, but it's another to lose all your savings as well, and worse yet, to end up in tremendous debt with no assets," Gianni declared. "However, that is merely my opinion, and I don't have the extra funds to invest, no matter how positive things look to be at this time."

"I do wish that Clarence had managed to join us. I told him just how significant this night was recognizing your achievements, Gianni. He's very keen that I should invest— heavily— and leverage as well. I'd have enjoyed listening to the two of you debate the matter," Bennett declared. "We're bringing C in to take care of our interests at L'Orté Point, so expect to see more of him. A and I might just purchase a place at Joel Bean's development on the Myakka River in Florida. The chewing gum heiress is building there, so it might be our crowd."

"Shall we retire to the Gentlemen's Lounge for a brandy or a sherry?" Andrew enquired, "Just last year, you would have required a physician's prescription. Things do change, sometimes quite rapidly." And with that, the trio withdrew from the dining room.

CHAPTER 34

1928-1929

Gianni was in Simcoe, where he rented a few rooms in a large home owned by an elderly widow of whom he was quite fond.

"Gianni, have you seen the new house?" Mrs. Harkness enquired.

"No, I've not taken note of any one in particular, but I've been spending a lot of time out on the Point. Where is it?" Gianni asked, curious about any change in the area.

Mrs. Harkness described the location to him, declaring that it would become the largest house in town. She was unable to recall the name of the owner, but said she'd heard that he owned other properties in the county, including a farm just north of Simcoe adjacent to that of her brother-in-law.

"Orville, that's my late husband's brother, says he's been approached, but he's not quite ready to sell. Orv's not been himself of late, so I told him he should consider selling. He's got no sons to take over the farm, and it's already too much for him to manage. He and Geraldine, his wife, could come and live with me in this big house," she observed. Then she added, "Of course I might need to chuck you out then, Gianni!"

They both laughed. Mrs. Harkness had already collected four cats and two dogs. She maintained a bird feeder in the backyard and looked kindly upon the squirrels who reaped the benefit of the seeds. She was a sweetheart, and Gianni was confident his place in the house was secure whether or not Orv and Geraldine made the move to Simcoe.

Gianni had been surprised to learn that the house, which had piqued Mrs. Harkness' curiosity the previous year, was the current residence of the Szabo family. He had been busy with construction and further sales on the Point and had failed to pay attention to the changes occurring in Simcoe. A quick search of the records confirmed that Peter Szabo was the owner.

Gianni had shifted his focus from Toronto to Hamilton and into the Niagara Peninsula. He had numerous business contacts in the bustling city on Lake Ontario, which was growing at a rapid pace. Gianni purchased a bottle of slivovitz from Arpad Szucs and made his way to the new Szabo residence.

It was a large house with a cement-lathe veneer rather than brick or stone. There was a lawn but no landscaping, no plantings, nor any kind of decoration. The house, trimmed in dark green, was situated on a massive corner lot and featured an expansive verandah along both of the street views. There was evidence of a cellar and three stories of rooms.

Gianni introduced himself to the young woman who answered the door and asked to see Peter. In turn, she identified herself to him as Erzsebet Szabo. Erzsebet invited him to take a seat in the parlour, directing Gianni to the room on the left of the entrance hallway. Then she disappeared. The house was an improvement over the one in Petrolia, but though it was much larger and, being new, in better condition, it was not well-furnished or particularly stylish. It was austere. From the parlour, he could see the dining room located deeper into the house. At the other side of the entrance hall there was a room that was furnished as an office. Gianni assumed that the kitchen was situated toward the back of the house, on the far side of the massive oak staircase. The floor plan was standard for that size of home, and Gianni had seen many.

In due course, Peter Szabo entered the room, looking much older and significantly heavier, but generally much as Gianni remembered him. "Gianni Sarto, how are you? I didn't expect we would meet again."

Gianni presented the bottle of slivovitz. "A gift to mark your move to Simcoe."

Peter's eyes brightened and narrowed, and he called out for Erzsebet, "Bring glasses for slivovitz." Then, turning to Gianni, he continued, "What is this? I hear you own the Point."

Gianni understood the need to tread carefully. "Yes, the German buyer decided to build at a different location, so I bought the Point from him about six years ago. Perhaps he thought it too much work, I really don't know. He kept it for four years before deciding to sell." Gianni had learned to lie effortlessly in the cause of business. Wanting to change the topic, he added, "So, what have you been doing these past ten years?"

At that moment, Erzsebet arrived with glasses for the slivovitz and Gianni noticed Peter's demeanour change in the young woman's presence. The difference in his body language was subtle, but very real. Gianni shifted uncomfortably in his chair and he could feel the hairs on the back of his neck begin to prickle.

Once she was again out of the room, Peter poured the slivovitz, prepared his pipe, and eventually the conversation resumed. "I think what we talk about that day at house in Petrolia. I sell everything—all equipment, house, land—and buy property around here and some in Niagara and Hamilton, farm for tobacco near here. Jozsef, my son, he find properties. Same as you for German. First we move Hamilton, but I no like there. Too big."

From his language, Gianni concluded this was not the first alcoholic beverage of Peter's day. "I believe I saw your son when he was just a boy that day in Petrolia. And the young woman, Erzsebet?"

"Wife."

"Yours?" Gianni said, incredulous.

"No, Jozsef," Peter stated, seeming to find humour in the presumption but it was a humour devoid of warmth.

The rest of the visit went well. Peter was well-satisfied with the explanation Gianni provided concerning activity at L'Orté Point. It made sense to Peter that Gianni would rent it out and that he was operating the lodge and selling lots for summer homes, all things which Peter had doubtlessly learned elsewhere. Gianni said nothing to contradict or embellish the stories circulating in the Simcoe community regarding L'Orté Point. It was important to him that Peter realize these were activities which Peter would have found unsuited to his own personality and that the sale of the Point had indeed been an excellent decision on his part ten years prior.

September and October brought significant upheaval in the world of finance; the results impacted every aspect of society. The bubble burst on Wall Street and those who had leveraged their stock purchases lost their assets in the resulting margin call. Some lacked the assets to make the margin call and those who were able to secure loans were now deep in debt, probably heavily burdened, and with little hope of recovery.

Gianni's lots had been selling well, but even his wealthiest clients were forced to tighten their belts. One after the other, like dominoes, the properties rapidly fell into foreclosure. Once again, Gianni found himself as the sole owner of L'Orté Point in its entirety. He planned to resell the lots—some already with cottages—once the economy stabilized.

The lodge continued to operate, providing accommodation and food to various paying customers associated with the Garners' enterprise. With his savings and the rent paid by the Garners, Gianni could continue operation of the lodge and weather the financial storm without difficulty.

CHAPTER 35

1930

Gianni's construction company had been contracted to paint St. Margaret's Orphanage that was located at the top of the escarpment at Hamilton. The orphanage's payment was due for the paint, which Gianni had obtained from a manufacturer he had sourced in the vicinity. He expected to receive a cheque from Sister Clotilde, so was surprised to see Monsignor Petek in the nun's office.

"Please take a seat, Mr. Sarto," the Monsignor began. "I presume you've come for your cheque."

"Yes, Monsignor, I have."

"Due to the current economic climate, our finances have suffered tremendously. I'm here today to evaluate the extent of the damage. Donations are down considerably, as you can well imagine, and soon we'll be struggling to have St. Margaret's continue to provide high-quality care for the orphans residing here. I'm hoping you might consider the paint job a donation so that we might forego payment, Mr. Sarto."

Gianni took his time in answering though he'd known immediately what his answer would be. "Well, the men who will be painting require payment, Monsignor. They, too, have mouths to feed. I have already acquired the paint for the job per your specifications. You had requested a high-quality lead-based enamel for durability. I had shown you the red label standard product as well as the blue label deluxe product. You selected the blue label deluxe, which, as I pointed out at the time, is the more expensive."

"Yes, I fully realize that. Isn't there something you could do to help us out? I know you've already made a donation, but—"

Gianni interjected, "I'll tell you what I can do for you, given the dire circumstances in which the orphanage finds itself. I will charge you a red label rate on the blue label paint. You'll get the deluxe, which I have already acquired for you, but I'll charge you for standard. I cannot do more. The workers must be paid, and certain costs for materials must be covered."

The Monsignor was delighted and so was Gianni. He'd never said that the deluxe was better than or even different from the standard. In fact, the two paints came from the same processing vats. Gianni had red labels and blue labels and selected between the two to match whichever the client decided upon. His men would be paid and he would also make a profit, just less than he had anticipated.

Sister Clotilde entered the room, and the Monsignor shared his good news with her. Gianni preferred to keep his distance from Sister Clotilde. It wasn't that the elderly nun's abundant and wiry chin hairs distracted him—which they did—but that her dentures were ill-fitting. As a result, conversation at a distance less than the width of the nun's desk resulted in one being caught in periodic cloudbursts of spittle. He moved his chair well-back from her.

Shortly thereafter, Sister Stanisia arrived—a tiny woman being swallowed by her habit and wimple. Known to the resident orphans as 'Sister Sneezy', she carried a tray with tea and biscuits. Once the diminutive nun had shuffled out, the Monsignor, Sister Clotilde, and Gianni continued their conversation.

"So, my regular donors are struggling, as are we all. Do you happen to know of anyone new to the area, Mr. Sarto? Someone whose finances might not have been so dramatically impacted."

Gianni sipped his tea and gave the matter thought. "Yes, I believe I do, though I'm uncertain how involved he may be with the Church. He might even be a Protestant, I really don't know."

"Oh, when it comes to caring for orphans, I can usually bridge that divide," the Monsignor said, boastfully. His past successes in such matters had earned him the honorific 'Monsignor'; he had so impressed the Bishop. He was eager to hear further details about this prospective donor.

The Monsignor struggled into the backseat of his henna red Ford Model-A town car. He was profoundly corpulent, and his robes added further to his difficulty. Moreover, Monsignor Petek disliked travelling in this particular car; the henna red clashed with the purple of his sash and was certain to give him a headache.

The Bishop had bestowed upon him the responsibility for finances pertaining to the orphanage run by the Sisters of St. Margaret. Things had been going well, and then— suddenly—all the finances had become submerged in the turmoil of the Wall Street crash. Not only had he lost money that he had invested, donors he had come to rely upon had lost significantly when the stock market dropped and as a result were now far less generous. Initially, Monsignor Petek had not realized the extent of the impact, nor the depth and severity of it, upon his finances—the finances that supported the Sisters and St. Margaret's Orphanage. The orphanage was a significant drain on finances. In good times, it was a significant draw, as donors could be counted upon to be generous in giving to care for orphans, but under the current conditions, not even orphans could be relied upon to generate a positive cash flow.

The Bishop was expecting things to continue as usual and Monsignor Petek had no choice but to seek out new donors in person, no matter how distasteful he found the task. The drive to Simcoe was far too long. As if in prayer, the Monsignor mumbled, "What I must endure, dear God!"

Peter Szabo had lived in Hamilton for a short time, and while the Monsignor had never met the man nor anyone in the family, it came to be whispered that Peter Szabo had considerable wealth. While the son, Jozsef, was more familiar to people in Hamilton, Peter had remained an enigma. Then they had disappeared, only to reappear in Simcoe. The Monsignor had been surprised and hopeful when Gianni mentioned Peter Szabo to him that day in the office. The parish priest in Simcoe had been asked for information on Peter, but beyond confirming that he owned the biggest house in town, little was forthcoming. While the young woman, Erzsebet, attended services quite regularly, Peter had attended only once, at Easter.

Having arrived in Simcoe, the Monsignor's driver pulled the car in front of the rectory. Monsignor Petek heaved a sigh of relief; he had survived the ordeal. His driver withdrew to obtain directions for the Szabo house from the parish priest. He dissuaded the priest from coming out to the car, saying that the Monsignor was on a very tight schedule—which he was. He would have said the same thing had that not been the case.

Shortly thereafter, the Model-A pulled in front of the Szabo house. The Monsignor was impressed and hopeful. The house was both new and large. The structure was devoid of embellishment, indicating to the Monsignor that the owner was a frugal man.

He had phoned ahead and wasn't surprised when Peter Szabo answered the door promptly. He was ushered into the parlour. A young woman—Erzsebet, he assumed—brought coffee and a prune-filled pastry but didn't join the men in the parlour.

"So, as I've explained, this current financial situation is threatening the good works of the Sisters of St. Margaret. The poor orphans, many having lost their parents as a result of the war and the epidemic, may now lose the roof over their head as a result of this economic disaster which has befallen us."

He could see that Peter remained untouched. Had he known the man, or observed the situation more closely, he might have realized that so far there was nothing in it for Peter himself. But Peter was quite prepared to address his own needs, given the Monsignor's failure to do so.

"Now, have little time and sometimes cannot move too good— still try go Church at Easter. But remember somethings from Church many years ago. You sell what called plenary indulgence?"

Monsignor Petek could tell that Peter was serious. *Serious* suggested that a donation could be secured if the Monsignor provided the right answer at this moment. He hesitated, determining how large a donation Peter might reasonably afford and be willing to give. He looked around the room, lacking in lavish decoration, and gave his answer.

Nevertheless, Peter was unmoved. The Monsignor was desperate. Then an idea occurred to him.

"Your house is very large, Mr. Szabo. Is it just you and your son, Jozsef, and the young woman?"

"Yes, Jozsef wife. She take care of house."

"Perhaps she could use some help to cook and clean and, if your health is sometimes poor, to take care of your needs. You may find it helpful to have a nurse."

"What you thinking," enquired Peter.

"A fourteen-year-old girl who is capable in the kitchen, and a ten-year-old who could keep house, do laundry, sew. I could provide you with a pair of Irish sisters. If you provide for them, you would have good help. They both speak English. Being girls, they don't require much food. I'm not suggesting you adopt them, not at all. Perhaps once a year—no more—and only if it's convenient for you, the local priest would drop by to say hello."

"School?" Peter asked, revealing an interest in the proposal.

"The age for leaving school in Ontario has been raised over the past several years from twelve to fourteen and now sixteen years, but there are exemptions for children who are already working, or who must stay at home. I think that definition applies here. Besides, as girls, they don't need much education beyond what they already have, or will learn, working here with Jozsef's wife to instruct them."

And so a deal was struck. Peter obtained his plenary indulgence and a pair of Irish sisters, while Monsignor Petek obtained his much-needed donation and reduced the costs to the orphanage by two mouths.

The men engaged in inconsequential conversation while enjoying Erzsebet's prune pastry. When the pastry was eaten and the coffee was drunk, Monsignor Petek arose from his chair, his girth somewhat enlarged, his purple sash taut, and took his leave through the front door to the awaiting car.

Inside the house, Peter Szabo was quite delighted with himself. He believed the plenary indulgence he had just purchased would save him from the fires of hell. With his advancing age, Peter was becoming increasingly anxious about the ramifications of his choices—just in case there were a God. With Erzsebet—and soon two more under his roof—well, now that he had a plenary indulgence, he was no longer concerned.

After collecting the plates and cutlery used by her father and the Monsignor, Erzsebet returned to her work in the kitchen. She had heard much of the two men's conversation. She resolved never again to enter a Church.

CHAPTER 36
1931

Gianni was at the wharf in Port Myer to oversee the loading of men, equipment, and supplies for the house he had decided to construct on L'Orté Island when he spotted a mahogany runabout docked nearby. Farther down the quayside, he spied a yellow Oakland roadster—Clarence's car—parked in the shade.

"That's not our barge you're loading up, is it Gianni?" Clarence barked, as he approached Gianni. Beside him stood a younger man who was shorter and carried less weight: Derwood Garner.

Gianni found a smile and applied it to his face; he decided to say nothing in response to Clarence. The barge, owned by a resident of Port Myer, was used by the Garners and Gianni in accordance with a rental agreement. The Garners claimed Monday, Wednesday, and Friday. Today was Tuesday.

"Derwood Garner, am I right? That makes you D. Welcome to the world outside Toronto!" Gianni smiled at the young man, who had attended both high school and university in Toronto and, having passed the bar exam in Ontario, was now employed at the Garners' Toronto office. "Your father must be very proud indeed."

"Gianni, our father speaks very highly of you." Derwood's eyes were clear and bright. There was no affectation. Gianni took an instant liking to the young man.

"I wouldn't have thought the activity at the Point required both C and D Garner. Or, is this just a look-see visit?"

"Right on both counts," Derwood answered. "And if I might enquire, what is it that you're building?"

"Oh, I've got a small island in the bay and I thought I'd put a house on it. Labour is cheap, and materials can be acquired at low cost, so I thought, why not? Mind you, I haven't got it all thought out yet."

"Something grand, though, I'll bet."

"I'm afraid you'd lose that bet, D. I've heard of too many grand projects that never house their intended occupants; they take too long to complete. I'm looking more to construct something that is . . . What would be a good word? . . . enough. I want something that is perfectly adequate, no more and no less."

Derwood cocked his head, thrown by Gianni's response. "How unusual," he muttered.

"So, D, will we be seeing more of you out here?" Gianni saw the young lawyer stand taller whenever he was referred to as D.

"I shouldn't think so. I'm charged with tending to all of the standard legal matters outside this venture. So, when you need a will or a trust and suchlike, see me. I'm not as colourful as my brother, but I am competent. My tastes just run counter to those of C in cars and investments."

Ouch, he thought. Gianni had heard that the elder of the two Garners had been heavily leveraged in the market, yet Clarence conveyed the impression of having rapidly recovered his finances. Perhaps the depth of his involvement had been greatly exaggerated.

Eventually Clarence, who had wandered off early in the conversation, rejoined them. "Are you planning to do your own stonework, Gianni? I hear that Italians are good for that."

"And red wine," Gianni answered, choosing to ignore the dig by Clarence. "Is that young Szabo by your runabout?"

"Yes, Jozsef. Do you know him?" Clarence asked.

"Actually, I don't think I've ever had occasion to speak with him, but I do know who he is."

"Yes, Jozsef keeps me apprised of the situation down here. He's a young man with a real future ahead of him."

"Did A and B ever buy that property in Florida at El Jobean?" Gianni queried.

"They did. They were staying at the hotel there while a Hollywood film was being shot, something with Tarzan, based on the book by Edgar Rice Burroughs," Clarence said, puffing up, as if this gave him greater personal significance.

"But apparently Joel Bean hadn't protected himself financially, as you did, Gianni," Derwood clarified. "The big investors from the north pulled out and the foreclosures fell to the banks, not Bean. I understand that he, like so many others, leveraged his purchase of the real estate. Now he's the proud owner of a hotel in a place with little reason for people to visit, though Father says that the fishing is excellent. It's no wonder Father is always praising you for your advice, Gianni," Derwood declared, much to Clarence's visible irritation.

"Perhaps he should consider something similar to your venture on the Point," Gianni suggested.

Clarence was dismissive. "No, Gianni, can you imagine having to transport the cargo all that way south?"

"Not from Canada, of course, but up from Cuba, and rum not rye," Gianni countered.

"Hmm," was Clarence's only response. They parted soon after.

Although he wasn't partial to the man, Gianni decided it was time for another visit with Peter Szabo. At his core, there was something profoundly wrong with Peter. It was, however, important for Gianni to keep himself well-informed because Peter's wealth made him an important person in the Norfolk County community and even into the Niagara Peninsula. On his next trip into Hamilton, Gianni visited Arpad Szucs at the tannery and picked up a bottle of slivovitz.

It had been over a year since he last visited Peter and clearly much had changed. The house and yard were in impeccable condition, contrary to Gianni's expectations. Much to his surprise, there were even flowers. Roses, hollyhocks, foxglove, delphiniums, carnations, and columbine grew in a carefully-tended decorative garden, providing a profusion of colour to what had previously been a drab exterior. Farther back on the property, he could see a vegetable garden. The young woman who answered the door at the Szabo residence was unknown to Gianni. Though plainly dressed, she was nevertheless strikingly attractive. Her thick auburn hair was braided and arranged at the crown of her head. Gianni struggled, trying not to lose himself in the depths of her green eyes. When she said her name was Annie, he thought it the most beautiful name he had ever heard.

She led him into the parlour, and as they passed by the other rooms, he could see that there had been some reassignment of their function. Through the large office on the far side of the entrance hall, Gianni caught a glimpse of a bedroom accessible through the office. It was from that direction that Peter emerged.

He had not aged well over the year and moved with some degree of difficulty. He was not jovial and looked barely approachable, though he accepted the slivovitz with some enthusiasm. The men shook hands and exchanged meaningless pleasantries.

"I met Annie at the door; have your son and daughter-in-law moved elsewhere?"

"No. Jozsef and Erzsebet, on next floor, work for me. Annie and Gracie on next floor above. Is Irish," he sneered. He removed glasses from a cabinet in the room and poured the slivovitz.

"Annie and Gracie . . . I don't recall them from my last visit, Peter. Where did you find them?" Gianni was determined to find out as much about Annie as possible.

"That Monsignor Petek, he arrange. Think two is too much. One enough. Gianni, you take one. I give you Annie. Now, sixteen years old—Petek not care. Eat too much, talk back—much trouble. Maybe alright for you. Jozsef no want." When it suited him, Peter would revert to a fractured English, further encouraged by the consumption of slivovitz.

"Well, I should speak with Annie first, so I know what she can do. Then I'll get back to you about this."

"Erzsebet and I going on little trip to doctor. When return, you decide. Until then, you visit with Annie here. She take care of house while Erzsebet away. Is good."

Gianni thought the entire matter was decidedly odd, but if it meant that he could visit with the Annie, he was more than interested in Peter's proposal.

Once he knew that Peter had departed on his medical trip with Erzsebet, Gianni frequently visited with Annie and her sister, Gracie. Immediately, he saw that Annie was smart and eager to continue learning. Conversation touched on the girls' family history and how they had come to be at St. Margaret's. He found himself drawn to Annie—the attraction was undeniable. However, he was roughly twice her age. He thought it impossible that she could find him attractive.

Gracie was just as smart, and the little girl was clearly a firebrand. She held strong opinions about everything. Knowing that she would need to remain in the Szabo household, both Annie and Gianni began to counsel Gracie, showing her how to deal with Peter or Jozsef when they became threatening rather than challenging them as was her inclination. Being clever, she caught on quickly.

Gianni invited the girls to join him on a trip to L'Orté Island. Recently, Gianni had purchased Bennett's old Ditchburn launch, the one he had seen in Montreal. He erected the canopy on the launch to protect the girls from the sun, and stowed the picnic lunch they had packed.

"So, will we be fishing?" Gracie asked, apparently relishing the idea.

"No, not today. I'm building a house on the island and I need to check on the men doing the construction. We can have a picnic there, but you shouldn't wander off. The island is just big enough that it might be difficult to find one another, even during the day, and we need to leave well before dark so we're not on the water too late." Gianni explained. "The men have a camp with tents, but we don't."

Gracie was disappointed. She had hoped to wander about the island for many hours and even try her hand at fishing. Gianni found her delightful and amusing. He thought she would make a wonderful sister-in-law, then he scolded himself. Annie was too young to think of in that way.

The girls were impressed with the large stone house. Annie noticed the variation in styling, though she didn't know what the various styles were called. One of the stonemasons, Darri, a recent immigrant from northern France, explained the Norman-styled pitch of the roof—useful given the amount of snow that accumulated on the island each winter. Another, Thomas, a jovial Brit from Bristol, showed them how the beams and stone-work meshed in the Tudor-styled wings and gables. They were particularly delighted to meet Connor, who hailed from County Wicklow in Ireland, and spoke to them about laying strong stone walls to stand against the winter winds on the bay. Then he showed them how to dry-stack stones to form a mortarless wall, a skill that took years to perfect. The men enjoyed displaying their skills for them, and the girls were an appreciative audience.

While Gracie and Annie set up for the picnic, Gianni had a talk with the various labourers, answering questions and working out details for the next phase. He returned to find the girls sitting quietly, their eyes closed. Gracie was petting a ginger cat—one of several brought to control vermin at the campsite. The girls were humming, and it sounded much like 'ah-when'. He hated to interrupt, but he was hungry.

After the meal, Gracie agreed to keep close to the building site, though out of harm's way, and promised to abide by Connor. Gianni took Annie for a walk, seeking the high point of the island. He enjoyed her company and thought that she might work for him as a secretary. He hoped that Annie would agree to abandon the Szabo household, leaving Gracie behind for a few more years—until she, too, would be old enough to come out from under the control of the orphanage system.

The time spent in Annie's company didn't seem sufficient, but Gianni considered the time of day and brought their walk to an end. They returned to the construction site.

"Oh Gracie, what have you done?" Annie exclaimed upon their return.

"Connor showed me which rocks were hardest, so I used pieces of the hardest ones to carve into some of the others. See?" Scattered about were large stones destined for flooring, some of which now displayed Gracie's careful carvings.

While Annie identified the pattern as an awen, the sisters spoke over one another in their efforts to explain its significance to Gianni. Annie expected him to be angry, but discovered that his response was some combination of interest and amusement. "I'll need to find some special use for these then, won't I?" He smiled warmly at the two.

CHAPTER 37

1932

Annie had remained at the Szabo house longer than she had intended and continued working for room, board, and little more. Her concern had been two-fold: Erzsebet and Gracie. Erzsebet had arrived home with bandages on her head, and she wasn't the same as before her trip with Peter. It was apparent that the medical intervention had been received by her rather than Peter, as they had assumed. Annie wasn't certain that Erzsebet could protect Gracie from Peter, and, until she was convinced otherwise, she was determined to remain.

Finally, the day arrived when Erzsebet, despite being substantially changed in personality—meaning she no longer displayed much of one—seemed clearly capable of looking out for the young teenager.

Annie had joined Erzsebet in the yard where she was tending the garden. "What are you doing out here?" Erzsebet demanded. "Never leave Gracie with the emperor."

"Oh, you mean Peter," Annie responded. "There's nothing to be concerned about; he and Jozsef have gone to the farm. I thought I'd come and see if I could help you. How are you doing, Erzsebet?"

"Good, better. Come with me, and I'll show you something." She led Annie toward the edge of the property and a shady spot near a stack of firewood. "There, see those mushrooms? That white one is called the angel of death. You don't want to accidentally put that into soup or gravy when you've been out collecting mushrooms. The emperor likes mushrooms very much." Erzsebet took the time to explain the physical characteristics, which could be used in identifying that particular mushroom.

"I think I would avoid mushrooms rather than chance picking the wrong one. The angel of death you say—sounds lovely." She meant it humorously and was pleased to see the corners of Erzsebet's lips curve upward, though the feeble smile failed to reach her eyes.

"Come see how the flowers are doing. What is your favourite kind?" Erzsebet asked.

"You've planted so many lovely flowers, Erzsebet, but if I had to pick one it would be the roses, especially the pink one. Perhaps we might make a rose jelly with the petals and rose hips. Which flower is your favourite?"

"I am drawn to this one, the foxglove. Never make tea from its dried leaves, or any part of it for that matter," she advised solemnly. "Even at night or with brandy mixed with it."

Their conversation continued in this manner for a time, as Annie tried to connect with any part of the old Erzsebet she had come to know.

A few days later, Annie left the employ of the Szabo household to begin work at L'Orté Point Lodge under Gianni's direction. She had room and board and a salary, some of which she put aside for a rainy day. She dreamt of the day Gracie would join her—as soon as Gracie turned sixteen.

"Just listen to me, Father; I know what I'm talking about. There are no roads on the property, so any vehicles only get as far as the west fence. That puts them a considerable distance from the lodge. Because it's isolated, the cops won't even care because there won't be noise complaints or such. And the police force doesn't have the boats for a water landing. I think anything they do have is on Lake Ontario—not up here on Erie. I tell you, we bring the girls in, maybe from Buffalo or Cleveland, so there's no reason for the local cops to get in on it, and we put them up at the lodge. We charge them for food and drink and accommodation on days they're not working—or all the time even. The clients can use the suites and entertain themselves with a bit of the usual fishing and hunting during the day. We collect on that as well. There's a fortune to be made."

"Clarence, I said no, and I don't know why I must repeat myself. That's not the kind of business I want to be a part of and I won't permit you to be a part of it, either. Besides, the lodge is Gianni's, and I seriously doubt he'd be a participant in such a scheme. Our agreement with him is solely for storage and transport of the liquor. That's it. And I don't want to hear more on the subject." Bennett Garner was noticeably irritated with his eldest son. "We all knew that Prohibition would come to an end someday, and that day now looms on the horizon. By the end of next year, there'll be no need for our product. We've made a tidy sum on this venture, and it's time to call it a day and walk away."

"My friends in the States . . ."

"Your friends in the States," Bennett boomed, "are thugs and gangsters. I've been telling you to keep your distance and just let the business run as any formal business deal does, but you've gotten your hands dirty, haven't you?" Bennett was fuming. The hour was late, and only he and Clarence were in the office. He didn't need to worry about being overheard and so could let loose upon his son. "I'm not sure which of the two of you is really the bigger dimwit. D is rather simple, but at least he's clean. You, on the other hand, have some smarts that you've used in all the wrong ways. You've sullied yourself to the point of having it affect your thinking, and I am thoroughly disgusted with you and your ideas on this matter. You want an easy profit that you can gamble away. What you should be aiming for—what I taught you to aim for—is a carefully structured profit that you spend wisely and reinvest with equal care. Gambling is for rubes. We Garners are above that, and I damned-well expect a son of mine to be above that!"

Meanwhile in Simcoe, Peter had just opened a bottle of slivovitz and poured some into each of two shot glasses on his desk. Jozsef had asked for time with his father, so the two of them could discuss serious matters. "So, what *serious* you want discuss?" Peter asked, contemptuously.

Jozsef outlined the brothel idea, much as Clarence had done with his father. The paternal response was much the same.

"Your lawyer friend fill head with shit. He smart, but stupid. You just stupid." Peter refilled his own glass. "Have big tobacco farm; have much land. Not making more land; someday, sell a bit. Brothel dirty business. I do this in Klondike; just try but don't like for business. Visit okay but business—no. Here police be too interested. Have money, gold. Hide in house. Maybe show you again sometime if you get smart. What you need more money for, eh?"

"Papa, I'm twenty-two years old! I need some freedom to make decisions for my future. I'm the one who found most of the properties you now have. I run a big tobacco operation. I deserve some security. You make promises, but I see nothing. You don't even have a will. You die, Erzsebet, who does nothing, gets half of everything. Man makes this success and woman—what does she know, especially now?"

Peter gave the matter consideration and instructed Jozsef to have Clarence Garner visit to discuss a will. Not the brothel. A will.

"You tell lawyer that money made by man is not for woman. Want will so Erzsebet not get. I work too hard. She maybe get married sometime, and then husband use my money. This I no want. I strong like bull; I not die for very long time. But see, now I make you happy, eh? Now you happy, now you go work."

"But, Papa, the brothel on the Point is a good idea, I tell you," Jozsef pleaded. "I can make us a lot of money."

Peter snarled, "You mention brothel once more and I leave money to Monsignor Petek or maybe Gianni Sarto. Lots of other people—so you just watch it." Jozsef was silent.

CHAPTER 38

1933

"D, I really appreciate you taking the time to come out here again."

"Well Gianni, I admit that I fancy getting in some fishing after we conclude the legal matters. Last time we managed to do both simultaneously, and we accomplished a significant amount, both legal and piscine."

"Well, I needed the privacy to be able to discuss things frankly with you and air some of my concerns. Being out on the water was an easy way to accomplish that. We'll go fishing after this matter is concluded, I promise. Let me get Annie."

Gianni's large stone house was complete—a unique and highly functional structure. The increased presence of Clarence and Jozsef at the lodge had tainted the environment there, and Gianni looked forward to the repeal of Prohibition in the States. Then the Garners and their enterprise would be gone from L'Orté Point.

When Gianni returned to his office with Annie, he found that Derwood had organized the various documents on the table, and three chairs had been placed at one end. Derwood took a seat at the head of the table, leaving Gianni and Annie to sit opposite one another to his left and right.

"Firstly, I need to be assured that each of you is here of your own free will because you are separate entities and can only speak for yourselves. If either of you wishes separate legal counsel, then please let's suspend these proceedings until you have received that counsel. Do either of you have any questions?" Derwood had focussed his attention on Annie as he said this yet he appeared surprised when she responded.

"I have a question," said Annie, adjusting her position and sitting more upright. "What would happen in the absence of all these documents? Not everyone takes such steps and I'm wondering what happens in such cases."

Derwood looked at Gianni, as if expecting him to provide the answer, or at least to offer a comment. Gianni was silent, and the corners of his mouth slightly curved upward.

"Well, Annie, such documents aren't really necessary unless there's something in the estate," began Derwood. "In their absence mayhem usually ensues as various interested parties make claims against the estate. Some claims may be justified, but greed often drives people to make claims that are not truly legitimate. It would be a matter for the courts to decide.

"In the absence of a will, The Public Trustee's office acts on behalf of the estate and the claimants have their lawyers as well. The office is generally under-staffed and over-worked. The process is often long and drawn out, possibly years—I've heard of one which spanned a generation, though that would be an extreme situation. It can be a long journey to a clear title. One reason for this is that the Public Trustee must first define the estate—the estate must be clarified, understood, defined—and that is done by collecting all the available documentation which identifies each asset of the estate. That's why marriages, births, land sales, and businesses are supposed to be registered. Ultimately, someone must search through all those files in order to understand the case before the courts.

"And I tell you, it's even worse if there's been a flood or a fire to destroy the archives or if the documents have been misfiled. That's one of the reasons I urge people to guard the notarized copies I provide. There were cases delayed as a result of the war as well, though that is now well behind us. When people get frustrated with the delays, they sometimes blame the lawyers, but I assure you that we are part of the solution, not the problem.

"Fortunately, some of the problems have been reduced now that certain guidelines are in place to provide for a surviving spouse and children in the absence of a formal will. However, the availability of the estate must still be established. The authorities cannot merely release assets before addressing any claims which have been made against those assets. The beneficiary receives the net proceeds, not the gross proceeds."

"Thank you Derwood," Annie replied, bringing Derwood's monologue to a close. "It's not something I've ever needed to be concerned with, so I was just wondering. You've answered my question.

"Now, please continue. I am in full agreement with you representing me in the presence of Gianni, Derwood," Annie affirmed. Gianni merely nodded.

"Fine then, the trust, Gianni—this puts all of your holdings under one umbrella. All of your investments of every kind are under this trust, which we refer to as the L'Orté Trust. The beneficiary of the trust may, at his or her discretion, direct any aspect of the trust. Should the beneficiary not be willing or able to do so, then it becomes the job of the trustee, currently, Garner & Garner, and specifically me as your current legal counsel, to ensure that the trust is managed in such a way as to protect the assets of the trust and provide for the beneficiary. At this time, the beneficiary is you, Gianni, so take your time in reading the document as if you weren't going to be making any of the decisions. By following these directions, would Garner & Garner's actions result in the outcomes you desire?"

"I'm a fast reader, D, and I've already examined this carefully. It's perfect. We'll take care of the signing all at once, if you don't mind. Connor and Darri are here and can act as witnesses."

"Now, I've made two wills for each of you, as per your instructions. And, of course, there are additional copies of each, which I'll have notarized and returned to you. So, in addition to the ones at the firm, which will be considered the originals, you'll have official copies to put into safekeeping and refer to, as you may require. The only difference between the two wills is the manner in which you are referred. In one, your marriage is acknowledged and in the other, it is not. The actual contents of the wills are absolutely identical. Gianni, you bequeath everything, including the trust to Annie. And Annie, you bequeath everything you currently have, or may acquire, to your sister, Gracie, to be held in trust for her until she attains the age of twenty-five, said trust to be managed by Garner & Garner, namely, me."

"And the aliases?"

"I've confirmed that a written affirmation on your part is required stating that you, Gianni Sarto, made those property purchases as Johannes Schneider and Jean Couture and at no time was anyone else involved. I've notarized copies of all the documents referring to you by those names and will file those with your affirmation. I don't think there are any reasonable grounds for dispute, but as I explained, that is not a guarantee that someone won't attempt to take the matter to court to pursue their own interests. It's just that I'm as confident as I reasonably can be that your estate would prevail."

"I understand, D. We do what we can. It's just that I have a bad feeling about this situation at L'Orté Point. I've got to be prepared. But no matter, I'll still be tense until the end of this year, at the very least. I'm happy to be married to my Annie, but I fear that such a change will be as a red flag to a bull for these people. Keeping our marriage quiet for a time will also protect Annie, I think."

"You could have taken this matter to another legal firm, Gianni. Would that not have simplified things for you, at least a bit?"

"A and B have been good to me these years, and I wouldn't want anyone poking around in their activities at the Point during Prohibition. A relationship with the likes of the business associates from Buffalo would no doubt be injurious to the firm. Appearances mean a lot to them. Some years ago they presented me with a gold pocket watch, in part because they couldn't bear to see me use the grey metal one I had, though they never said as much. If something were to happen to me—and I'm not saying that I think it's in the cards—at least the proceeds of all my work will go to the one I love, my Annie."

One particularly pleasant day in September, Gianni received a letter, signed by Clarence, and requesting a meeting with him at L'Orté Point Lodge two days later. No mention was made of who else might be in attendance, nor what the topic of the meeting might be. Gianni could only guess. His initial reaction had been to ignore the letter, then he considered suggesting an alternate location, such as the Toronto office of Garner & Garner. Ultimately, he decided to stand his ground and face Clarence. He hoped that Clarence was as smart as Bennett thought he was.

L'Orté Point

"Annie dear, you might want to tie down your hat and bundle up tightly to keep from feeling the cold and damp. Even though it seems warm now, once we get out onto the water, you'll feel the chill."

She stood on the dock that jutted out from the deck surrounding L'Orté Point Lodge, where she had spent a few days working in her capacity as lodge manager. She handed him a leather train case, which she had packed with a change of clothes and personal items. Gianni took her hand as she gingerly stepped into the Ditchburn mahogany launch. In that touch, he could feel the trust she held in him and she, the concern and care he felt for her.

He checked the fuel gauge, primed, then started the boat's engine. It was quiet, yet powerful, in the manner of its owner. Giovanni Sarto had recently celebrated thirty-three years on this earth, and he was successful—set for life a full two years before the target deadline he had given himself. The launch he had admired at the Port of Montreal years ago was now his. Bennett thought Gianni should buy a new one, now that his finances were healthy, but Bennett didn't understand the significance that owning this particular launch held for Gianni—how it made him feel each time he looked at it.

He looked toward Annie and placed his arm around her shoulders, drawing her in close. He would do what he must to protect her. He had felt like that from the moment he first laid his eyes upon her.

Gianni had been too busy and too focussed on his plan to acquire the Point and develop the lodge. He had made the mistake of trusting Bennett Garner's judgment too much. *But how does one trust, just a little? What is the proper measure of trust?*

Annie had just begun to shiver, though ever-so-slightly, by the time they reached the island and docked in front of what had come to be called the manor house. Gianni laughed when he first heard the phrase, and now he merely shook his head whenever anyone referred to his sturdy stone house in that manner. Connor lived on the island with them and was there to meet the launch as they docked.

Between Connor and Gianni, Annie was conveyed safely from the launch to the dock along with her train case. Gianni had planned to remain in the launch and merely turn it once again toward the Point. Instead, he followed Annie out and onto the dock. Tonight, it was particularly difficult to part, and they both felt the tension in each other's body. In their final embrace, she heard him say, "Remember, I love you. When this is over, we'll bring Gracie home."

It was quiet at L'Orté Point Lodge when Gianni returned. He had not wanted to involve any of his guests—some of whom were also potential buyers of the lots, which were again available—so had arranged for them to spend the day and one night at Niagara Falls. There wasn't the usual coterie of Clarence's workers, just a few of the regular Lodge staff. He dismissed them for the night, and they retired to their accommodation, happy to have some free time for a game or two of towie.

Gianni heard the motor cut out. The sound of the runabout was unmistakable; Clarence had arrived. And with him was Jozsef.

He invited Clarence to join him in his office. He had coffee to offer him, and they both knew rye was available. His shoulders relaxed somewhat when Clarence accepted the coffee without comment. The situation required a clear head, not one clouded by alcohol.

"You suggested we meet, so here we are, C," Gianni stated, sipping his coffee. "Is there something you want to discuss?"

As he had with his father, Clarence outlined his new plan for L'Orté Point Lodge post the repeal of Prohibition. Gianni had heard it all before; the details varied, but not by much.

"You can make a fortune with this, Gianni."

"I don't need a fortune, Clarence, just enough to provide for those who are my responsibility. Perhaps you're more worldly and I might be rather unsophisticated, but your idea is just not for me. I'm sorry to disappoint you. I know this is important to you, but I just can't do it."

"After all Garner & Garner has done for you over the years, Gianni, I'd think you'd be more grateful."

"Clarence, you know that's not the way it works. The firm hired me to do a job, which I did and for which I was paid."

"You wouldn't have this lodge if it weren't for the firm."

"You could say that neither of us would have any of this if not for Prohibition. Remember that the venture in which you've been involved for the duration of Prohibition had a start and, as we expected, an end—neither of which either of us can influence. I have a contract with the firm—well, technically, John Taylor does—to provide certain services. I do that for a fee, which is also laid down in that contract. I would have been prepared to extend the contract, but that opportunity has been lost to me as well, not just to your firm and to you."

"We're different, you and I, Gianni," Clarence observed. "I want it all, and you don't. Why? I don't understand how you can *not* pursue such an opportunity. The chaps from Buffalo are living a life that's exciting, while you're here with a rock house you call a manor, and you're trying to sell pieces of a sand-spit. They've got it all planned out, and I'm going to be a part of it. I just thought I'd give you this chance to benefit as well, considering that my father is so gung-ho about you."

"I don't know why I don't perceive things as you do, Clarence. Perhaps it has to do with losing both parents in a flood of molasses when I was eighteen, perhaps not. We make plans and decisions based on the best information we have at the time. For some reason, I'm drawn in a different direction from you."

Clarence stared intently at his empty cup; he was mulling things over. He walked across the room to get himself another cup of coffee and to take a bit more time to reconsider. He said nothing.

"I hear you became quite the baseball fan when you were in Buffalo," Gianni suddenly said.

"Hmm-m."

"Consider this, Clarence: the first All-Star Game in baseball occurred at Comiskey Park in Chicago on July sixth of this year and Babe Ruth essentially won the game. Then there's that twenty-nine year old player for the Phillies, Mickey Finn. He isn't selected to play in the game. He must have felt bad about that."

"I'm not following."

"But he got to listen to the game and experience the excitement, so that's good."

"No, I don't think that's tremendously great, Gianni; he was denied an opportunity to play in a historically significant game."

"But it was because the very next day, Mickey Finn died. At the age of twenty-nine. An ulcer."

"Oh. I missed that."

"And you also missed one helluva hurricane that hit Florida yesterday. I wonder how Joel Bean is doing."

Clarence went quiet, apparently giving the matter some additional thought. Eventually, he spoke. "Look, clearly you don't want this deal, and I can't get it without your agreement.

I can't see a partnership between us working," Clarence reluctantly admitted, his shoulders slumping in resignation.

They shook hands and left Gianni's office, bumping into Jozsef—bottle in one hand and cigarette in the other. Jozsef had been eavesdropping.

"Oh no, this isn't over. I'm tired of getting pushed around. Clarence, draw up a contract or better still, a purchase agreement. Let's say *ten dollars*." Jozsef was agitated.

"My answer to you, Jozsef, is *no*," Gianni said, tiring of the discussion. "Clarence and I have come to an agreement. Time for the two of you to discuss your available options. Perhaps there's another opportunity you can pursue with your American friends."

Clarence stood back, watching. He felt the matter with Gianni had been concluded. Although it hadn't been settled in the manner he'd have preferred, he had agreed. The idea was dead. Reluctantly, he had come to realize it was the only reasonable response to a very disappointing situation.

He was wondering how he might begin to explain this to Jozsef and discuss alternatives to their plan, given that the man was angry and fuelled by alcohol. He was still wondering when Jozsef suddenly changed his grip on the bottle of rye, swung it hard, and hit Gianni in the left temple. The impact of the bottle caused a skull fracture, driving the bone inward and lacerating an artery. As the bottle broke, a shard of glass was launched toward Clarence, barely missing his eye but cutting the bridge of his nose.

Clarence was shaken; he had never been comfortable or confident in situations involving physical altercation. While he tended his wound, gently wiping away the blood with his fine linen handkerchief, Gianni lay before him, crumpled on the floor and bleeding from his head wound. Drifting in and out of consciousness. Dying.

Clarence couldn't bring himself to deal with Gianni's wound—there was blood. "He's dying. Do something," he finally urged Jozsef, while remaining rooted where he stood. "You did this. Do something!"

And Jozsef did. Using a piece of the broken bottle as a blade, he severed Gianni's jugular. Gianni Sarto was dead at thirty-three.

Initially, Clarence was horrified by this outcome. Then a calm overtook him and he declared, "This will all work to our advantage, Jozsef. You take care of the body while I give this some thought. I doubt that Gianni Sarto bothered to have a will. With him dead and without next-of-kin, the property will be dealt with by the Public Trustee. I can make this work. Yes, indeed."

Jozsef looked out over the water—its dark depths holding tight to secrets while ripples on the surface teased with glints of reflected moonlight. He paused, and reversed his course, turning his back to the boathouse.

He dragged Gianni's body back along a wooden walkway to one of the storage sheds holding the next shipment destined for the States. He unlatched the door and helped himself to a bottle of rye. Gianni's suit jacket had ripped open and the gold pocket watch in his vest caught the reflection of moonlight. Jozsef's eyes lit up, and he greedily claimed his prize. "This calls for a celebration," Jozsef shouted.

"I have no candles; I have no cake; I have no firecrackers," Jozsef cried out. "Gianni, you celebrate with me—you will be my candle! Celebrate with me, Gianni!" he exclaimed, splashing rye over Gianni's body, lying cold on the walkway.

Jozsef stumbled back down the wooden dock to the boathouse where he located a can of gasoline. With the can in his hand, Jozsef returned and began pouring gasoline over Gianni's body, thoroughly saturating the area. Then he randomly tossed the container in further celebration. The remaining gasoline streamed from the can as it sailed through the air, hitting the door of a nearby storage shed, where it continued to empty.

Jozsef withdrew a cigarette from its pack, lit it, and dropped the burning match onto the body. He was ill-prepared for the sudden *whoosh* as the saturated clothing caught fire. Alarmed, he panicked and disposed of his cigarette, throwing it down where it found a small puddle of gasoline pooling on the wooden walkway to the second storage shed.

Jozsef's eyes went wide with amazement. His celebratory flames danced and he began to dance with them. "Look what you do, Gianni!" he called out, his eyes blazing. But not all of the heat radiated from Gianni's body or even from the burning wooden walkway. Jozsef had unwittingly spilled some of the flammable liquid on his trousers. He tried to extinguish the flames by beating them and brushing them from his clothing, but succeeded only in spreading the flames to his shirt sleeves. He could smell burning flesh and it was his own. The fire grew rapidly in intensity, the flames leaping and igniting additional wooden structures, moving inland toward the remnants of Peter Szabo's old logging operation and the new cottages built by Gianni. Frantic, Jozsef ran toward the boathouse and managed to extinguish his personal blaze in the foul water of the bait tank. Burned, wet, and largely unclothed, he stumbled inside and barely managed to secure a place with Clarence in his runabout. Jozsef winced in pain as he settled into the runabout. Then he located the bottle of slivovitz he had stashed in there and drank deeply. In his hand, he held his reward: the gold pocket watch.

The fire burned throughout the night and engulfed all of the buildings, including the boathouse. In the process, the remaining Ditchburn mahogany runabouts were lost as was the rye stored in the sheds. The extent of the devastation presented a significant loss to the Garners, though officially a loss to John Taylor whose name marked all the agreements. The community to the west of the lodge had worried the fire might reach them, but Gianni had begun to clear the way for development of the golf course, and the clearcut acted as a firebreak, preventing the spread of the fire beyond L'Orté Point.

When the authorities finally investigated, they found a single body charred in the rubble—Giovanni Sarto.

"Where Jozsef?" Peter demanded from his bed. "Jozsef!" Jozsef had been missing for several days and Erzsebet could offer no explanation. Inexplicably, Peter blamed her for his absence.

"Why don't you ask fancy lawyer?" Erzsebet mumbled, her voice trailing off. She chewed her lip and continued her chores.

Despite concern for her own medical condition, Erzsebet had been nursing Peter through what appeared to be a bad cold, made worse by his ongoing breathing problems. The doctor had visited and recommended plenty of fluids: soup, tea, and the like. He had also provided a prescription for brandy, though alcoholic beverages were now readily available without one. Despite the care he received, Peter was not doing well. He was plagued by gout, emphysema, and the doctor suspected kidney and liver problems. Nevertheless, the doctor was optimistic he would recover. *Strong like bull*, Peter repeatedly boasted.

L'Orté Point

Gracie was relieved that Erzsebet was taking care of Peter. He was vile at the best of times, yet managed to become even more so now that he was ill. All of his energy was channelled to that end rather than toward his recovery.

Erzsebet took steps to keep the news concerning L'Orté Point Lodge from Gracie but was unsuccessful. A letter arrived for Gracie, and Erzsebet had been tending Peter when the postman delivered it:

> *My dearest Gracie,*
> *I must share some very bad news with you. There was a horrible fire at the Lodge and Gianni was killed. I thought you should know. I can't bear to think of it. It pains me so that he will never have seen his child.*
> *I am staying at the manor for awhile, at least, but eventually I'll be moving from here and going back to St. Margaret's where Mam worked. As I am with child, they have agreed to let me return, and give birth in their infirmary, I think, as a courtesy to her memory. Connor has agreed to remain with me here and transport me to the convent. If at all possible, I'll visit with you before I leave the area. There is much to discuss, but there will be time later.*
> *Please give my love to Erzsebet. Take care of each other. (Just think, in the spring, you'll be an auntie!)*
> *With much love, your sister,*
> *Annie*

"Erzsebet!" Peter called out again and again; his mood was vitriolic. His bedroom was on the main floor, just off his office. It was convenient to the kitchen, and Erzsebet was thankful that she didn't need to climb the stairs to serve him. Her pregnancy was more advanced than originally thought, and she found her increased size and weight cumbersome.

"You wanted soup. You told the doctor you wanted soup. I'm making soup. Mushroom, your favourite. Soon."

While the small pot of soup simmered on the stove, the water evaporating, concentrating the flavours, Erzsebet prepared a special tea for him—an infusion made the same way as she might make, for herself and for Gracie of chamomile or mint. She had collected a large quantity of special leaves over the summer and had carefully dried them. Erzsebet always took great care with food preparation. She went into Peter's office to retrieve a bottle of slivovitz.

From his bedroom, Peter continued his tirade, but Erzsebet and Gracie ignored him. "Slaba," he shouted, demanding Gracie's presence for no particular reason.

Gracie and Erzsebet looked at one another and neither moved toward Peter's bedroom. Erzsebet had taught Gracie well. "Do you think the emperor will get tired and stop all the hollering?" Gracie asked.

"I think he'll stop," came Erzsebet's flat reply. She ladled the soup into a bowl and placed it on the tray with a spoon and napkin. Then she took the long-steeped infusion, sweetened it with a bit of honey, and poured it into a small teapot. In another spouted container, she poured a generous amount of slivovitz. Both the infusion and the slivovitz were placed on the tray with a teaspoon and a cup and saucer.

When Peter had been given sufficient time to enjoy his liquid meal, she returned to his bedroom. "How was your soup?" Erzsebet enquired as she readied to remove the tray.

"Taste not good," he answered, but that was often what he said in response to such questions, though he rarely left food uneaten.

"And the tea?" she pressed.

"Slivovitz good." Peter responded. "Bring bottle and glass."

Erzsebet did as he requested. Then she returned to the kitchen. "Bring in the laundry, Gracie. It should be dry." While Gracie tended to the laundry hanging from a line in the yard, Erzsebet cleaned the kitchen, disposed of the waste, and washed and dried the dishes, returning them to their proper locations on the shelves. The task she had set for herself was complete. She and her unborn child would both lose their father this night.

PART III

CHAPTER 39

2015

The interior of the barge was surprisingly luxurious and spacious. The decor was shabby chic, which provided the appropriate ambience for a European river barge. Eve was most enthusiastic about the decor, so Kent remained silent on the subject. The friends disappeared into their cabins to prepare for dinner.

The second to emerge found Lucy pondering the metal box they had discovered buried at the manor house. It remained locked.

"Want me to cut off the lock?" Albin asked her.

"Yes, please." While Albin removed the lock, Lucy cleaned her Claddagh ring, taking special care with the small heart-shaped emerald. As she slipped the ring on the little finger of her left hand and positioned the heart to face inward, she thought again of Gracie.

She didn't open the metal box until all seven of them were present and enjoying their aperitifs. Eve brought her Punsch. After a moment's hesitation and a sip of Punsch, Lucy opened the box.

Inside, she found a grey metal pocket watch sitting atop an envelope and some documents. She put the envelope in front of herself and placed the pocket watch and the documents in front of Kent who sat across from her. The large envelope bore Irish stamps and was thick with papers. It was addressed to 'Miss Betty-Lu Taylor', and the return address revealed that it had been sent by Gracie.

"Gracie must have sent this to me when I was just a little girl. I can't make out the date on the postmark. I really don't remember it at all—and she never mentioned it to me." Carefully, Lucy opened the unsealed envelope, removed the sheaf of papers, and quickly scanned their contents. "Oh, it's a little story composed by Gracie. How cute! It's called *'Connor the Cat Visits Canada',*" she squealed in delight.

"Tell us a story, Lucy," Yoichi called out. There was friendly encouragement from the others.

"Okay, I'll read it to you. Rather than illustrations, she's attached photos. I'll describe them instead of passing the little book around. Okay, here goes—ready children?"

There was cheering to welcome the fun as the little group got into the spirit of the moment—and their aperitifs.

"The first photo is of a cat. *Connor the Cat is a ginger cat. Connor the Cat is an unusual cat. Connor the Cat is a magical cat. Connor the Cat is an adventurous cat.*"

"Oooh, the tension builds—" Yoichi called out. Donald playfully shushed her.

"The second photo is of a big tree with a hole near the ground. *Connor the Cat lives in a tree cave—a hole at the bottom of a very, very big, and very, very old tree.*"

"The third photo is of a wall of stacked stones—"

"That's a mortarless wall and requires quite a skill to accomplish. There are a lot of them in Ireland and some are very old," Kent informed them.

"Boo-oo, I was just getting into the plot. You're ruining the story." This time it was Donald being silly. Kent pretended to pout.

"Now children, behave yourselves," Lucy said, continuing to read aloud, "*Connor collects stones. Connor carefully stacks the stones on top of one another. Connor is building a wall. 'Ah, when this job is done, I shall be safe,' says Connor. When the final stone is put into place, Connor hears a magical sound. 'Whoosh', and the job is done!*

"*'This wall will keep me safe,' says Connor. Connor climbs to the top of the wall and walks it in a full circle. With each step, Connor leaves a paw print behind. Connor's paw print looks like this—*"

Lucy paused. "Heh—there's a drawing of an awen. I had wondered why there was an awen marking the ceiling in the garage. Maybe my dad helped Laszlo with the vault and marked the ceiling. If so, this story was written before 1983, and that might be why I don't remember it."

"What's the rest of the story, Lucy?" Kent asked. The mood of the room had turned somber.

"*Connor likes to climb the very, very big and very, very old tree. The first branch on the tree is named Italy. Connor likes Italy.* There's a photo of—I think it's Gianni.

"*Another branch on the tree is named Ireland. Connor likes Ireland.* I think this photo must be Annie.

"*On the other side of the tree there is a big, old stump of a branch named Hungary. 'I'm not hungry,' says Connor. Connor doesn't understand. Connor is scared of that branch. It is brittle and dangerous. Connor stays well away from that branch.*

"There's no photo for that part.

"*One day, Connor climbs all the way to the highest branch. This branch is named Canada. Connor likes Canada very much. Connor can see the stone wall encircling the tree.*

"*Connor sees that beyond the wall there is water. All around—there is water. Connor is on an island!*"

Quiet filled the room. Then Kent spoke, "Lucy, I think you should look at this. One of the documents from the box is a marriage certificate."

"My parents?"

"No."

The old certificate was brittle and discoloured with age. She handled it with great care. It affirmed that a marriage had taken place between Giovanni Sarto and Annie Hogan. *Had Gracie known?* She showed the document to Donald, wondering why he hadn't discovered this information.

"Somehow this marriage was never recorded, or perhaps it was removed from the records. If it had been there, I would have found it. Some sort of bureaucratic bungling, perhaps?" Donald suggested.

"Or, maybe someone was paid to look the other way and not enter the information into the records?" Lucy suggested. *Even when you think you know; you don't—not really.*

Lucy was moved by the find. Trying to retain her composure in front of her guests, she announced that she wouldn't be digging through the remaining few documents just then but would wait until tomorrow. And at that moment, Elinor announced that dinner was served.

The night air was chilly in September, so they dined inside rather than up on deck. The fish course featured the perch caught earlier that day by Donald and Albin and the two men were noticeably pleased with their first-time success. Helen, already impressed with Elinor's skillset, was further impressed with her ability in the galley. The two women had a lot in common.

"Sunset occurs just after seven o'clock tonight and there's a lunar eclipse of the blood moon, which should be readily visible just after sunset. It'll take about two hours. That's why I picked September 27 for our little outing." Lucy announced. Eve and Yoichi both asked why it was called a blood moon, and Lucy explained, "Something to do with the amount of moonlight filtering through the atmosphere, as I understand, resulting in a reddish hue during the eclipse, but otherwise it's just a big harvest moon."

After the meal, they bundled up and took their Irish coffees to the upper deck where lounge chairs had been set out for them. A huge harvest moon hung in the cloudless sky above them. Lucy leaned against Kent and sipped her coffee as they watched the moon gradually disappear, then reappear. When fully eclipsed by the Earth, the moon displayed with a reddish corona. Helen and Albin pointed out various constellations, and they were able to enjoy the star-studded night sky without interference from city lights. Even Yoichi was impressed with the celestial display.

Just as Lucy was beginning to feel the chill and considering her retreat into the main lounge, Kent's phone rang. As he answered it, he moved inside. Lucy followed close behind and, by the time she was inside, Kent was handing his phone to her. "Lucy, DS Kovacs needs to have a word with you, Eve, and Albin."

When her conversation concluded, she passed Kent's cellphone to Eve, who shortly thereafter passed it to Albin.

Donald, Yoichi, and Helen found this to be decidedly odd. "What's up?" Yoichi was the first to ask. "Not to pry, but all four of you look stunned."

"Julius Roman is dead. He was found in his cell. It's being investigated. Might be a suicide," said Kent, impassively. "DS Kovacs wanted to tell each of us and answer any questions we might have, because we were Julius' victims."

"You really think it was suicide? Maybe the mob didn't want him to talk," Yoichi suggested, while enjoying her second Irish coffee.

A sudden chill ran through Lucy and she leaned toward Kent for warmth. "And that's why there's a blood moon tonight," she softly whispered.

EPILOGUE

A year later, the official report was released concerning the death in custody of Julius Roman. It acknowledged that he had been found unresponsive in his jail cell, where he was being detained while awaiting trial. After guards performed CPR, he had been transported to the hospital while in cardiac arrest. He was pronounced dead at eight o'clock the night of September 27, 2015. On his death certificate 'homicidal strangulation' is given as the cause of death.

The Crown Attorney's Office requested a full investigation by the OPP and RCMP concerning the circumstances of his death. There were several violations of normal jail procedures the night it occurred, including malfunctioning cameras and guards who were derelict in their duties. They have since been charged.

However, no one has been charged in the death of Julius Roman, or in having made his death match a suicide by hanging. His claim to having evidence against organized crime figures and powerful people in Canada, and in other countries has caused much speculation and resulted in many conspiracy theories concerning his death.

The death of Lucy's father, John Taylor, formerly known as Janos Szabo, remains recorded as a drug overdose. As a result of Julius Roman's death, all charges against Julius were withdrawn, including those to which he had confessed. Therefore, the records concerning Lucy's father could not be corrected to acknowledge that it was a murder by drug overdose.

Lucy improved security at L'Orté Park and subsequently sold it to a non-profit, with the requirement that a plaque respecting Gracie remain in a place of honour in the reception area of the residence. The new owners had suggested it be placed in the exercise room, but Lucy remembered how much Gracie had disliked chair yoga.

Kent and Lucy completed their arrangement with the province of Ontario regarding L'Orté Point and L'Orté Island. The Point became a nature reserve owned by the province. Property taxes on the island were waived in anticipation of it eventually becoming the property of the province upon their deaths. They decided to build a self-contained green residence on the island with a studio for Lucy and lots of guest rooms, and they were taking their time carefully investigating the old manor house. They had already discovered several additional boxes, but these had not been hidden—and they were empty. Lucy reasoned this had been the source of funding for her education, first boarding school and then university. Many questions remained unanswered, but she was content.

Lucy wasn't sure what she wanted to do with the two sleep-paintings, so they remain covered and stored in her studio. To date, there hasn't been a third.

People were shocked when Juliette retired from Garner & Garner many years earlier than expected, and her exodus caused substantial upheaval at the firm. There were unsubstantiated claims that her health was in jeopardy. Some said that she was abroad and travelling the world. No one has been able to contact her to confirm.

THE END

COMING SOON

Look for the sequel to *L'Orté Point*, expected to be released in 2022. **Cow on the Ice**, is a bittersweet romantic mystery/thriller—a matter of revenge, greed, longings and losses. Lucy and Kent are vacationing in Europe—and dangers lurk, both at home and abroad.

J. A. Gibbens

GENERATIONS*

Andrew Garner
Bennett Garner
Peter Szabo

Clarence Garner
Derwood Garner
Annie Hogan
Gracie Hogan
Gianni Sarto
Jozsef Szabo
Erzsebet Szabo

Goldie Szabo
Janos Szabo/John Taylor
Laszlo Szabo

Juliette Garner
Lucy Taylor-Gillespie
Paul Szabo

*Though not exhaustive, this list is intended to provide assistance by clarifying the relative positions of certain characters through time.

GLOSSARY

acres vs hectares Canada began to introduce the use of the metric system to the general population April 1, 1975. Before that date, the Imperial or British system was commonplace. It persists within the older population as well as in certain applications, specifically measures employed when dealing with the USA. The US customary system of measure, which is used within the USA, is similar to the British system in certain, but not all, respects. (Note: 1 acre = 0.4 hectares; 1 hectare = 2.5 acres, approximately)

Carolinian A horticultural subzone of the deciduous forest region in which plants considered indigenous to the Carolinas in the USA are also found to be indigenous to the islands and north shore of Lake Erie in Canada, due to the moderate temperature of the region.

cazzo Italian, a vulgar interjection that is the equivalent of damn, shit, or fuck in English.

coglione Italian, slang for 'testis'; used to say that someone is an idiot, a prick, or to express extreme annoyance.

Crown Attorney	In Canada, this is the prosecutor of court cases.
da	Irish, diminutive of 'daidí', which in English is 'dad'.
dumbom	Swedish, meaning 'silly'.
ER	Emergency room (of a hospital)
étendre	French, 'to stretch or extend', also as a movement in ballet.
fouettés en tournant	French, 'whipped turning', a ballet move usually performed as a series and in which the dancer turns on one foot while thrusting the other outward and inward at each revolution.
frisk	Swedish, meaning 'not ill', rather than 'well'.
grand allegro	French, ballet term referring to spritely, fast or brisk steps, performed with the greatest control while achieving great heights or distance.
grand plié	French, ballet term for a full bend of the knees bringing the thighs parallel with the floor.
Harkness, Ontario	Fictional, see Map B or Map C.

hectares vs acres	Refer to "acres vs hectares" above.
Janus	Roman god; fictional mob term.
Jiyu Ki Do Ryu	Style of karate which translates as "Way of the Free Spirit".
Latte, Quebec	Fictional. There is a town of the same name in Italy, near the border with France.
loonie	Nickname for the Canadian one dollar coin, so named because it features the form of the common loon, *Gavia immer*.
L'Orté Point	Fictional, see Map C.
mam	Irish, meaning 'mom'.
Menj föl és manadj ott	Hungarian, translates into English as "Go upstairs and stay there."
ninny	Swedish, meaning 'foolish person'.
OPP	Ontario Provincial Police
plenary indulgence	Plenary indulgences have been used within the Roman Catholic Church since the end of the eleventh century. An indulgence is applied in lieu of doing a penance for sins that have been confessed. While Pope Urban II instituted this for those who had participated in the Crusades, later it was

plenary indulgence (continued)	made available to those who could not go on the Crusades, but instead made cash contributions to the Church. This was seen as the selling of indulgences. There was a misunderstanding among many of the faithful that a plenary indulgence took time off one's sentence in Purgatory since there was always an expression of days associated with plenary indulgence. However, the Church intended for the number of days to reflect days worth of penance, not days of torment in Purgatory. Therefore, the purchase of a plenary indulgence became seen as a way to facilitate one's entry into Heaven, a "get-out-of-jail-free" card.
Port Myer	Fictional, see Map C.
RCMP	The Royal Canadian Mounted Police are the national police force in Canada. A branch of the RCMP, the Criminal Investigation Branch, is similar to the FBI in the USA or MI5 in the United Kingdom.
slaba	Hungarian, meaning 'weak'.
stor i orden	Swedish, translates as "big in the words," an idiom meaning "all talk."
towie	Card game developed in France in the 1930s.

CPSIA information can be obtained
at www.ICGtesting.com
Printed in the USA
LVHW101139081122
732650LV00002B/218